Sheep's_Clothing

Sheep's_Clothing

JOSI S. KILPACK

DESERET
BOOK

Salt Lake City, Utah

Library of Congress Cataloging-in-Publication Data

Kilpack, Josi S.

  Sheep's clothing / Josi S. Kilpack.
    p. cm.
    Summary: Fifteen-year-old Jess, the oldest of seven children, feels like a loser until she makes a new friend in an online chat room, but when "Emily" turns out to be a sexual predator who abducts her, the FBI, her parents' emergency training, and the prayer of her Mormon community help her to survive.
    ISBN-13: 978-1-59038-746-7 (pbk.)
    [1. Online chat groups—Fiction. 2. Kidnapping—Fiction. 3. Christian life—Fiction. 4. High schools—Fiction. 5. Schools—Fiction. 6. Family life—Utah—Fiction. 7. Mormons—Fiction.] I. Title.
    PZ7.K55915She 2007
    [Fic]—dc22   2007002447

Printed in the United States of America
Malloy Lithographing Incorporated, Ann Arbor, MI

10   9   8   7   6   5   4   3   2   1

To parents everywhere,
especially mine,
who loved me despite myself

Acknowledgments

As always, it took a village to get this story right. Thank you to my sweetie, Lee Kilpack, for his help with the original idea and continuing story from day one of this project. Thanks to my dear friend Julie Wright, for the months of brainstorming and support, along with Tristi Pinkston, Bob Bahlmann, Heather Moore, and Shirley Bahlmann for their priceless feedback. Thank you to BJ Rowley for his excellent editing skills at the end and for the details about toilets and contacts I would never have known otherwise. Thank you to Willard Boyd Gardner for help with the details about police work, and thanks to my writing groups—Logan, Utah: Janet Jensen, Arianna Cope, and Carole Thayne; and Willard, Utah: Anne Ward, Jody Durfee, Ronda Heinrickson, and Sheryl Compton—for the months of feedback that helped me get things fine tuned.

Big thanks to the talented staff at Deseret Book: Jana Erickson, product director; Jay Parry, editor; Sheryl Smith, designer; Laurie Cook, typesetter; and Lisa Mangum, editorial assistant. It has been an absolute joy to work with these individuals, and I can't thank them enough for all their efforts in this book's behalf.

Hugs and kisses to my family for all their enthusiasm and support, especially my husband, who is always the first to tell me that I can do anything. He is my foundation. Thanks to everyone who has taken the time to tell me how another book I've written has touched, entertained, or edified them. You can't know the difference you make. And, of course, thanks to my Father in Heaven, for all of the above and so much more.

Prologue

January 22nd

The invincibility and insecurity of adolescence had made everything so easy. They had met through a website used mostly by teens, mybullet-inbored.com. So many young girls looking—searching—for someone to make them feel special.

If only Terrezza hadn't led him on. He'd been so careful, building her trust, and assuring himself that she was the one. And then she betrayed him just when he thought she finally understood. She tried to leave after he'd worked so hard for them to be together. She wouldn't even give him a chance to make things work, and he'd known from the beginning that he could never let her go home. If she would have just accepted his love, and loved him in return, they could have been so happy.

He parked the car, then went around to the trunk, scanning the area to make sure he was alone. But January in Alberta, Canada, kept very few people from coming this far out of town. Plus, night was gathering fast. After opening the trunk he hefted his load onto one shoulder. Though it was not an official landfill, that detail hadn't stopped the residents of Jasper from using this place for years. Old appliances peeked out of the snow, and the corners of black garbage sacks fluttered in the wind. He navigated the unsavory and uneven ground in order to reach the middle. He wouldn't risk leaving her on the outside edges where she could be easily discovered.

An old stove sat at an odd angle toward the middle of the area, and in the gathering grayness of evening it looked like a tombstone silhouetted against the sky. That's where he would leave her. When he reached the stove, he hefted the body, wrapped in a blanket he'd bought at a second-hand store that morning, and laid it on the ground.

"It could have been different," he whispered, his words carried away by the wind. He wanted to see her again, look at her face, but he resisted. She was dead. He needed no more reminders of what could have been. Obviously, she wasn't the one.

Turning around, he headed back toward the car. It was forecasted to snow that night and all the next day. He was counting on the snow to eliminate the need for a burial. As he walked, he reflected on the years that had led up to this, all the girls he'd met online, all the opportunities he'd been afraid to pursue in person. But now he needed someone to share his life with. It wasn't about the thrills anymore, the explicit online chats he'd been having with girls for years—it was about love and having a life with that special someone. He'd been wrong about Terrezza, but he wouldn't make the same mistake again.

Back at the cabin, he packed his things and circled the date March 22 in his planner. That was exactly two months away—plenty of time to make a new game plan, plenty of time to analyze what had gone wrong and mourn Terrezza properly. After all, he loved her.

It was hard not to be discouraged. *It's okay*, he told himself as Canada disappeared through his rearview window. *You'll love again, and next time everything will be perfect.*

——Original Message——
From: emjenkins000@yahoo.com
To: jjk_hollywood@hotmail.com
Sent: Tuesday, March 21, 9:03 PM
Subject: Hi

Jess—

i just ran across your bored on mybulletinbored.com and thought i'd say hi. my name is Emily and i live in pennsylvania—go flyers! do u like hockey? i play the piano too and also love the mountains like u do. just thought i'd pop in and say hi. i'd love to be e-pals. tell me more about yourself.

Emily

———————

With all the children finally down for the night and the dishwasher started, Kate dried her hands on a dish towel and scanned the now-clean kitchen. With six kids, a clean kitchen was a rare enough event to deserve the notice, and since overcoming a particularly nasty bout of the flu the previous week, Kate was still catching up around the house. Lying in bed and having life go on around her had been absolutely miserable. The kids had caught it, too. Luckily, they recovered better than she did.

Kate turned off lights on the way to her bedroom, then shut the door, and the day, behind her. As she crossed the room to her jewelry box, she took out her earrings, glad she'd felt well enough to go to Enrichment that night even if the presentation hadn't been one of the better ones. Rather than being inspiring, it made her feel guilty for all the things she didn't do right. She hated that.

Brad was brushing his teeth in the adjoining bathroom and winked as she began getting undressed. She smiled and modestly turned her back to him. After seventeen years and six children, she no longer had the same confidence in his seeing her body that she'd once had. He always said she was beautiful, of course, but what else could he say? And even if he *had* made peace with the differences—thirty-five pounds in all the wrong places—she hadn't.

"How are you feeling?" Brad asked after spitting into the sink.

"Tired," Kate answered. "But good. Thanks for coming home early enough to run the kids around. I was glad I got to go."

"Did you see that note from Caitlyn's dance teacher?" Brad asked while rinsing his toothbrush. Kate had been home for almost an hour, but with family prayer and scriptures, bedtime, and half a dozen end-of-day necessities, they hadn't had a chance to talk much.

"Yeah," Kate said as she fastened the last button on her pajama top and turned to face him again. "I kept telling her she'd get in trouble if she didn't follow the dress code—hopefully she will now."

"What was Enrichment about?" Brad asked, surprising her. He didn't usually ask about those kind of details.

"Womanhood," Kate said. "Being a good woman, a good member of the Church, and a good mother. It was good, but the kind of presentation that makes you feel like you're not doing nearly enough."

Brad laughed and filled up a paper cup with water. "Well, it sounds like of all the Enrichments you could have missed, this one would have been it. You've got that whole womanhood thing down."

Kate smiled at the compliment. "Except I can't seem to get my teenaged daughter to say four words to me most of the time, and Keith's teacher sent home yet another note about him talking too much and not turning in assignments. He might just flunk out of the second grade."

"Everybody deals with that stuff. Jess is quiet—she always has been—and Keith is the class clown like *he* always has been." Brad swished his mouth out one final time. "There's no such thing as a perfect parent."

Kate nodded. She knew that, but still, she *wanted* to be perfect. Overall, she was happy with her mothering, but there was always something she felt she should be doing better. Maybe everyone felt that way.

She passed Brad in the doorway of the bathroom, and he wrapped an arm around her waist and stole a kiss. She wriggled away, shaking her head at him. "Stop it," she said with a laugh.

Brad got into bed, but she could see his reflection in the mirror as she wiped the mascara from her eyes. His dark hair and brown eyes both contrasted and complemented her fair complexion, blue eyes, and red hair. Their children were a grab bag of features and coloring from the two of them, and with each pregnancy she and Brad had wondered what this newest addition would look like.

"By the way, your mom called again," Brad said, watching her.

Kate felt her smile fade, but she quickly pasted it back on and continued her skin-care regime. She'd heard it said that every person has two chances at having a family—the one you're born into, which is beyond your control, and the one you create, which is entirely up to you. She was very proud of the family she had created. Glad to have a second chance. The reminder of that first family, if you could call it that, was not necessarily a welcome one.

Brad continued. "She was wondering why you didn't call her back last week."

Kate shrugged. "The message didn't sound all that important." But she

3

did feel bad. She could be hard on her mother, but was she any better when she ignored her mom's efforts, trite and lacking as they were?

"It's been months since you talked to her."

Kate looked at him in the mirror. "I know. Did you tell her the kids and I have been sick?"

"Yeah," Brad said.

Kate let out a sigh. "I'll call Mom back tomorrow." The irony, however, was that she and her mother really had nothing to talk about. Two very different women, with different lives, different ambitions. It was hard to believe they were even related sometimes, and the conversations always felt choppy and strained. She was glad Brad said nothing more, letting the subject drop.

When her face was slathered with moisturizer, Kate shook one of her antibiotics from the prescription bottle before popping open her case of birth control pills. She noticed she was on her last one and made a mental note to pick up her next round from the pharmacy in the morning. She filled a paper cup with water, swallowed the pills, and found herself wondering if she wanted to start another month of birth control. She glanced at Brad in the mirror. Was he ready to discuss Thompson number seven?

After five perfect pregnancies, her last one had been different. She'd been put on bed rest for her blood pressure, then hospitalized, and even with that intervention, Chris was born a month early. Luckily, the complications were only on her side—Chris had been fine. However, the doctor had said the same problems could arise if she got pregnant again—but he'd said it as if the idea of having seven children wasn't a consideration anyway. For most people, it wasn't. Even Brad was willing to stop. But Kate had spent her childhood dreaming of siblings, of dinners at the table, and being a part of a real family.

When she met Brad—who was one of seven children—Kate determined that even though she hadn't had it for herself, she desperately wanted a family like that for her children. His siblings were his best friends, and his parents were amazing people. Brad's mom was more of a mother to Kate than her own mother had ever been. Being a part of them had been like coming home for the first time in her life. They both wanted that sense of family, that knowledge of belonging to so many people, for their own children.

They had Jess right away, and Kate loved being a mom. But she had to work while Brad finished school, and it was heartbreaking to leave Jess with Brad's mom every day. They decided to put their family on hold until Kate could stay home. When Brad graduated with his CPA three years later, they made up for lost time by having five kids in ten years. With Brad's mom to mentor her through it, Kate's joy in motherhood just kept growing.

Jess would be sixteen in a couple months—a young woman, soon to be an adult. The baby of the family, Chris, was eighteen months, more and more independent and less and less the little boy for whom Kate was the center of the universe. Possible complications or not, the kids weren't getting any younger, and neither was Kate. She'd also felt sure for months now that they were ready to invite one more spirit into their home. She wouldn't feel this strongly if she wasn't meant to have just one more child. Would she?

She looked at Brad's reflection again. He was laid against the pillows, his eyes closed and his face relaxed. He let out a breath, the kind of breath that testified of the long hours he was working, with it being tax season, and the evening he'd just spent alone with the kids. Probably not the best time to bring up the idea of having another one. She'd need the right moment, and until then she'd pray that his fears of what might or might not happen wouldn't overshadow the family they'd always planned on.

She flipped off the lights. They were so busy these days that the time to just be together, be a couple, seemed to slip away from them more often than not. Nights when they actually went to bed at the same time seemed few and far between. But she was feeling better and didn't have a science project to help with tonight. Brad wasn't at the office getting just "one more thing" taken care of.

"It's dark," Brad said as she made her way toward the bed, using his voice as a compass.

Kate smiled to herself, glad that even after seventeen years the world could still stop just long enough for the two of them.

2

——Original Message——
From: jjk_hollywood@hotmail.com
To: emjenkins000@yahoo.com
Sent: Wednesday, March 22, 4:18 PM
Subject: Re: Hi

Emily,

I'd love to be e-pals too. What's it like in Pennsylvania? I'm afraid I
don't know anything about hockey—sorry. I don't think it's very popular
here in Salt Lake. I looked at your bored too. You're older than me, I'm
just a sophomore but I'm almost sixteen. What are your favorite sub-
jects at school? I love Math and Biology—I'm thinking I might be a
chemist one day but I can't take Chemistry until next year. Anyway, I'd
love to know more about you. Do you have a boyfriend?

Gotta run, I need to help my mom with something.

Laters,
Jess

_____

Perfect," Mom said. The three ponytails Justin had put into her hair
flopped to the side when Mom cocked her head. Mom's auburn
curls looked ridiculous held up by the pink and red barrettes. Jess let go of
the picture frame she was helping set straight and took a step away from

the wall. Mom cocked her head to the other side, the ponytails flopping again. Didn't Mom care that she looked like an idiot with her hair like that? Jess hoped no one came to the door.

Jess still didn't understand why Mom needed her help in the first place, but sometimes it seemed like Mom just asked for help for the sake of asking. Jess was already in a bad mood, since Britney, her *supposed* best friend, had ditched her for lunch again. She really just wanted to veg out today.

Keith and Justin came running through the back door, waving sticks as if they were swords and yelling at each other with screechy pirate-like voices. Both Jess and Mom had to move out of their way.

"Gosh, you guys, go away!" Jess said when Keith's swipe of his "sword" nearly took off her head.

"Be nice, Jess," Mom said, still looking at the frame. "Some day your brothers and sisters are going to be your best friends."

Jess bit her tongue to keep from saying, "Yeah, right." Since Mom didn't have any siblings, she had no idea how annoying they were. Jess didn't say anything out loud though, not wanting to invite a lecture. She contented herself with making a face at the retreating backs of her brothers when Mom wasn't looking.

"Do you like it?" Mom asked. Jess turned her attention to the picture they'd just hung. It was a needlepoint Mom had done of the Jordan River Temple; that's where she and Dad had been married. Their wedding date was stitched across the bottom—ten months before Jess had been born. She wasn't quite a honeymoon baby, but close enough to count. That's what Mom always said. Jess didn't want to think about that stuff—it gave her the creeps—so she thought only about the picture. It was nice, for needlepoint, and Mom had been working on it for over a year. But Jess liked the wreath that had been there before.

"It's nice," Jess said, then felt bad when Mom's face fell a little bit. She *had* worked really hard on it, and she always made a big deal when

Jess did well at something. "I mean, it's really nice," Jess corrected, then worried she'd showed too much enthusiasm. She had to be careful or Mom would offer to teach her how to do it for the hundredth time.

"I could show you how to do needlepoint," Mom said and Jess smiled. It was kinda cute how Mom always wanted to show her how to do the stuff she never learned to do as a kid, but Jess wished Mom's idea of quality time was taking Jess to a movie or something. Jess didn't like all that crafty stuff Mom was into. "Ya know, my mom never did stuff like this. I had to learn it on my own."

Bummer, Jess thought sarcastically, *since needlepoint is such an important life skill.* It was okay for Mom to do it—she was old—but the last thing Jess needed was needlepoint to make her even more weird.

It was a challenge to find just the right amount of disinterest without hurting Mom's feelings. "Maybe sometime," she said, not making eye contact and wishing she could just get back to her game. Jess got forty-five minutes of free time on the computer every day, and she still had fifteen minutes left—she'd paused the timer and was anxious to get her time in before one of the kids needed the computer. Homework always took precedence over free time. Mom had been sick last week and Jess hadn't gotten much of her time. *That* had been totally lame. Jess had to make dinner almost every night last week *and* do the laundry—all of it. It *was* cool to make all her favorite dinners, but Jess was glad Mom was finally feeling better.

"You can go finish what you were doing," Mom said in that tone that always made Jess feel bad, even if she was sure she hadn't done anything wrong. Mom lifted her hands to her hair and *finally* started undoing Justin's hairdo. "I think I've been pushing myself too much," she said. "And I'm just wiped out today. Can you help me with dinner before we go to gymnastics?"

Gymnastics, Jess thought darkly, wanting more than ever to lose herself in the computer game for a little longer. "Yeah," Jess said, but she thought Caitlyn ought to help with dinner since Jess had done it so much last week. But even though Caitlyn was the next oldest, she was barely twelve. Still, it didn't seem quite fair.

Sharla came upstairs whining about Justin having played in her room while she'd been at school. Then the phone rang. Jess made her escape.

"Thanks, Jess," Mom said on her way to the phone. "You can have another half hour on the computer before we get started."

Sweet! Jess thought. *At least there were perks now and then.* Jess sat down at the computer, wondering if Emily would write back soon, then felt lame for being so excited that someone other than spammers had noticed *her* bored. She had barely reset the timer and gotten back to her game when the computer dinged, announcing she had an e-mail. When she saw it was from Emily she broke into a wide smile. Maybe Emily needed a friend as bad as Jess did. Jess hit reply, then put her fingers on the keyboard and started typing.

3

—–Original Message—–
From: emjenkins000@yahoo.com
To: jjk_hollywood@hotmail.com
Sent: Wednesday, April 12, 11:13 AM
Subject: Helloooooooooooooooo

Jess—

where are u girl? it's been like three days since you wrote to me last. yr
not mad at me r u? i'd just die if u were mad at me. do you have gymnastics today? i'm so sorry. that sucks yr mom makes u go even though
u hate it. remember my cousin Colt—like my best friend in the whole
world. He's moving to florida. i'm so bummed. i'm going to be so lonely
without him. i wish u were here. u would understand, wouldn't u? can u
believe we've been e-mailing for three weeks? weird. anyway, rite back, K

what's it like having such a big family? do u like it?

Em

———

Brit," Jess called, holding her books against her chest and hurrying
toward her friend. They only had one class together this trimester
and hardly ever saw one another these days. Britney turned, her long
blonde hair swishing through the air like a shampoo commercial. She
smiled when she saw Jess and waited for her to catch up. Their

friendship often felt like that these days: Jess trying to catch up. Unfortunately, Jess felt like she was always lagging behind no matter how hard she tried.

"I didn't see you at lunch," Jess said, annoyed that she was a little out of breath from running a whole ten feet. She had to talk loud to be heard over the voices of the thousand other students at her high school.

"Yeah," Britney said. "Candace asked me to go to lunch with her. I tried to catch you this morning to let you know, but you were already gone. And then I had to hurry out of computer class cause I'd left my English book in Candace's car."

Jess wasn't sure how Britney had missed her that morning, since their lockers were in the same hall and Jess had seen Britney talking to her friends. But that kind of thing had been happening a lot lately. Ever since Britney made track team, she had all kinds of new friends. But Jess didn't want to come across as a whiner. She shrugged to emphasize it wasn't a big deal. "No biggie. I just wanted to make sure you hadn't gone home sick or anything." It sounded lame, even to herself, but Jess had never been very good at coming up with things off the top of her head. They walked a few more steps, Jess dodging this way and that to avoid collisions with students coming the other direction. She noticed the crowds seemed to move out of the way for Britney, so she stuck closer to her and was able to benefit from the parting sea of students.

"I have a track meet tonight so the coach gave us an hour to go home, get some food, and then come back. Do you want to walk home together?"

"Sure," Jess said, hoping she didn't sound too excited. They used to walk home together every day, but it had been weeks since Britney had had a practice-free afternoon. They arrived at Jess's locker, and Jess started turning the lock.

"Great, I'll be right back," Britney said. Her locker was at the other end of the hall.

But Britney didn't come right back. She was stopped by Micah, a boy

Britney'd had a crush on all year. Once she finished flirting with Micah, one of the other girls on the track team caught up with her, and Jess watched from her locker as Britney laughed and talked about things Jess probably didn't know anything about. She tried not to let it bother her— she really did—but it was so hard. Jess wanted to have exciting things to talk about. But Jess had never been as social as Britney was, and all she had to talk about was piano, which no one cared about besides her parents. While she waited for Britney the social butterfly to take a breather, Jess organized her locker, rearranging the pictures taped inside. Most of them were of her and Britney, though she had the school photos of some of her other friends as well. Would she be a total nerd if she sat down in the hall to start working on her math homework while she waited?

"Sorry," Britney said a few moments later. Jess smiled and shut her locker. She'd been ready to go for almost ten minutes.

"That's okay. Who was that you were talking to?" Jess asked as they pushed through the big glass doors. Most of the students had left, but a few stood in clumps talking or waiting for a ride. It wasn't too cold for April, and though the sky was overcast, at least it wasn't raining.

Britney went on about *all* her new friends, what events they ran in track, what grades they were in. Many of them were seniors. Jess didn't even know a senior, other than the ones she went to church with. Jess's jealousy grew, but she tried not to show it. When Britney finally ran out of things to brag about, she asked Jess how life was.

"Good," Jess said, searching for something exciting to talk about— anything that was new and interesting. Emily—why hadn't she thought of that sooner? "I met this girl through mybulletinbored.com. She's really cool."

"You met her online?" Britney asked, raising eyebrows that looked shapelier than they used to. Why didn't Britney tell her she'd started waxing her eyebrows? Jess raised a hand to her own bushy red eyebrows, then lowered it. She didn't need any more self-defeating thoughts at the moment. But she liked that she'd got Britney's attention.

She shrugged as if she'd met lots of people online. "Yeah, she's really great. We have so much in common." *Would Britney be jealous of that?* Jess wondered.

Britney was quiet for a few seconds, and Jess felt the glimmer of victory until Britney spoke again. "Doesn't that like, freak you out? I mean it could be some psycho. My mom made me watch this *Dateline* thing where they catch all these guys that try to hook up with teenagers—talk about creepy." Britney's tone was much closer to disapproval than envy.

"She's not a psycho," Jess said, rolling her eyes to emphasize how ridiculous it was. "She's a junior and she's cool—she lives in Pennsylvania."

"You don't really know who she is," Britney said as if she were talking to her little brother. "Sure, I use the bored too—but only with kids I know from school."

Jess bristled. "Forget it." They walked in silence for several seconds.

"So," Britney said as if she'd been searching for another topic to talk about. They didn't used to have that problem, and Jess didn't understand why things had changed so much between them. If they were really best friends, wouldn't they still have a hundred things to talk about? Britney continued, "How's that quilt you've been doing with your grandma?"

Jess smiled. "Great, I'm going to her house on Saturday to put it up on Grandma's frame now that all the piecing is done. It's so cool, though, I wish I could keep it."

"That's cool," Britney said, but she didn't ask any more questions, and Jess felt dumb for acting so excited. She'd noticed that the popular girls never acted excited about anything except clothes and boys. "How's gymnastics?" Britney asked after another awkward pause.

"Horrible," Jess said, her mood further darkened just thinking about it. Up until now she'd been able to forget it was Wednesday—or as she thought of it, humiliation-in-spandex day. "I so wish my mom would let me quit."

"Come on," Britney said, playfully nudging Jess with her shoulder. "It's good you're doing something."

Jess turned to look at her friend. "What's that supposed to mean?"

Britney's face flushed. "Uh, nothing, just that gymnastics is your thing, ya know?"

"It's not *my* thing," Jess said. "It's my mom's thing." It had always been Mom's thing. She wanted Jess to have all the opportunities she didn't get. It never crossed her mind that Jess wasn't her—that she didn't care about the same things Mom cared about. But Jess hated complaining about it, especially since she lost every argument she ever started with her mother.

"Well, yeah, but you don't *really* want to quit, do you? I mean, you're really good and you can do back handsprings and stuff."

Not very well, Jess thought. Especially compared to the twelve-year-old toothpicks in her class. "You know I hate gymnastics," Jess said, disappointed that she had to remind Britney of that fact. She'd only complained to Britney about gymnastics for the last three years. "I'm the fattest girl in the class, and it's awful."

"Well, maybe you should lose weight. My mom just lost ten pounds. She could give you some tips. In track, every pound makes a difference. Lael, she's a senior, you don't know her, but she gained like six pounds last summer and lost almost two full seconds on her hundred meter."

It was Jess's turn to blush. She couldn't believe Britney was saying this. She felt tears prick her eyes. Even though Britney was perfect, cute, thin, and popular, she'd never once flaunted those things in front of Jess. Until now Jess had assumed Britney didn't really care. "I forgot something at school," Jess said quickly, turning around so Britney couldn't see the tears she couldn't seem to blink away.

"Oh," Britney said in surprise, stopping on the sidewalk. "I'd go with you, but I've got to get home and then get back to the school."

Jess hadn't stopped walking. "No big deal," she said over her shoulder, ten feet now between them. "Good luck at your meet." Her voice cracked on the last word, but she hoped she was too far away for Britney to notice.

"Thanks," Britney called back. "See you later."

Jess just nodded and kept walking. As soon as she turned the corner and was out of Britney's view, she leaned against the fence and wiped at her eyes. Some other students passed her on the sidewalk, giving her weird looks, so she hurried further down the street and ducked into the covered parking area of an apartment building. It was empty except for a few cars and an orange cat that huddled in the corner, assessing her level of threat. Apparently even it didn't want anything to do with her, and it ran out of the parking garage, disappearing into some bushes.

Jess took a breath, hoping to calm herself down, but a sob broke from her throat instead. Why didn't she have cool friends like Britney did? Why wasn't she outgoing and popular? Britney used to understand her. Jess could talk to her about anything. What had changed? How come every time they were together lately Jess felt as if Britney were doing her a favor?

She dropped her head and gave in to the tears. She hated being such a loser.

4

——Original Message——
From: jjk_hollywood@hotmail.com
To: emjenkins000@yahoo.com
Sent: Wednesday, April 12, 2:58 PM
Subject: Re: Hellooooooooooooooooo

Em,

Sorry I didn't get back to you sooner—we got new internet service and so I couldn't get online. I'm not mad at you but I'd GET mad at you for reminding me about gymnastics except that Britney already did. I'm sorry Colt is moving—I have a ton of cousins but they live all over the place and I'm not that close with many of them. I'm bummed for you big time. I wish I had a guy cousin I was close to—I bet that would make me a lot more comfortable around the boys at school.

I told Britney about you today and she got all freaked out, said you might be some kind of psycho. She also told me I'm fat and should lose weight—nice huh? I told her you were way too cool to be some weirdo. Like I wouldn't know!! Sometimes best friends are way overrated but I still hope she does okay at the meet tonight. Go Warriors!

A big family is okay. The little kids are always getting into my stuff and I have to help out a lot, but I think it will help me be a better mom one day. AND I have my own room—which none of the other kids have except Chris, but he's still a baby. So it's okay, I guess.

I've had a really lousy day, today—how about you?

Laters,
Jess

———————

He smiled as he finished reading the e-mail and opened a new browser window on his computer. In the search field he typed in Utah+high school+Warriors, then he hit Enter. It took less than five seconds for the computer to show him the first of a few hundred thousand listings that included all three words. He scanned the page and opened a link that looked promising. "Weber Warriors," he read aloud as he scanned the page. But the school wasn't in Salt Lake, and she'd mentioned a few times that it was. The Weber High School Warriors were several miles north, near the city of Ogden. He went back to the Google search and clicked another link. "Taylorsville Warriors," he read out loud, his eyes darting to the address and then to the map of Salt Lake he had open on his desk. Taylorsville was a suburb of Salt Lake. He opened the "Sports" tab on the website and clicked on "Track" from the menu options. He scanned the individual events until he found the current date: "April 12— Warriors face off against East High Leopards at the East High track— 5:00. Events will include the 100 meter dash, 200, 400 . . ." He stopped reading and laughed out loud at his success. He opened the document titled "Jess" on his computer and added this information to the growing list of details she was slowly giving him.

He was getting closer.

5

—Original Message——
From: emjenkins000@yahoo.com
To: jjk_hollywood@hotmail.com
Sent: Thursday, April 13, 4:02 PM
Subject: Britney

Jess—

ya know, you've talked about britney a lot and i'm not convinced she's as cool as u think she is. i mean she's kinda ditched u for the track team and now she's all freaked out because u e-mail me? that's just lame.

as for internet freaks, i think that's mostly just stuff parents make up. i mean i've never known anyone that's had something weird happen—but my aunt met her husband online and they are such a cute couple. he's a lot older than her, but it works out so great for them cause he can buy her great stuff and he's so much more mature than the other guys she'd date. In real life they would have never met—the computer was like destiny for them. i think online is a great way to meet people—u don't have to play games, ya know? u can just be yrself without anyone judging u. if u ask me britney is just jealous with a capital J.

i have two little brothers and a little sister and I think it stinks to be the oldest. my mom always makes me take care of them and help out and they don't have to do anything. and she acts like that's just my job, ya know, like having all these kids was my idea. i don't think our moms have any idea how lucky they r for all our help. we have so much in common. i'm so glad i found yr bored.

Em

PS—i've attached some get-to-know u questions, i can't wait to read yr answers!

————————

"You know I would love to tend her," Kate said into the phone while she stirred the spaghetti sauce she'd been simmering all day. It was the same recipe Sister Erickson had made for Enrichment—was it really three weeks ago?

"If you're sure," Julie said, still vacillating.

"Bring her over or I'll never talk to you again—I need my baby fix!" Kate said with sarcastic force.

Julie laughed. "Okay, see you in a bit. Thanks."

Kate hung up the phone. Not only was Julie her best friend, something Kate hadn't expected to find as an adult, but the friendship had rubbed off on their daughters. Britney, Julie's daughter, was more outgoing, but Jess did better in school, and their differences seemed to balance each other out perfectly. Kate glanced at the clock. Jess had come in from school and gone into the study while Kate was on the phone. The other kids would be arriving any minute. Justin was running and doing a somersault onto the couch over and over while shouting "Geronimo!" each time. She smiled at him and wiped her hands on a dish towel. She could watch him play for hours—except she'd never get anything else done if she did.

"Jess," she called out, loud enough to be heard over Justin's play.

"What?" Jess called back.

Kate kept talking while heading toward the study. "You were late getting home."

"Yeah, I forgot something. Sorry."

"Julie's bringing over baby Sheila while she takes Braxton to get his cast off. The kids will be home in a minute, and Chris will be awake as soon as they come in. Can I count on your help today?" She reached the study and stood in the doorway.

"How come I always have to be the one that helps? Why can't Caitlyn do it for once?" Jess said.

Kate lifted her eyebrows, surprised at Jess's response. Usually Jess agreed to help out; she seemed to like it. "Caitlyn is only twelve and she needs just as much help as the others do," Kate explained.

Jess pursed her lips but didn't say anything else. Kate wondered at the attitude, but decided not to dwell on it. Fifteen was just a hard age.

Taking advantage of the semi-peaceful house—a rare occurrence— Kate leaned against the door frame and watched her daughter. Jess was almost Kate's height these days—five foot six—but instead of Kate's fair complexion and blue eyes, Jess had Brad's olive skin and dark brown eyes, which were unusually striking on a redhead. Kate would have loved to have skin like that—still would. Jess had gotten her braces off two months earlier, and since getting contacts last summer, her eyes were no longer hidden behind the glasses she'd worn since she was eight. She was on her way to becoming a very pretty girl. Jess looked up to find her mother standing there.

"What are you working on?" Kate asked, eyeing the computer with something akin to trepidation. Kate had attended college when computers were still young, and she'd been too busy with other things since then to really figure them out. Brad had helped her set up an e-mail address last year, but she rarely used it. Real life took place around the kitchen sink, not the Internet.

"Homework," Jess answered.

"What homework?"

"I have to do a report on Bangladesh," Jess said, still clicking. Kate took a couple of steps closer and saw a website with all kinds of geographical information. In her day, she had to go to the library and use an encyclopedia she couldn't check out. It was amazing how times had changed.

"For what class?" Kate said, trying to open up a dialogue.

Jess looked up at her mom with an unspoken "duh" on her face. "Uh, geography, Mom."

Kate looked down, wanting to reprimand Jess for talking to her that way but not wanting a confrontation. Kate loved her kids, but thus far she was not a fan of the adolescent phase. Give her potty training or stranger anxiety any day of the week over the moodiness of a teenager. However, Jess was a lot better than most teens she knew, and Kate reminded herself of that often.

"Everything okay?" Kate asked, though she didn't expect much of an answer. Kate hadn't forgotten what fifteen was like, so caught up in yourself that the other people in your life seemed far away. In order to keep Jess engaged in the family she made a point to ask for Jess's help as often as possible. It ensured that she and Jess had continual interaction; and if nothing else, Jess would know she was needed. So far it seemed to be working. Jess was an excellent student and did her part at home without too much complaint. Most women with kids Jess's age didn't have it half so good.

"Fine. I get twenty extra credit points if I turn this report in before Friday. I really want to get it done tonight." She looked up and met Kate's eyes. "Do I have to go to gymnastics?"

"You know the answer to that," Kate said. They'd invested in gymnastics for almost a decade, and Kate kept hoping that one of these days, all the practice would pay off. She also hoped the exercise would help her oldest daughter shed the extra fifteen pounds that had plagued her since reaching puberty. Other than walking the few blocks to and from school, gymnastics was all the physical activity Jess had in a typical week. "Just because it isn't always fun, doesn't mean it's okay to quit."

"But Mo-om," Jess whined, "I'm not any good at it and I hate going—I'd rather do this report."

"You're good as long as you're trying," Kate said with a sympathetic smile. Kate would have done anything to have a mother who supported her the way she supported her own children, but she realized not knowing the alternative made it impossible for Jess, or any of the kids, to understand. "We've talked about this before—you're committed until the end of the year."

Jess's face fell, and she looked back at the computer. Jess had loved gymnastics until right around the time she started high school the previous fall. Kate talked her into giving it one more year, and though Jess didn't complain out loud, Kate knew she wished she'd been allowed to quit. It was so hard to know if Kate was doing the right thing by making her see it through, but with the year almost over, it seemed ridiculous to pull Jess out now.

Kate walked into the room and smoothed her hand over Jess's hair. Even though Kate was now happy with her own hair color—the nice dark auburn she'd prayed for all through high school—she still battled the curl. Jess's hair was just like hers had been, though Jess never made a big deal about it. She wasn't too particular on girly things like clothes and hair. "When you take a shower tomorrow morning you ought to use my new conditioner. It's been great at keeping my hair soft, and it really cuts down on the frizz."

"Okay," Jess said. Apparently surrendering the argument about gymnastics, she leaned over to pull a book out of her backpack.

"You've got a few minutes until the bus drops the kids off." Kate left the room and turned her attention to Justin, who was still playing in the living room. She knew where she stood with the little kids, and she tickled him until he was laughing so hard he could barely breathe.

The house was instantly transformed into the Thompson's House of Noise and Confusion when the three kids in elementary school came through the front door. Julie dropped Sheila off a few minutes later, and, despite the chaos, Kate's heart melted as she took Sheila out of her car seat. Julie had her two older children, Britney and Braxton, early in her marriage and then couldn't get pregnant again. At least, not until a year and a half ago, years after she had given up. Surprise! There were thirteen years between Sheila and Braxton. Sheila was six months old and perfectly content to be held and bounced while Kate and Jess helped supervise the kids with chores and homework.

"Jess, you're wonderful," Kate said, giving her oldest daughter a shoulder hug once the last of the homework was returned to the backpacks and the kids had scattered. "You can get back to your report now—but thanks for your help." Chris had awakened and was emptying magazines out of the rack by the fireplace.

"You're welcome," Jess said and hurried back to the study.

"Can I hold baby?" Justin asked when Kate finally sat down. Kate had thought he was downstairs with the other kids.

Kate looked at her four-year-old and smiled. "Sure," she said. "Come sit by me."

He scrambled onto the couch and held out his arms. Sheila was sucking on her pacifier, and it bobbed up and down as her wide blue eyes scanned their faces. She was such a mild-mannered baby. "Now let me put her in your arms. Make sure you keep this arm under her head—good." Justin smiled and stared into the baby's face. Kate drank in the nostalgia of the moment and felt her heart ache at the idea of having to give Sheila back in a little while. There was nothing like a baby.

Chris hurried over to them, and Kate hoisted him on her lap. He looked at the baby in Justin's arms with suspicion, causing Kate to laugh and squeeze him slightly. He needed a little brother or sister so he'd understand there was plenty of love to go around.

Kate didn't want too much space between Chris and the next baby—the last baby. It had been hard on Jess when Caitlyn came along. It still seemed to be hard for Jess to fit with the rest of the kids. When Jess was an adult, the years wouldn't matter so much, though the idea of Jess being a grown woman brought on a little spasm of fear. What would Kate do when all her kids grew up and left home? She couldn't imagine it.

"All done," Justin said, interrupting Kate's thoughts. She hurried to shift Chris to one side and take the baby as Justin scrambled off the couch and ran downstairs. Chris scowled at the infant now in his mother's arms and jumped down to follow his big brother, leaving Kate alone with Sheila for the moment.

Kate sat back against the couch and adjusted the baby so she was holding Sheila close against her chest. "You're just the very cutest thing in the whole world," she cooed, receiving another smile for her efforts.

Dinner was looming and she had laundry that needed to be put in the dryer, along with a dozen other things to do, but for now she just absorbed the baby—the smell, the feel, the perfection of her.

I'm so ready for one of my own, she thought to herself. A wave of warmth ran through her body. She'd been prayerful for weeks, gearing up. But she could feel that today was the day. It was time to talk to Brad.

The phone rang and Kate sighed. She'd known the peace wouldn't last very long. With Sheila still in her arms she went to the phone, scowling at the caller ID when she recognized her mother's number. Why was she calling again? She usually went three or four months without her pointless phone calls. But if she didn't answer, Mom would just keep on calling until she and Kate talked and her mother could put her conscience to rest for another few months.

Kate shifted Sheila to one arm and picked up the phone. "Hi, Mom," she said into the receiver, keeping her voice light.

"Katie," her mom said as if they were the best of friends and talked every day instead of three times a year. "I might be moving to Utah. Gary has a job offer in Ogden. Wouldn't that be great?"

Kate's stomach sank. Ogden was thirty miles north, but Kate didn't know if she was up to having her mother so close by. "Wonderful," she said. *Just wonderful.*

6

Journal entry, April 13

Remember me? Yeah, well I got in the habit of writing every day when I was working on my Faith project for Young Women's but, well . . . ya know. So what's new with me? Absolutely nothing!! Maybe that's why I don't write. I'm still the fat girl in gymnastics, the only kid at school with fluorescent hair (that doesn't dye it to be that way) and Britney and I almost never hang out now that she's on the track team. Oh well, just cause we've been best friends all our lives doesn't mean we're going to stay that way forever.

BUT I've met this way awesome girl through mybulletinbored.com. Her name is Emily and she lives in Pennsylvania. She's not Mormon, but super nice. We've been e-mailing for a few weeks. She just "gets me" ya know? We have so much in common and in some ways it's easier to be friends with her than even Britney cause I can tell her anything and it's not like she's going to tell anyone else. We talk about all kinds of things—boys, home, school. She's like really into hockey and wants to be some kind of scientist when she grows up—right up my alley! It's almost like she's an older sister I never had. It's nice to feel like someone likes me for who I am.

I'll be finishing up my Good Works project for my Young

Womanhood award, so I should get it next month. I'll be so glad to be done with it!!

Well—that's about it.

me

————

Kate was putting the finishing touches on her grocery list when she heard the garage door open. *Good,* she thought with a thrill in her stomach and a nervous smile on her face. She'd been gearing up for this conversation all afternoon, but wished the butterflies had gone to bed when the kids did. Why was she so nervous?

"Hi," she said when Brad came in.

"Hi," he replied as he set down his laptop case and shrugged out of his jacket, throwing it over the back of one of the kitchen chairs. He gave her a hello kiss that she wasn't sure even touched her lips. "How are you?" he asked.

"Good," Kate said, adding light bulbs to her list and scanning it one last time. She was sure she was forgetting something—but what? "I saved you some dinner."

"Oh, I grabbed a hamburger on the way home," he met her eye apologetically. "I should have called."

Kate smiled and shook her head. "It's not a big deal," she said.

"I'm going to that Houston conference," Brad said shaking his head and getting a drink of water. "I had so hoped they'd just pick a few people, but they're sending most of the associates."

Kate made a face. He didn't have to travel often, but he hated it when it was required. So did she. "When?"

"April 29th through May 4th. I left the paperwork at the office. But it's another one of those Sunday through Thursday conferences, which means I fly out on Saturday. I hate that."

"Me too," Kate said, sharing in the depression. It completely

destroyed the weekend leading up to it when the conference started on
Sunday, and Brad didn't like breaking the Sabbath. "How was the rest of
your day?"

Usually both of them answered that question with very few words.
Brad surprised her by telling her all about it. She did her best to pay attention but found her mind wandering, then felt guilty for it. She followed
him to the bedroom, turning off lights as they went. Once in their room
she climbed onto the bed, sat cross-legged, and smiled as Brad finished
talking about his evening while changing into his pajamas. Last summer
he'd taken up bicycling, and though he hadn't ridden much during the
winter, it had still paid off. He'd dropped fifteen of the thirty pounds he'd
gained since their marriage. She should really follow his example and
work toward getting in better shape herself. But if she were going to have
another baby, it didn't make sense to lose the weight now.

"And how was your day?" Brad asked as he pulled a T-shirt from the
closet.

She had planned to bring up the baby conversation right away, but
was suddenly nervous, so she quickly thought of something else to talk
about. "My mom called. She might be moving to Ogden. Gary has a final
interview with a company out here."

"Really?"

Kate shrugged and picked at the bedspread, "I'll believe it when I
see it."

"I think she wants to be closer to you," Brad offered. "She's getting
older. It's not such a surprise that she's wondering what she's done with
her life."

Kate shrugged again, pretending it didn't matter. Her mom, Joy, was a
real estate agent, first in Utah when Kate was growing up and now in
Oregon, where she'd moved a few years ago with her latest husband. She
was very successful in her career, and though Kate's father had been a
bum, Joy's next three husbands had been relatively good guys. She also

looked wonderful for her age, which was very important to her, but when it came to the things that made a difference—children and family—they'd always been at the bottom of her list. Kate had grown up knowing that if her mom could relive her life, Kate wouldn't be part of it at all. But Kate had made her peace with that a long time ago . . . at least she'd tried to.

"She spent my childhood pushing me away. I don't feel like I need her anymore." As soon as she said the words, she knew they came out too harsh. She looked up at Brad, waiting for him to make a comment. She reminded herself that Mom had done the best she could, just as Kate was doing now. Kate could only hope that her best would be a *lot* better than her mother's ever was.

Brad pulled the T-shirt over his head and didn't respond. She searched for a new subject to discuss. "I got to watch Julie's baby today."

Brad accepted the not-so-subtle change of subject and smiled at her knowingly as he smoothed the shirt over his stomach. "I bet you loved that."

Kate nodded. "I did. In fact, it got me thinking . . ." Her voice trailed off as she looked at him, a huge smile on her face.

Brad paused in the process of stepping into his pajama bottoms and looked at her. "You've got to be kidding."

Kate lifted her eyebrows and felt her smile falter. She'd prepared herself for some hesitation, but not hostility. "What?"

"Please tell me you're not saying you want another baby."

Kate tried to laugh off his attitude. "What's so bad about that?"

Brad let out a breath and pulled his pajama pants on. "Do we live in the same house? The mere idea of throwing another baby into the mix fills me with unmitigated dread."

"Funny," Kate said in response to his sarcasm. "What about that big family we always wanted?"

"We've got it," Brad said as he plopped into bed, causing her to bounce a few times. His face turned serious. "After last time . . ." he said, his voice softer. He looked away, then met her eyes again. "I thought this decision was made."

"Well, we certainly haven't made any *absolute* decisions, you know that, the last time we talked you didn't shoot it down."

"I guess it's been awhile since we discussed this," he said in a tone that communicated the fact he'd rather they still weren't talking about it. "The doctor was very clear about what to expect should you get pregnant again, and as far as I'm concerned, that's all I need to know. It's not worth the risk."

"It was one doctor, and he only said there was a *chance* I'd get toxemia again."

"A chance is too much," Brad said with resolution. He put his arms behind his head. "And we have six kids already—six wonderful, happy, healthy kids."

"We've always wanted seven."

Brad looked at her, his expression sympathetic and yet determined at the same time. "Just because there are seven in my family doesn't mean we have to have the same number."

Kate shrugged, feeling talked down to. She still wanted seven.

Brad continued, "I don't think you can possibly understand how scary that was for me. You could have died."

"But I didn't even come close, and lots of women get toxemia." He didn't say anything when she stopped talking, so she continued, meeting his eyes, hoping he would see in hers just how badly she wanted this. "You *really* don't want another baby?"

"It's not about wanting anything," Brad said. "It's about making reasonable decisions. But, now that you mention it—things *are* nice right now, Kate. Chris sleeps all night, Jess is almost old enough to drive—why mess with that?"

"Because of those very things," Kate said. Maybe his hesitations were a sign of his lack of faith in her ability to handle it, rather than just concerns about the pregnancy itself. Maybe if she could convince him she was up to it, he'd change his mind. "Jess is such an incredible help, and Chris is getting older and more independent. God's given us one window of opportunity to have children, and it's running out." She sensed he wasn't happy with her answer when he looked away.

"It seems to me that God closed that window when the doctor told us not to have more children, Kate." He looked back at her. "I really thought you felt that way too. I figured that's why you haven't brought it up."

Kate blinked, and searched for what to say next. How could she make him understand how important this was to her?

Brad spoke before she could come up with a rebuttal. "We've been commanded not to run faster than we have strength, and I feel our obligation is to the kids we have."

"Yes," Kate said, bristling at the absoluteness of his last comment. "But I feel there is one more of *them* up there."

Brad let out a breath of frustration and got up from the bed. He turned to the window while she followed him with her eyes. "Kate," was all he said. Nothing more, but in her mind everything else he'd just said cycled through. She really hadn't expected this and wished she'd prepared some better responses to his concerns.

She got out of bed and walked over to stand behind him, wrapping her arms around his waist. He covered her hands with his own, and she rested her chin on his shoulder, staring out the window with him and trying not to panic. The wind was blowing the swings back and forth, and she watched the rhythm and tried to relax.

"Let us get a second opinion," she whispered. "I'll find a specialist."

He didn't respond.

"Please, Brad," she begged. "I understand what you're saying, but I can't give up this easily. My family is everything to me, and I'm aching for one more baby."

Brad remained silent for several seconds; then he let out a breath of surrender. "Someone that will be honest," Brad said, as if he feared she'd pay off an OB/GYN to lie about something like this. "But you need to know, Kate, that right now, I'm against this."

How could she be so sure and he feel so differently? She wondered if perhaps she was wrong. Was she confusing spiritual impressions with her own desires? But she chose to focus on the fact that he'd agreed to a second opinion. That was something.

Brad turned in her arms, facing her, his arms resting on her waist—or what used to be her waist anyway. "Not everyone gets everything they wish for, Kate. Maybe you need to make peace with that."

Kate swallowed, trying to adjust to his feelings while keeping them at arm's length. She just couldn't believe she was finished having children. "But we'll get a second opinion before we decide," she reminded him. "I respect your feelings, Brad, but I'm aware of my responsibilities to this family. I don't make this decision lightly."

He pulled her to him, so that her face rested against his chest. She had the feeling he didn't believe her. But she knew she was right about this; she could feel it. Somehow she'd have to help him feel it, too.

7

——Original Message——
From: emjenkins000@yahoo.com
To: jjk_hollywood@hotmail.com
Sent: Monday, April 17, 10:15 PM
Subject: Take my cousin please!!

Jess,

i'm so depressed. i can't believe colt is gone already, it happened so fast.
i wish u knew him, he's such a great guy. i'm worried about him down
there all by himself, and so i had a question for ya. i wonder what u'd
think of e-mailing with him? he's going to college in the fall so he's not
real motivated to make friends for the last few months of school, but
knowing both of u the way i do i just know u guys could be great
friends and i talk about u so much that he feels like he knows u already.
u always say how yr nervous around guys—this might be just the ticket
for u to get used to talking to one. he's really cool and i'm kinda worried
about him, ya know?

please, please, please, please, please—it would make me soooooooooooo
happy. his e-mail address is coltinator_51@yahoo.com and i know he'd
love to hear from u.

anyway—i was thinking some more about britney. have u ever thought
that maybe she doesn't take the time to know u anymore? like because
u've been friends for so long she just expects that u'll always be there?
but then again if she wasn't totally snobbing u, maybe u wouldn't have

time for little ol' me. i couldn't handle that. u're like one of the best friends i've ever had and britney's an idiot to not see how totally awesome u are. there's just something special about u. i can't believe she doesn't see that. i feel like I've known u forever. oh, why can't u live in pennsylvania? (r u tired of me saying that yet :))

what's your mommy dearest making u do for her today? :) i swear u should get paid for everything u do to help her out.

Emily

———————

Monique Weatherford stared out her kitchen window. It was a beautiful spring day, but she busied herself with other things to keep from thinking too much about what the day meant. She made breakfast for her husband, the silence stretching between them like ice on Lake Michigan in winter. Perhaps words would be strong enough for them to walk across that ice, meeting in the middle, but did they dare risk it? The words had been dwindling these last few months until there was simply nothing more to say. Today, especially, offered no reprieve.

Harrison left for work, and Monique let out a sigh of relief to be alone again. Alone was easier these days than together could possibly be. Monique cleaned the kitchen, moved on to the laundry, and then got into the shower. She'd taken a part-time job at the library a few months earlier. It wasn't fancy—she just shelved books. But no one tried to talk to her there, other than asking if she knew what aisle they would find *Sushi for Dummies* or some other hard-to-catalog book. It was too hard to stay home alone all day . . . waiting. She'd considered asking for today off, but then she would have to explain why, and she didn't know what she'd say. Again, the words might support her, but then again, they might not.

She patted her hair dry, the tiny braids falling to her shoulders, parted down the middle. The hair closest to her scalp was getting nappy and outgrown. She'd need to go get her hair done soon. She stared at her round face in the mirror, dark eyes framed by a chocolate complexion, and remembered this day one year ago—the last birthday. She was glad she'd made such a big deal of it.

"Where are we going?" Terrezza had asked after Monique picked her up from school and they didn't head toward home. They'd had a difficult year, but Monique was determined to believe the worst was behind them and make the most of the day.

"You're sixteen years old," Monique had said with a broad smile. "Sixteen and never been kissed."

"Mo-om," Terrezza said, looking out the window.

"Pretend with me, please."

Terrezza laughed—that boisterous laugh too big for her body that made it impossible for people not to smile with her. "Okay, for you I'm sixteen and never been kissed. So where are we going?"

"Raquel's."

Terrezza's eyes went wide. "Raquel's?" she repeated. "No way!"

"Way," Monique said. "You can get whatever new style you want— maybe those long braids you've been wanting. You can even get those blonde streaky things if you want. And a pedicure." Personally, Monique thought blonde looked odd on women of color, but a woman's hair reflected her mood or personality. At sixteen, Terrezza was old enough to appreciate that. If she thought blonde streaks helped tell the world a little about her, Monique was willing to give in. She usually braided Terrezza's hair herself—but not this time. Perhaps never again, now that her baby was so grown up.

"Holy cow!" Terrezza squealed. "Really?"

"My baby is sixteen. In a few more years you'll be gone, and I'll have the house to myself—it's something to celebrate, don't you think!"

Monique's blood ran cold at the memory of those words as she stared into the sink. She told herself that Terrezza had known she was kidding—

they joked that way all the time. But it still sat in her stomach like a stone. The year leading up to that birthday had been a doozy. Terrezza had fallen in with some bad friends, was arrested for shoplifting, and was suspended for having marijuana at school. Monique had quit her job as manager of a jewelry store so she'd be home more often.

But even with Monique home, Terrezza was cutting school. She even ran away one weekend, throwing Monique and Harrison into an all-out panic. But she came home two days later, was grounded for three weeks, and promised she'd never do it again. Things got better, and her sixteenth birthday had been a day of gratitude for both parents. Terrezza was back on track and doing great.

Or so they thought. Eight months later, with things getting tense between her and her parents again, Terrezza went to the mall and never came home. Her car was found the next day with a note saying she needed a time-out and had gone to Danyelle's. They didn't know a Danyelle, and they hadn't heard from Terrezza since that day. No phone call, no clues. She was gone.

Monique looked at her reflection in the bathroom mirror again and said what she said nearly every morning. "I would do anything," she whispered. "Anything to have you home again."

The words melted into the walls. No one answered back. Terrezza had been gone four months and eight days. Though the police had done some looking around, they lost interest quickly. Terrezza had a history, and everyone—even Monique and Harrison—had to admit that in all likelihood she'd run away again.

And yet, it didn't feel right. She'd been doing better. And none of her friends—not even the loser ones—knew where she might have gone. She was gone for Christmas, New Year's, and now Easter and her seventeenth birthday.

Monique finished her morning routine and left for work, almost disappointed that she wasn't any more depressed today than she had been yesterday. Maybe depression itself had limits.

At a staff meeting that afternoon the employees were asked to write up a one-page job description. It was necessary for some grant the library was applying for. Monique took notes, finished her shift, and returned to her empty house, wishing the other kids were still living at home.

Jamie, their oldest, lived in New York and worked at a bank while attending NYU. She rarely called home anymore. Karl, the proverbial middle child, was living with friends across town, drinking too much, and threatening to marry his girlfriend. He'd been attending Ann Arbor with a major in computer science but dropped out after Terrezza's disappearance. Each of them was trying to make sense of what had happened to their family—each of them avoiding one another as if to ignore the reminder of what they'd lost. It wasn't that they had ever been particularly close, but whatever bonds they did have seemed to have dissolved as the weeks and months since Terrezza's disappearance passed them by.

Monique wasn't hungry and had no one to cook for, so she sat down at the computer to type up the job description. It took several seconds to figure out how to even turn the thing on. Terrezza had been the computer administrator in their home. Monique had heard once that her generation were like technology immigrants, whereas her children's generation were natives. She had no doubt that was true. The kids could make the computer do amazing things. Monique was lucky if she could find the print command all by herself. When she managed the jewelry store she avoided most of the technology, leaving that to the younger employees. Since working at the library she'd had to become more comfortable with a keyboard, but it was still intimidating.

She opened Microsoft Word and was reminded why she avoided *this* computer specifically. Terrezza was still in it. Her files were there—titles like "If I Had Pink Eyebrows, What Would They Say?" which had been an assignment for her creative writing course. There was something titled

"Buddhism in the Modern World" for her world studies class and one titled "The Fibula Connected to the Patella" that must have been biology related. Terrezza had always had a way with words—and the files still waiting in the computer attested to it. Monique told herself not to, but she couldn't help it. She clicked on a report titled "Appendicitis"—it was a report Monique didn't remember Terrezza working on. She wanted to hear her daughter's voice through the words of her silly report, remember that Terrezza had once had a life full of mundane topics to stress about. Where was she now? What was she doing? Was she thinking about home today?

Monique furrowed her eyebrows when the document opened. It had nothing to do with appendicitis. In fact, it looked like instructions for some kind of computer program. Why was it in a document titled "Appendicitis"?

She told herself she didn't know enough about computers to warrant concern—but she couldn't help it. She hurried to the kitchen and picked up the phone, calling her son's cell number. It went to his voice mail.

"Hi, Karl, I wondered if you could come help me with the computer. I found something that looks kind of weird. . . . Uh, . . . anyway, give me a call."

8

——Original Message——
From: jjk_hollywood@hotmail.com
To: emjenkins000@yahoo.com
Sent: Tuesday, April 18, 1:50 PM
Subject: Re: Take my cousin please!!

Em—

Now, tell me the truth, is Colt a total nerd? Not that I'm NOT a nerd, but still. Is he super annoying? I have five little brothers and sisters—I have no more room for annoying in my life!! But if he's not totally lame, then yeah, it might be fun. I know you two are really close, so that's a good thing. I've never e-mailed with a guy before. I've GOT to get a new picture for my bored!! You haven't showed him my old one have you? If he sees my picture he won't want anything to do with me.

I'm in Computers and I only have a minute so if I just stop typing you'll know that the teachers ba

———

Jess hit send and swallowed as Mr. Paxton crossed to his desk. She hadn't seen him come back in and could feel his eyes on her. Had he seen her send the e-mail? She didn't dare look up. She quickly closed her e-mail program and went back to the project she was working on, building a website. After almost a minute she felt herself relaxing. If he hadn't said anything by now, she must have gotten away with it. She felt a little thrill of victory, even if her heart was still racing at the mere consideration of getting caught.

Jess finished her project a few minutes later, and raised her hand so that Mr. Paxton would check it on his computer. It was ironic that Spyware, the big, bad threat of Internet users everywhere, was put to consensual use here in school. It allowed Mr. Paxton to keep vigilance over every computer in the lab. After a minute an IM popped up—that's how Mr. Paxton communicated with his students.

> **Mr. P:** Good site, but if you use class time for personal
> e-mails again I will put you on a blocked computer.

Jess felt her cheeks heat up and she looked around as if he'd said everything out loud. There were two blocked computers at the far side of the room. They were specifically designed to keep kids from getting online, and only troublemakers—kids that looked up porn or abused their Internet privileges—were sent there. She swallowed her embarrassment and wondered what she should do. Jess had never gotten in trouble in class before. Should she pretend she didn't know what he was talking about? Should she apologize? Picturing herself sitting at a blocked computer, with everyone smirking at her, caused her heart to race all over again. Another IM message popped up.

> **Mr. P:** Do you understand?

Jess swallowed again and held back the tears, reprimanding herself for being such a baby. Most kids got in trouble all the time. They'd just roll their eyes or shrug their shoulders. Why couldn't she be like that? Why did she have to feel things so much? She hurried to reply before he had to ask her again. He must think she was such an idiot.

> **JessT:** I understand, I'm so sorry. I promise I'll never do it
> again.

She barely had time to take a breath before he wrote back again.

Mr. P: Good. You're an excellent student, Jessica, I expect better from you.

Now she felt even worse. She looked up and could see Britney watching her from her computer across the room. "What's going on?" Britney mouthed, but Jess just looked away, trying to duck behind her computer monitor so that Britney couldn't see her face.

JessT: Okay. I'm sorry.

When the bell rang a minute later, Jess bolted for the door, wanting to put as much distance between her and Mr. Paxton as possible.

"Jess," Britney called. Jess had already cleared the classroom. A hand grabbed her arm. Jess stopped but didn't turn around; she probably looked like a total nerd for hurrying out of the classroom so fast. She felt tears come to her eyes again. *Not now,* she told herself. *Not in front of Britney.* She blinked quickly and for once wished Britney was off with her new friends somewhere. She was ignoring Jess more and more all the time— why not now?

"What's going on?" Britney asked.

Jess had no choice but to turn around, but she wouldn't meet Britney's eyes. She tugged at the hem of her T-shirt. "Nothing," she said, looking at the ground.

"Jess," Britney said in a tone that sounded so much like Jess's mom that Jess looked up. "Your face was like beet red," Britney said, a laugh in her voice. Jess felt her cheeks heat up again. "And I've known you for, like, forever, so what happened?"

"I just sent an e-mail. Mr. P caught me."

Britney laughed again and Jess wanted to melt through the floor. "Is that all?" she rolled her eyes. "Everyone messes around when he leaves the room—it's one of the perks of being online in the middle of the day."

Jess just nodded. She knew other people broke the rules, but she didn't know anyone that had been caught. Was she the only one stupid enough to be noticed? Was she once again out of the loop like she always was?

"What did he say to you?" Britney asked. She started walking and Jess walked with her, though she really wanted to be alone.

"He said he would put me on a blocked computer if I did it again."

"Are you serious?" Britney said, and Jess began to feel like maybe Britney was being sympathetic. But then Britney laughed again.

"What's so funny?"

Jess and Britney both swung their heads around at the same moment. Nick Tolson was walking behind them, hurrying to catch up. He was a junior, totally ripped and with long brown hair. He was on the basketball and track teams and lots of girls said they only went to the games and meets to watch him. It just so happened that because Jess took so many advanced classes, Nick was in three of them—including her computer class. Jess sat just two desks away from him, not that he'd ever noticed her before. Jess tried to stand up straighter, hating how she felt like such a frump next to Britney.

"Mr. P caught Jess sending an e-mail. He said if she does it again she'll get a blocked computer." Jess tried to smile, as if she thought it was kind of cool to get in trouble. But then Britney finished. "Would that be hilarious? Jess over there in a corner all by herself."

Nick laughed. Britney laughed. Jess was frozen. Britney was making fun of her? Nick saved her from having to respond by ignoring her completely. He looked at Britney, "Are you coming to Spring Fling with us?"

"Oh yeah," Britney said, flashing her beauty queen smile. "I'm totally there."

"Sweet," Nick said, and passed them by, calling out to someone farther down the hall. Britney turned back to Jess as if nothing had happened. "Well, I better hurry to my next class," Britney said, already moving down the hall. "Catch ya later, Jess."

Jess just stood there. It took all her energy to keep from crying. Kids rushed by, hurrying to class, and she reviewed what had just happened. Was Emily right about Britney? Was Jess holding onto a friendship that had played itself out already? The thought gave her a pit in her stomach, but she couldn't ignore what had just happened. Jess would never have done something like that to Britney. Never. And Britney was going to Spring Fling with Nick Tolson? Neither Britney nor Jess were sixteen yet. They used to whine about the fact that they'd never get to go to dances their sophomore year thanks to their families' rules about not dating before sixteen. But Britney was going?

The bell rang and broke the spell of self-recrimination. Jess hurried down the hall, around the corner, and into her next class. At the doorway of the classroom she realized she hadn't stopped at her locker to get her book, which meant she was unprepared. But she was already late and the teacher had seen her; in fact, the entire class was looking at her standing in the doorway.

"Jessica Thompson," the teacher said, smiling at her sarcastically as Jess's face grew hot for the third time in ten minutes. Nick Tolson was in this class too, and he smirked, leaned over to a friend, and whispered something. Jess had no doubt it was about her. "How nice of you to join us," the teacher continued. "Why don't we start by having you work out this equation on the board?"

9

——Original Message——
From: jjk_hollywood@hotmail.com
To: emjenkins000@yahoo.com
Sent: Tuesday, April 18, 2:55 PM
Subject: You'll never believe what happened!!

Em—

Today was like the worst day of my life, you'll never believe what
Britney did to me. I so wish you lived here, that we went to the same
school. It's so not fair. But I think you were right about her. She was so
rude to me today. It happened after computer . . .

———————

Hey, Jess," Kate said when Jess entered the kitchen. She'd immediately gone into the study when she got home from school and Kate
was surprised she was out so soon. Sometimes Kate worried Jess was on
the computer too much, but they had a really good virus blocker thing
installed when they got the new Internet hookup and that made her feel a
lot better. And with all the advanced courses Jess took, she was always
loaded with homework. Kate wondered if she should cut back on the
forty-five minutes of free time.

Kate didn't look up from the dough she was shaping into rolls. The
kids would be home any minute, and she wanted to get the rolls covered
and out of the way before they came in. Honestly, it was like opening the

floodgates when they got off the bus. Not that she minded, but it did necessitate a certain amount of forethought. When Jess didn't answer, Kate looked up at her daughter. "Everything okay?"

Jess went to the fridge. "Yeah," she said. But something was off in her tone and Kate furrowed her brow. So many teenage emotions to try to make sense of. Poor Jess.

"Are you sure?" Kate asked. She shaped the last roll, covered the pan with a flour sack towel, and put the pan on top of the stove. She washed her hands while waiting for Jess to respond. When she didn't, Kate tried again. "Is there some secret password that will get you to open up?" she asked playfully.

Jess looked over her shoulder and met Kate's eyes. "Open Sesame," Kate said, making a popcorn-popping-on-the-apricot-trees motion. The water from her freshly washed hands splashed, causing Jess to pull back. "Or Abracadabra or maybe chocolate cake." She smiled at her own humor, but Jess looked at her like she had flowers growing out of her head and turned back to the fridge. Maybe that kind of thing didn't work so well with teenagers. So then, what did?

Jess finally turned back and shut the fridge with her foot, a yogurt in her hand. Kate opened the silverware drawer and handed Jess a spoon. "What's the matter?" she asked, choosing the direct approach over the cute one this time.

Jess looked up at her with an expression that almost convinced Kate she was going to say something. "You know you can tell me anything, right?" Kate kept her face soft and open so as to be encouraging. She also fervently prayed that whatever Jess had to say would be something she could answer. But just as Jess opened her mouth the front door burst open.

"Mom!" Keith yelled. "Justin fell on his scooter and he's all bloody!"

"What?" Kate said. Justin had been downstairs watching cartoons only fifteen minutes earlier. She untied her apron as she ran for the door, remembering that Justin had been asking to ride his scooter all afternoon and Kate had kept telling him she'd go outside with him in a minute. Apparently the minutes had dragged on too long.

Sure enough, he was in the driveway screaming his head off—she wondered why she hadn't heard him from the house. She scooped him up and hurried back inside, trying to calm him down and convince Keith that his brother's leg did not need to be amputated while Caitlyn and Sharla trailed behind her. By the time he was bandaged up and the other kids were calmed down, Chris was awake. Kate fed the toddler, supervised homework time, continued to comfort Justin, and before she knew it an hour had passed and it was almost time to leave for Keith's karate. That was when she remembered Jess.

"Jess," she called, feeling horrible that their moment had been interrupted. She checked the study, but Jess wasn't there. She hurried downstairs, while hollering for Keith to get ready. They needed to leave in five minutes. The door to Jess's room was closed and Kate couldn't hear any sound behind it. She turned the doorknob quietly and pushed the door open a few inches. Jess was on her bed, the covers pulled up to her chin, her face toward the wall. Kate opened her mouth to say something, but then realized from the rhythmic breathing that Jess was asleep. She cocked her head to the side sympathetically and then pulled the door closed. On her way back upstairs, she made a mental note to find a chance to talk to Jess later.

"Caitlyn," Kate said as she got to the top of the stairs. "You get to watch the kids today while I take Keith to karate, okay."

"Really?" Caitlyn said, her eyes lighting up. "You'll let me?"

Kate was surprised by the reaction, but remembered Jess being similarly excited when Kate had started leaving her with the kids a few years ago. She wasn't nearly as excited these days. Kate hadn't even considered having the two older girls take turns. Caitlyn wasn't nearly as responsible as Jess was, but it was time she learned. Kate had often felt that Jess was responsible because as the oldest child she'd always had responsibilities. Surely that same theory could be applied to all the kids.

"It's about time," Kate said with a smile. "Don't you think?"

"Yes," Caitlyn said, punching the air. She turned to Sharla and made a prima-donna face. "Now you guys have to do everything I say."

Kate scowled. *Maybe this wasn't such a good idea.*

10

From: emjenkins000@yahoo.com

To: jjk_hollywood@hotmail.com

Sent: Tuesday, April 18, 8:15 PM

Subject: Re: You'll never believe what happened!!

Jess—

britney is totally lame. do u want me to come down there and bust her kneecaps—or better yet her nose? then maybe she'll realize she isn't so perfect. that totally sucks she did that to u. i told u she was lame. i'd do anything to be there right now. we could make a list of 100 things to hate about britney. i'm so sorry. did you e-mail colt yet? i promise he'll make u feel so much better!

Em

———

Jess's first piano teacher had told her that she'd be fresher and able to concentrate better if she practiced her piano in the mornings. That was nine years ago and even though Jess had been through three teachers since then, she liked doing piano first thing—and after so many years, the other kids slept through it. Last week her teacher had assigned her to learn *Rhapsody in Blue* by George Gershwin; it would be her recital piece next month. It was hard, but she was making progress. It was fun to be good enough to play pieces like this.

She heard Mom get up a few minutes into her practicing and start moving around in the kitchen behind her. Jess's piano was Mom's alarm clock. After a little while Jess could smell pancakes. She looked over her shoulder to verify that her nose was not deceiving her. Mom never made pancakes on a school day.

The timer on the microwave dinged, announcing that her practice time was over, and Mom turned it off. Jess finished the line she was on, then turned off the piano light and got up. She was still in her pajamas and didn't need a mirror to tell her that her hair was a mess.

"You're sure making progress on that piece," Mom said, smiling—but in a contrived way that made Jess distrustful. None of the other kids were up yet, and Jess kind of wished they were. She didn't want to talk about yesterday anymore and had a feeling that's what the pancakes were all about.

Mom took two golden pancakes from the griddle and put them on a plate. Jess's stomach growled and Mom smiled. Jess considered saying she wasn't hungry so as not to be tricked into saying anything, but she loved pancakes. She sat down and Mom put the plate in front of her.

"So," Mom said, sitting down across from Jess with her own plate. "What happened yesterday?"

Jess shrugged, but she was tempted. She remembered when she was little and would climb up on Mom's lap and listen to stories, or the time in third grade when she accidentally swore at a kid at school and the teacher sent a note home. Mom had gotten mad at first, but then Jess had started crying and Mom held her for a long time, at least until one of the little kids interrupted them. Jess liked those memories, but they seemed like a long time ago. Mom was busier now; she had more kids. Jess didn't think what she had to say was very important, and it was hard not to think Mom would feel the same way. And yet, Mom *had* made pancakes.

"Come on, Jess," Mom said. "You seemed upset."

"Well," Jess said, pouring syrup on her pancake but not meeting Mom's eye. Then she looked up, and the next thing she knew she was telling Mom what happened. She told her what Britney did, about being late for class—everything. She didn't cry though, and she was glad for that. When she finished, Mom was nodding.

"I'm so sorry that happened," Mom said, but her voice had a diplomatic tone to it and Jess felt misgivings about having said anything at all. "But I'm sure that Britney didn't mean it like that. She *is* your best friend, Jess. I'm sure it was just some kind of misunderstanding." She paused and took another bite of her pancake. Jess couldn't believe what she was hearing even though it had been exactly what she'd expected. Mom swallowed the bite and continued. "I mean, in the halls with so much happening, it's hard to interpret things." Then she looked at Jess with a different expression. "What concerns me the most is that you would be sending e-mails in class—why would you do something like that?"

Jess felt a fire in her stomach. How could she be so stupid as to tell her mom anything? She should have known she would never understand. She looked back at her plate and shoveled the rest of her breakfast into her mouth. All Mom cared about was Jess being the good girl, doing what she was supposed to do. Well, maybe Jess was tired of living her life for everyone else. Maybe she was tired of being nerdy and frumpy and so thoroughly out of it.

"Jess," Mom said. "I asked you a question. Why would you break the rules and who were you e-mailing anyway?"

Jess looked up and scowled at her mother, but Mom didn't even flinch. "Never mind," she said, standing up. "I shouldn't have even told you."

Mom stood up too. "Of course you should. You can always talk to me."

"Talk to you?" Jess said. "So that you can get mad at me?"

"I didn't get mad, I just—"

"Forget it," Jess said, heading for the stairs. "I need to take a shower." She hurried away before Mom could say anything else. Emily was so right. No one else cared.

11

Jessica Thompson
English, 6th hour
Limerick in 5 minutes Assignment
April 19

There once was a girl with red hair
Who wondered if she was still there
When others walked by
She started to cry
Cause life, it just wasn't fair

C- *A limerick is supposed to be funny, Jessica, not sad. These
timed assignments are tough. Better luck next time.

_____

A C-minus?" Sarah said, shaking her head and making her glasses wobble. Jess knew from years of four-eyed experience that Sarah needed to get the frames tightened, but she didn't say so. Sarah wasn't the type that cared. Sarah's goal in life was Harvard, and she couldn't care less what people thought of her so long as she eventually got a scholarship. Jess ate lunch with her and some of the other smart kids from her classes almost every day now that Britney had her other friends. Jess wished she had half of Sarah's confidence. "I used the same limerick I wrote in 7th grade and got an A." She rolled her eyes. "It was about a fly that gets attracted to some honey—you know, like that saying, 'You catch more flies with honey.' Want to hear it?"

"Sure," Jess said, taking another bite of her lasagna while wondering if she'd ever gotten a C- on anything before today. Sarah only got to the second word of her limerick before Britney suddenly appeared on the bench next to Jess, with her lunch and everything. Sarah shut her mouth and scowled. She had no patience for the snobby kids, and she'd told Jess more than once that she considered Britney a snob. Lately, Jess had started agreeing with her.

"Hey, Jess," Britney said, smiling widely. Her hair was all curly, the top pulled away from her face. She was so pretty. Britney looked across at Sarah. "Hi, Sarah."

"Hey," Sarah said. She scooted her tray closer to Clarisse, who was talking to Mike, effectively abandoning Jess.

Jess braced herself. She had gone to school early so as not to have to walk with Britney and then made a point of ignoring her at school.

"You okay?" Britney asked as she opened her brown lunch sack. Britney always brought lunch from home. She said school lunch was too fattening. Jess glanced at their thighs, pressed against the bench. Hers were easily twice the width of Britney's. Maybe Britney was right about school lunch. Then again, who cared if Jess was skinny?

Jess just shrugged.

"What's the matter?"

Jess considered her options. She could pretend everything was fine, like she normally would, she could just be snotty until Britney figured it out, or she could be direct and get it over with—something that went completely contrary to her nature. She asked herself what Emily would do, and that gave her confidence. She took a breath, but didn't make eye contact—that was too much. "You can honestly tell me you don't know?"

53

"I honestly can," Britney said, her voice contrite. "You've never been like this to me before."

"Yeah, well, you've never made fun of me in front of someone else before either. And you didn't even notice?" Jess shook her head and took another bite of lasagna while Britney processed the comment.

"Jess, what are you talking about?"

Jess finally looked up at her. "Yesterday—after computer class—Nick. Ring a bell?"

"You mean when I said you'd get sent to the blocked computer if you sent another e-mail? You're mad I told him you got in trouble?"

"No, when you said 'Wouldn't that be hilarious? Jess over there in the corner all by herself.' You might as well have said 'Hi, this is my loser friend Jess' and in front of Nick Tolson, of all people." She shook her head. "I would never do that to you."

"Jess," Britney said, her voice whining. "I didn't mean it like that. I only meant that since you're the smartest kid in the class it would be so ironic if you of all people ended up on the blocked computer. I wasn't making fun of you."

"Yes, you were," Jess said. "It was embarrassing, especially in front of *him*. He didn't even know I existed until then, but now he knows I'm a big nerd."

"Nick?" Britney asked. "He knows you exist. He said it's his goal to beat you on the next math test—he even knows your student number, 161, because it's the only number that's always ahead of his on the score sheet Mr. Knox posts after every test. He says it's cool that you're so smart."

Jess turned to look at her in surprise. Someone, let alone Nick Tolson, thought she was cool? "Really?"

Britney smiled. "Yeah, he thinks it's amazing that a sophomore beats every junior and senior in that class. He knew what I meant when I said that about the blocked computer—you can even ask him. But I swear I didn't mean to be rude."

Jess went back to her meal, unsure what to do next. But the success of being so open gave her the confidence to continue. "Ya know, Brit, I'm real good at school and all, but I still feel like a little kid when it comes to making friends and stuff. You're like this super popular girl and I'm this red-headed nerd. It really hurts when you rub it in, especially to your new friends."

Britney put her arm around Jess's shoulder and gave her a hug. "I'm so sorry," she said softly, her voice all sweet and syrupy. "I really didn't mean to make you feel bad, and I'm *not* super popular—not by a long shot. I'm like the slowest girl on track, and it's so embarrassing." She dropped her arm from Jess's shoulder and went back to her sandwich.

Britney was bad at something? Jess didn't believe it. "But you know how to talk to people and everyone likes you."

"Everyone likes you too, Jess, but you're really shy and you don't involve yourself very much."

Yep, I'm a loser. "I don't know how."

"Just be Jess," Britney said with a bright smile. "You're my best friend, Jess, 'cause you're awesome. You're funny and nice and cute."

Jess made a face. She knew the cute part wasn't true. She was a loooong way from cute. Britney continued. "But you don't let people know you, and if you did, they would all love you like I do."

Britney made a good point. Jess *was* shy and she didn't include herself. But when Emily e-mailed her she'd been herself and Emily really liked her. Maybe Britney was right—but it was still hard to forgive her so easily.

"In fact," Britney said, "you heard Nick talk about Spring Fling, right?"

Oh, good, Jess thought, *she was going to rub that in too. Some apology.*

"Well, see, it's this big group of kids, mostly sophomores but some juniors too. Most of us are on the track team, but we're inviting a bunch of friends cause some are like me, not sixteen yet, and can't go on a real date. So we're all going to the dance together, just friends, and Jenny Lunt, she has like this huge house and her parents are going to borrow a bunch of tables from their church so we can have a big dinner there."

Jess turned to look at her. "And your mom's letting you go?"

Britney nodded. "She talked to Jenny's parents and everything, but she insisted on driving me to the dinner, then from the dinner to the dance." She paused and rolled her eyes. "I know, so lame, but at least I get to go. We're going to get a big group picture and maybe if you came, you and I could get our own picture together, you know Best Friends Forever—our first high-school dance."

"You're inviting me?" Jess said in shock. "Your friends are okay with that?"

"Well, yeah," Britney said. "Girls are inviting girls and boys are inviting boys, so there's no dates-on-the-sly, ya know, and I want you to be the person I invite." She grabbed Jess's arm and smiled wide. "Our first dance—wouldn't that be awesome?"

12

——Original Message——
From: jjk_hollywood@hotmail.com
To: emjenkins000@yahoo.com
Sent: Thursday, April 20, 5:46 AM
Subject: dance

Emily,

Update: Britney apologized. I totally ignored her yesterday and so when
she asked me what was wrong I told her. She felt really bad and said
she was sorry. I was glad—I mean I totally get what you mean when you
say she doesn't understand me, cause I know she doesn't, but without
you living closer I need some friends around here, right? And my mom,
she makes me so mad! I was so close to telling her what happened
Tuesday but BIG SURPRISE we got interrupted. Then yesterday morning
she tried again, and I told her and BIG SURPRISE she ended up getting
mad at me!!! She like totally defended Britney and said I misunderstood
her and got mad that I sent an e-mail during class time. You're right—
she so doesn't get me.

So I took your word for it and e-mailed Colt those get to know you
questions you sent me awhile back—with my answers of course. I hope
he e-mails back but I totally understand if he doesn't. I mean I am a
sophomore and the picture on my bored still shows my braces. I REALLY
need a new picture. If he says anything to you, tell me okay? I'm so
nervous.

Britney is going to Spring Fling with a bunch of other kids. Spring Fling is the last formal dance of the year—it sounds so fun. She asked me to go—dang I sooooooooo want to but I know my mom will say no. Do your parents make you wait until you're sixteen? I think it might just be a Mormon thing. When's your birthday? Mine is May 17.

Anyway—gotta get off the computer and get going on my piano—I got up early to write you back since I'll be at my grandma's all afternoon finishing the quilt I'm making. I hope Colt e-mails me back soon.

Jess

―――――

Kate consciously stopped her hands from fidgeting with the cord of her purse and took a breath. Why was she so nervous? It had been a week since she and Brad had first discussed having another baby, and as promised she'd made an appointment with an OB that specialized in high-risk pregnancies. Brad had hoped to make it, but even though tax day had been last week, he was still crammed trying to catch up with quarterlies. So she was here on her own, waiting for the dreaded second opinion.

She heard the door open behind her and stood up. Since this was only a consultation, she was in an actual office rather than an exam room. It gave the appointment a formal air that didn't help with the nervousness she was feeling. The doctor, Dr. Lyon, looked up from the chart in his hands—likely the medical records she'd authorized he could receive—and smiled. Kate smiled back.

"Have a seat," he said as he made his way around the desk and sat down. He continued scanning the papers, and Kate returned to her chair. He was about Kate's age, but his hair was turning silver at the temples.

He looked up and smiled again. "So, you're here to get your fortune told."

Kate hadn't thought of it like that. It made it sound mystical and edgy. She shifted in her seat.

"I'm kidding, but you are here for a second opinion, correct?"

Kate nodded.

"And Dr. Carmichael is your regular OB?"

Kate nodded again.

"I received your records but haven't spoken directly with Dr. Carmichael."

"Good," Kate blurted out, then felt silly. "Sorry."

Dr. Lyon laughed. "Why don't you tell me, in your own words, what happened with your last pregnancy."

"Okay," Kate said. "I was fine until about thirty-two weeks, when I started getting headaches. The doctor said I had pre-something, or toxemia, so I was put on bed rest and had a home-health nurse come take my blood pressure every few days. I felt okay though."

She hoped that telling him she felt okay would make an impact, but his expression was impassive. "At thirty-six weeks I had to be hospitalized because my blood pressure was getting higher and they couldn't bring it down. The next day they induced labor. Four hours later Chris was born healthy and strong with no problems whatsoever." She smiled to emphasize the happily-ever-after part.

Dr. Lyon nodded. "Do you always have such fast labors?"

"Yes," Kate said, as if it were a badge of honor. "My first baby, she's almost sixteen, was eight hours, and every baby has been a little shorter. Perfect deliveries. Perfect babies. My mother-in-law says I was just made for childbearing."

"And what did Dr. Carmichael tell you about any future pregnancies?"

Dang! She'd hoped he wouldn't ask, though that seemed silly. She had no doubt he knew all this. "He said that the complications—toxemia— could happen again."

"Did he explain why toxemia, or preeclampsia, is such a serious complication?"

"Uh," Kate searched her memory but couldn't bring anything up. "I'm sure he did but I can't really remember. I really felt okay, other than the headaches."

"The reason your blood pressure went up was because your body was having a kind of reaction to the baby. The pressure builds up in your circulatory system and causes all kinds of problems. For instance, you probably did a urine test right before you were sent to the hospital, and it probably said you had proteins in your urine."

Kate nodded. She did remember that.

"That's because your kidneys were unable to filter correctly—it's early stages of kidney failure."

Kate furrowed her brow. Kidney failure wasn't good. Dr. Lyon continued. "Had they not induced labor, your body would have responded to this sloppy circulating and intense pressure by attempting to thicken your blood, sending out mass amounts of blood platelets—the part of the blood that forms clots, to close a wound, for example. But this influx of platelets into the compromised bloodstream causes hundreds, thousands, hundreds of thousands of blood clots to form in the veins all over your body. It only takes one to travel to your brain and cause a stroke or a seizure, both of which are extremely serious complications for you and your baby."

Kate swallowed. A stroke. Had they told her that?

"Mrs. Thompson," the doctor said. "You probably know other women who have had preeclampsia."

Kate nodded.

"And you likely don't know of anyone that's had a stroke."

That was true. She'd never heard of anyone having a stroke.

"But that doesn't mean it doesn't happen. You have an excellent doctor, and he did everything right. You were otherwise healthy and you have good deliveries—you are a success story. But that doesn't minimize the risk."

"But you say all this as if I will for sure get it again."

"You've had several children—that's a risk factor. You're close to forty years old—another risk. You've had toxemia before—yet one more risk. Your chances of getting toxemia again are high."

"How high?"

"I'd say you have a 60 percent chance of getting it, but if you do, it will likely be worse than it was last time and will likely manifest sooner in the pregnancy."

"How could it be worse? If I'm monitored and medicated, then when it gets bad enough we can induce labor again—right?"

"Probably," Dr. Lyon said, leaning back in his chair. "But what if it manifests itself at thirty weeks, and you have to deliver your baby two weeks after that? Even with weekly appointments you could be okay one day, and the next day your body could start reacting, and the only actual cure is to have you deliver your baby."

"But last time I had headaches. That's what got the doctor's attention. If I had a headache I'd go in."

"You might not get headaches this time," Dr. Lyon said.

Kate swallowed, not wanting to get emotional, but this was . . . huge. "So you're telling me that I shouldn't have another child."

"No," Dr. Lyon said, causing Kate's head to snap up. "I'm telling you to make an informed and educated choice. If you were determined to get pregnant again, I would recommend you lose some weight first and get in as good physical shape as possible—some studies have shown that optimal health seems to lessen the risk of preeclampsia in some cases. I would tell you to follow a strict diet and plan on partial bed rest by your fifth month to take any pressure off your heart. You would have weekly appointments from that time on, with the added stipulation that you monitor your blood pressure at home on a daily basis. Once you hit thirty weeks, I would see you twice a week, and you would be on full bed rest—that's allowing only two vertical minutes every three hours every single day. It would mean finding care for your other children, and depending a great deal on your husband, and it would be difficult both lifestyle-wise and emotionally. After the baby is born, you'll need to take it easy for another six weeks in order to get healthy again."

Kate absorbed this as best she could, but among the details was hope. This could work. She could make arrangements; she could learn to take her own blood pressure. "And if I could do all these things, then you think I could do this?"

"As long as it's clear to you that doing all this still guarantees nothing," he sat back in his chair and looked at her. "You need to understand that regardless of all the things we may do, the monitoring, and the medications—you are taking a risk both for yourself and your baby."

Kate looked at her hands and tried to absorb it all objectively. The fact remained, however, that she felt that they could make this work. Dr. Lyon seemed very competent and she would do everything in her power to ensure things went smoothly. She wouldn't take extra risks and she'd follow his instructions to the letter. Dr. Lyon continued.

"I have to tell you, Mrs. Thompson, that it's women like you that gave me this." He pointed to the silver hair at his temples. Kate couldn't help but smile even though she knew she was being reprimanded. "But I have treated hundreds of women in your situation, and if you are determined, and I have a feeling you are, then I could help you—with the understanding that both you and your husband are perfectly clear on the risks and the requirements of seeing this through."

"So the first thing I need to do is lose some weight," she said.

Dr. Lyon nodded. "At least twenty-five pounds," he said. "And I'd need to do blood tests before I gave you the green light, to be sure that you have no other issues going on."

Kate nodded. She could do both of those. She mentally canceled the shepherd's pie she was planning on making for dinner. A nice chicken salad would hit the spot just as well.

"And," Dr. Lyon added. "I'd want to discuss this with your husband."

13

——Original Message——
From: emjenkins000@yahoo.com
To: jjk_hollywood@hotmail.com
Sent: Thursday, April 20, 7:52 PM
Subject: Re: dance

Jess,

britney—being nice—i don't buy it. i'd be careful if i were u, cause she's so totally two faced that u can't trust her. but i am glad yr feeling better. y do u even want to go to the dance with her? believe me once u get to know colt u won't want to ever see another boy as long as u live.

my parents didn't let me date til i was 16 either, so it's not just the mormon thing. It's a good rule i think—y date if theres just one person made just for u?

i can't believe yr mom did that, i mean i can, because she's just that way—always paying more attention to the little kids and ignoring u—but how horrible to get mad at u for something Britney did. I'm so sorry, Jess. how do u stand it? it must make u feel horrible that yr so unimportant to her. u know she'll say no if u ask her about the dance and u might even get another lecture. i'm so sorry—sometimes families are more hurtful than helpful, ya know?

i was invited to go to the movies with a friend today and my mom won't let me cause she has a meeting and i have to baby-sit. it makes

me so mad. she doesn't even care that i have no life. i feel like a
servant.

Em

————————

"Did Chris finally fall asleep?" Kate asked when Brad came into the
bedroom that night. Jess was still baby-sitting for the Jensens, but it
was almost ten o'clock so she should be home any time.

"Finally," Brad said, his frustration evident. She'd offered to put Chris
to bed, but Brad had assured her he had it covered. Kate appreciated the
help, but it also made her uncomfortable, as if he were helping out
because he thought she needed it. With her current goal to convince him
she had this motherhood thing wrapped up enough to make room for one
more, she wanted to prove herself.

Kate finished putting away the laundry she had folded on their bed
while Brad went into the closet and began getting undressed. "So how was
the appointment today?" he asked.

Kate took a breath. "Good," she said, keeping her tone upbeat and
light. "He seems like a wonderful doctor."

"What did he say?"

"Well," Kate said, picking her words carefully. "He said that, like Dr.
Carmichael said, there is a risk, but," she hurried to add before Brad cut
in, "he gave me some specific requirements I would need to meet and he
was really quite positive."

Brad came out of the closet, undoing the last button of his shirt and
shrugging out of the sleeves. "Really?"

It wasn't an excited "Really" as in, "That's really great!" it was more of
a "Really?" as in, "I don't believe it." Kate hurried to strengthen her case.
"Yeah, he even pointed out that though I know a lot of women who have
had toxemia, none of them has ever had a stroke."

Brad's eyebrows went up. "A stroke?"

Oops. "Well, that is a risk—but really only for women who aren't otherwise healthy or don't take their condition seriously. I'm neither of those things. He gave me a play by play of how the pregnancy would be handled and really educated me on the condition. But he also said there is almost a fifty percent chance that I would have no complications at all, that this pregnancy would be just like my first five."

Brad turned and disappeared back into the closet. She heard the hangers move on the rack and bit her lip, praying for him to be open-minded about this. Brad returned with a T-shirt in hand. "So what was the play by play?"

"Well, I need to lose some weight and get in shape; then he will monitor me really closely. I would need to be careful, take my blood pressure at home, and plan ahead. But I can do all that stuff. Julie already said she'd help with the kids if I needed it."

"You talked to Julie before you talked to me?"

Double oops. "She watched the boys for me, so we talked about it when I picked them up."

Brad let out a breath. "I wish I could have been there."

She didn't like his tone. "What, you think I didn't ask the right questions?"

"I think you want this so badly that you can't be objective."

"What a horrible thing to say!" Kate shot back.

"Well," Brad said, shrugging one shoulder and looking at her. "This is what you want, you meet with the doctor, and he basically tells you everything you want to hear—what am I supposed to think?"

"You're supposed to trust me," Kate said, but she was squirming. She wasn't telling Brad everything the way Dr. Lyon had told it to her. "And you're equally unable to be objective because you *don't* want this."

"Which in and of itself ought to mean something," Brad countered in sharp tones, putting on his T-shirt. He took a deep breath, and when he spoke again his voice was softer. "What about us, Kate? What about just enjoying this life we have right now, not adding another baby to it. Can't you just be happy with what we have?"

Kate was saved from having to come up with an insufficient answer by Chris's wails. She'd never been so happy to hear a cranky toddler. "I'll get him," she said quickly, making her escape. Brad didn't try to stop her.

Several seconds later, she lifted Chris from his crib and held him against her chest, his cries turning to whimpers as she rocked him in her arms. In another year Chris wouldn't even be in a crib; he wouldn't mold into her the way he did now. Thinking about it filled her with such sorrow. No more babies. Ever? She simply couldn't imagine it. Brad had no idea how important this was to her. Chris shifted in her arms, reaching a chubby arm around her neck, and she nuzzled her face into his curly blond hair. *How can I not have more of this?* she thought as tears filled her eyes. *How can I give it up?*

She heard the front door open—Jess—and listened to her and Brad have a muffled conversation. Eventually they both went downstairs. Presumably to watch the news. Kate put a now-sleeping Chris back to bed.

She shut the door to her bedroom behind her a minute later, glad to be alone. Kneeling by the side of the bed, she pleaded with the Lord to soften her husband's heart, to help him understand. Had he any idea how eternal his decision was?

It seemed like hours before he came to bed. Kate pretended to be asleep. Friday morning, they were cordial to one another, but things were tense, each of them waiting for the other to make the first move. The drawback of not fighting very often was that when they did, they were sorely out of practice.

"Mom?" Jess asked the next morning after she finished her practicing.

"Yeah." Kate didn't look up from the dishes she hadn't washed the night before. She was tired and frustrated by the argument. She even felt a little sick to her stomach. What a great way to start the day. She couldn't remember the last time she'd been in such a bad mood.

"Um, Britney is going to Spring Fling with like this huge group and she asked if I can go too, so can I?"

"What's Spring Fling?" Kate asked, putting a cup in the dishwasher only to realize the dishes already in there were clean. Great. Which ones had she just put in?

"It's the last dance of the year," Jess said. "It looks so fun and there are no couples or anything—just a big group."

Kate tried to tune in, but her thoughts felt far away. "You're not sixteen, Jess; you know the rules."

"Well, I'll be sixteen in a few weeks, and Britney's not sixteen until July and her mom's letting her go."

"That's her mom, not your mom," Kate said, paying a bit more attention now. What was Julie thinking, and why hadn't she told Kate? She'd have known the issue it would create for Kate when Jess's best friend got to go.

"Mom, please," Jess begged. "Julie's going to drive us everywhere, and we're having dinner at one of the girl's house with her parents there and everything. I promise you it's just a group."

"A group *date*," Kate said, inspecting a handful of silverware before realizing she should just run the load again. Washing already clean dishes made her feel wasteful and intensified her frustration.

"No, Mom," Jess said with enough venom in her voice to get Kate's full attention. Kate looked up in surprise. Jess never talked to her that way. "It's *not* a group date; it's a group *of kids* going to a dance. That's all. Why do you have to make such a big deal about it?"

"I'm your mother," Kate said, putting one hand on her hip and staring Jess down. Jess didn't react to the power stance Kate was going for. "It's my job to make a big deal out of things, and it *is* a group date and you are *not* going because you are *not* sixteen."

Jess stomped her foot and Kate was further surprised by the attitude. Caitlyn was the one with dramatic reactions, not Jess. Kate was in no mood for Jess's . . . mood.

"That's so not fair!" Jess said loudly.

Ha! Jess had no idea what fair was. "And I so don't care," Kate returned with sarcasm that may have been a bit too thick. Jess's eyes hardened and Kate attempted to redeem herself. She softened her voice and tried to repair her expression. "Look, I know you want to go. I know it's hard that Britney gets to, but—"

"Whatever," Jess said, narrowing her eyes. "I knew you'd never let me go. I told her all you cared about was rules and that it didn't matter to you one bit that I'd be the only loser not there. Ya know, I do have a life, Mom, and you're doing a really good job of ruining it!" She turned and stalked down the stairs. Her door slammed several seconds later, causing Kate to jump.

"What was that?" Brad asked, coming out of the bedroom, tying his tie.

"Nothing," Kate said, going back to the dishes and feeling horrible about what had just happened. Yet she didn't want to bring Brad into it. She was embarrassed at how she'd handled it and didn't feel up to taking on his judgment. "Jess is being moody."

"That's not like Jess," Brad said, as if this were the most dramatic thing that had ever happened in the Thompson household. He really was out of it around here.

"She's fifteen," Kate said, reminding herself that this kind of thing was normal teenage pushing-the-boundaries stuff. "Now and then it comes out."

"Well, is she okay?" Brad continued as Chris started crying in his room. Kate let out a groan. She'd hoped after last night that he would sleep in today. *Thank you, Jess.* Kate looked up at Brad, shifting from feeling bad about Jess to being angry about last night. Anger was easier. "If you're so worried about her, then go check on her yourself. Chances are I can't be *objective* enough to make the right decisions anyway."

"Nice, Kate," Brad said, giving her a disappointed look and turning back to the bedroom while she turned toward Chris's room. Between last night and this morning she'd never felt so unappreciated and dismissed. He really had no idea what she did for this family, did he? The good news was that unless a train drove through their living room, the day couldn't get much worse.

14

——Original Message——
From: jjk_hollywood@hotmail.com
To: emjenkins000@yahoo.com
Sent: Friday, April 21, 7:47 AM
Subject: Re: dance

Em,

I should have listened to you. I asked my mom about the dance and she totally shut me down. She wouldn't even listen to me and told me flat out that she didn't care how I felt. I mean, you're right that she's always way more into the little kids than me, but she's never told me to my face she doesn't care about me. She tried to apologize when I came back upstairs but like she always tells me, you can't undo everything. I just wish she cared about me a little bit. The dance is going to be soooo great, and I don't get to go.

I came to school early and I'm on the library computer—I don't dare try and send e-mail during computer class anymore. Anyway, I hope you have a better day than mine has started out being. Colt must think I'm the loser I really am cause he hasn't written me yet. Oh well, he probably saw my picture on my bored. I'm not surprised. I really think Britney is trying hard to be a good friend, but I can see what you mean. It's hard for me to trust her like I used to, but . . . yeah.

Laters,
Jess

Monique stared at the ceiling, too worked up and excited to sleep. After she had left Karl several messages, he had finally showed up last night to check out the funny document on the computer. She'd had time to feel like an idiot by then, but it only took Karl a few minutes of clicking the mouse and typing in commands to figure out that her first impression had been right. It *was* a program of some kind. Monique called the detective who had headed up Terrezza's case more than four months ago. He came over that morning and Monique called in sick to work. Together Detective Simmons and Karl had gone over the information with a fine-toothed comb. Not only was the document instructions for loading a program, but it was an instant messaging program, and some of the conversations had been saved in other documents titled *research* and *notes*. The detective only read a couple of the saved messages before taking the computer to the station and letting them know he'd call them on Monday.

Harrison had been working. When he came home, Monique told him everything. His expression hadn't changed, and he'd said nothing. It made her uncomfortable that she understood why he reacted that way. Hope was hard.

Karl hadn't understood though. He'd stormed out of the house, not giving Monique a chance to thank him for all he'd done. To Karl, his father's reaction was one more piece of evidence proving that Harrison didn't care. But Monique knew that in her husband's mind it was just common sense not to get too excited. To get excited meant he had to risk something, and he didn't have anything left that he could afford to lose. Both of them had dwindled to merely existing these last few months. If this came to nothing, after getting her hopes up, she had little doubt that she would break in two.

They'd gotten ready for bed in silence—that ice between them still fragile and untrusting. But she couldn't sleep. She was still too worked up. What if they found her? What if Terrezza actually came home? Perhaps she'd been tricked by this computer person—brainwashed. Certainly her experience would have been horrible. Monique couldn't think too long about that. Instead, she focused on a vision she'd created in her mind of seeing Terrezza step out of a police car after they found her. The joy of that moment would be absolutely incredible, and all this worry and stress would become insignificant.

She felt Harrison shudder in his sleep, reminding her that she needed to rest as well. Rolling onto her side, she turned her back toward her husband and closed her eyes. He shook again. She paused, then slowly turned to face his back. A sob escaped his barreled chest. She laid a hand on his shoulder, unsure what to do with his emotion. Her touch seemed to unleash his demons, and he began crying without reserve. It tore down the last of her own emotional defenses. Tears filled her eyes and spilled down her cheeks. She clung to his back until he rolled over and wrapped his big arms around her. They both gave in then, crying like scared children, huddled together in the dark. What would Monday bring? Where would it lead them?

15

——Original Message——
From: emjenkins000@yahoo.com
To: jjk_hollywood@hotmail.com
Sent: Saturday, April 22, 9:07 AM
Subject: yr mom

Jess,

yr mom isn't just lame, jess, she's mean. how horrible for her to not even discuss the dance with u. yr like the dream daughter in every way. first making u go to gymnastics, and now this? it's horrible. that's sad and im so sorry. u deserve so much better than that. make sure u never tell her about me—she'd probably ground u from the computer for the rest of yr life if she knew u had someone who cares about u as much as i do.

i haven't heard from colt yet but i'm sure he'll write u back. u and colt will get along great. u have so much in common. do u IM—cause i have a great program i can send u that can be hidden on yr computer so yr mom would never know—i think she's the type that would freak out. let me know if u want it. the fact is that the only way yr ever going to have any freedom is if u find it yrself. yr mom doesn't understand what it's like to be a teenager—u have to experience life, not live in fear of it.

Emily

At thirty, he realized he was destined to live his life alone. The same descriptions he'd endured in high school still followed him—weird, stupid, strange. Even if grown women didn't say it out loud, he knew that's what they thought of him. But with computers helping them get to know one another, he realized girls actually liked him. All kinds of girls—young, beautiful, so full of life. He'd never felt so good about himself, so powerful and secure, as he did when he discovered his first chat room. After so many years of loneliness, he was able to find the girl of his dreams—over and over again.

At first all he wanted to do was talk. But the confidence was intoxicating and soon he wanted to be more important than anything else in her life.

He loved them—he loved all of them—but after Terrezza he realized that it took a special kind of girl to love him back. It still hurt that Terrezza wasn't the one. But he recognized his mistake. She was too headstrong, too aggressive—that's why he'd looked for a different kind of girl this time. Sweet, innocent, trusting. He couldn't afford to be wrong again.

He opened one of his e-mail programs and scowled. No messages. Janeece hadn't written to him in over a week, and the last two e-mails he'd sent to Roxi had bounced back. He took a breath, calming himself, and reminding himself to be patient. He knew that was the only way this would work. Patience was everything, and he wouldn't end up like one of those guys caught by *Dateline*. He was smarter than that. There were three girls still e-mailing consistently—all from separate accounts so he didn't mix up the details of their lives. They were getting more comfortable with him, sharing more, getting closer. That's what he wanted.

But it was time to step things up now that each of them was anxious to find out who Colt was. Just the way he'd planned it.

16

——Original Message——

From: emjenkins000@yahoo.com

To: jjk_hollywood@hotmail.com

Sent: Saturday, April 22, 2:05 PM

Subject: check out these boreds

Jess,

check out these boreds. they are awesome. i wish i had a boyfriend, don't u? i wonder sometimes if i'm missing the very best part of being a teenager—being in love. I know u have yr religious ideas, and i really respect that, but sometimes don't u just want to . . . i don't know—be special to someone?

colt called me and said he'll be writing u soon—he's still getting settled and their computer isn't hooked up yet. he's excited to get those get to know u questions. Speaking of boyfriends . . . u two are like made for each other!!

so do u want that IM program? colt and i use it all the time and it's so nice to chat back and forth.

Em

She said no?" Britney said, hanging the dress on the door of her closet so Jess could see the whole thing. She'd gone shopping that morning and called Jess as soon as she got back.

"I told you she would," Jess said, looking at the dress with more envy than she could have ever imagined. She wanted to cry, and yet pretended she didn't care. She'd been excited when Britney invited her over, but now she wished she'd stayed home. It had been such a lousy week already, and then Mom cut her off from going to the dance—the one thing that could have made things better. She felt like she had a giant L printed on her forehead. Britney got everything she wanted, and Jess never did.

"Maybe my mom could talk to her," Britney said.

Jess shrugged and flopped back on the bed, mostly so she didn't have to look at the dress anymore. "I doubt it will help. My mom loves rules, and this is a rule. You better just hope she doesn't talk to *your* mom." Britney came to sit on the edge of the bed and Jess looked up at her. "She might convince your mom of her evil ways."

Britney laughed and Jess smiled. It was nice to make Britney laugh.

"My mom sucks," Jess said, surprised at her own anger, but not really feeling bad about it. Emily agreed that Mom was unfair. She'd even said she was mean, which was hard for Jess to think about—*oblivious* seemed like a better term—but it did seem mean that Mom didn't care how Jess felt about anything. Almost as if Mom didn't even like her.

"Now come on," Britney said, standing up and going back to the dress as if it were a magnet. Jess propped herself up on one elbow, looked at the dress again, and felt the jealousy come back full force. The dress was turquoise, with a fitted bodice, thick cap sleeves, and a sheer shawl that wrapped around the shoulders and tied in the back, like a jacket. Britney would look like Miss Teen USA in it. "Your mom's not that bad," Britney continued. "I really think she just needs more time to think about it."

Jess was instantly annoyed by the comment. Was Emily the only person in her life who cared about how other people treated her? "Oh, well, thanks for being so understanding," she muttered, drawing Xs over the flowers on Britney's bedspread with her finger.

"What? Your mom's way nice," Britney said, looking at Jess again. "Remember that time she did our hair all fancy and put on makeup and served us our own tea party? That was so fun."

"That was like four years and two kids ago," Jess reminded her, her mood getting darker by the minute. "She's become a lot less cool since then. Trust me."

"Well, what about your dad?" Britney suggested. "Maybe he would let you go."

Jess opened her mouth to say he wouldn't, but then reconsidered. *Dad,* she thought to herself. *Why hadn't she thought of that?*

17

From: jjk_hollywood@hotmail.com
To: emjenkins000@yahoo.com
Sent: Saturday, April 22, 9:17 PM
Subject: Parents! Who needs em!!!!

Emily,

I'm baby-sitting tonight and the kids finally went to bed. The Hutches have a way nice computer—it's awesome!

There is really no reason for me NOT to do that IM program you were talking about. You're right that I have no freedom unless I find it myself. Did I tell you we got the times for my gymnastics performance this week? As if not going to the dance weren't bad enough. I'm going to look like such an idiot—talk about feeling like garbage. I'm so glad I have you to talk to about this stuff—it seems like I can't talk to anyone else anymore. Even though Britney tries to understand, she just doesn't quite get it.

I did get to look at those boreds—holy cow! I can't believe what some kids will take pictures of themselves doing. I would never do that stuff and yet my mom won't trust me to go to a dance with a bunch of friends. I would like to have a boyfriend, but it's not going to happen. No guys like me, but I'm really excited to get to know Colt. He sounds really cool. But he hasn't e-mailed me so he probably thinks I'm a total loser. Sorry. I'll play around with the IM and let you know how it goes.

Britney's dress is so hot I could barely look at it! She's so lucky. I wish I had her mom.

Jess

———————

Brad tried to enjoy the basketball game Saturday night, but the tension in the house made him uncomfortable. Yesterday, he'd called and made an appointment with Dr. Lyon for next Thursday. He had a very strong feeling that Kate was warping what the doctor had said to fit her own agenda. Yet he felt horrible for doubting her.

The more he'd thought about their situation, the clearer it became in his mind. Yes, the health concerns were huge, but he also felt more and more of a desire to move on from this stage of life. Kate had been pregnant or breastfeeding for most of the last thirteen years—Chris had only been weaned six months ago. In a couple years they would have no diapers, no more nap schedules. They could take family vacations and he and Kate could go on regular date nights instead of random celebrations of birthdays and anniversaries. Heck, they had their own built-in baby-sitter with Jess, but Kate was anxious about leaving the little ones with her for very long or at night. He really wished he'd made it to Kate's appointment with Dr. Lyon. Whatever it was that had kept him from going didn't seem half as important now, and he wanted to kick himself for not making it happen.

One week from today he would fly to Houston for his conference. He hadn't been looking forward to this trip, but now he wondered if the timing would be a good thing. He'd talk to the doctor on Thursday, then have a few days to process what he'd learned and come up with a game plan. Even if Dr. Lyon confirmed that Kate was exaggerating what he said, it wouldn't be easy to resolve things with Kate. They were both seeing it from opposite sides of the equation—could they find a middle ground? He groaned. Everything was so complicated.

After several minutes, Jess came downstairs and sat with him. She'd been at Britney's most of the day, and then she went baby-sitting for a family in the ward. As the oldest of six, she was a baby-sitter in high demand. He put an arm around her shoulders and gave her a little squeeze. Some of his fondest memories were snuggling with her on the couch when she was a little girl. They'd watch movies together, and she'd squeal when he tried to rub his "scratchy face" against her cheek. He missed those days and wondered when life had become too busy for him to connect with his children. Then again, back then they had only Jess. Nowadays it was a rare occurrence for him to have alone time with any of the kids, and he knew he needed to work on changing that.

"Dad?" Jess said after a minute or so, and a sweet layup by Johnson. That man could move.

"Yeah, Jess," he said, though his eyes were on the game. Denver stole the ball and he gritted his teeth; the Jazz should have expected that.

"I know how important it is that I don't date till I'm sixteen, but can I please go to the dance? It's just a big group, and everyone else is going."

Brad furrowed his eyebrows and looked at his daughter. "What dance?"

Jess looked up at him. "Mom didn't tell you about it?"

Brad shook his head, wondering why Kate wouldn't have mentioned it. Then he turned down the TV and gave Jess his full attention. "Why don't you tell me about it."

First, she told him all about the dance, but he sensed that though the dance was definitely an issue, there was more to it than that. He asked questions about other aspects of her life, and for the next ten minutes listened as Jess opened up like none of the kids ever had to him before. She told him about Britney making the track team and finding a whole bunch of new friends and of how badly she hated gymnastics. "I'm such a loser,

Dad," she said as she started winding down. "And now I have this chance to be with new kids, and spend time with Britney, and Mom said she didn't care about any of that stuff."

"She told you she didn't care?" Brad asked, wanting to make sure before he gave his blood permission to boil. Was he so distracted by other things that Kate would talk to their kids that way and he'd have no idea?

Jess nodded. "And I explained the whole thing, how it wasn't a date and I turn sixteen two weeks after the dance anyway—she said no to everything."

Brad nodded and Jess stared at her hands in her lap.

"Let me talk to your mom about the dance," Brad said. He hated the way Jess looked unsure whether or not she should have said so much. He'd do anything at that moment to make her feel better. "I can't promise you anything, but I can try—okay?"

Jess nodded, but her shoulders slumped. Brad took it as a sign that she thought he was powerless against Kate. On impulse he added, "And if you want to, you can quit gymnastics." He regretted it as soon as the words left his mouth. That was a pretty big promise to make, and yet maybe this was the right tack to take. Maybe he needed to take back some of the power, since Kate seemed to have no problem making the dance decision without him.

Jess looked up at him, her eyes wide. "Really? Right now?"

Brad nodded. "You need to understand that your mom kept you in there because she wanted you to have the opportunity—she never had the chance to do that kind of thing and she wants to give it to you guys. She doesn't want it to hurt you."

Jess nodded, but Brad wasn't sure she believed him. As it was, he couldn't quite understand how Kate could not know how miserable Jess was in gymnastics. He knew she'd wanted to quit last summer and Kate had helped her change her mind, but Kate hadn't said anything about Jess not liking it. Or maybe, like Jess said, Kate just didn't care. It was hard to think of Kate that way, but over the last few days he'd seen a side of Kate he hadn't noticed before. Was it an agenda? Or just determination to have her way? He wasn't sure, but whatever it was, this seemed to give further evidence of it. "I'll call the gymnastics studio Monday, okay? You don't have to do that final performance," he continued.

Jess smiled. "Thanks Daddy," she whispered.

Brad pulled her into a hug and held on tight. "I love you, Jessie," he whispered into her hair. "Being a teenager is a hard thing, but please don't forget how truly wonderful you are and how much we love you. It's going to work out, okay?"

Jess pulled away, her face—and he hoped her heart—lighter. "Okay."

Brad waited until he heard her bedroom door shut before turning off the TV—the game now in the fourth quarter—and heading upstairs. Kate was at the kitchen table working on some stupid handout that the kids in Primary would destroy tomorrow. She had time to do that, but not talk to him about their daughter?

"Why didn't you talk to me about the dance?"

Kate looked up at him with a confused expression. "What?"

"Jess just told me about your argument yesterday. Why didn't you talk to me?"

"Well, we already made the rule together years ago," Kate said, seemingly innocent about any offense she may have caused. "She's not sixteen."

"Kate," he broke in. "We're supposed to talk about this kind of thing. We're supposed to be a team."

Kate let out an exasperated sigh as if to say she did not have time for this. "Jess is a fifteen-year-old girl who—"

He cut her off. "Who is feeling overall lousy about herself, feels like her best friend has left her behind, and gets a stomachache every time she thinks about her gymnastics performance. Did you know she spent last week's gymnastics class hiding in the bathroom? That's how embarrassed she is. She told me she thinks of herself as a loser. What's more, you don't care, and you told her so."

"I do care," Kate replied, her eyes wide with surprise. She finally put down the marker in her hand, her eyes narrowed. "And I apologized for the comment I made about not caring. I haven't been feeling well and—"

"That's no excuse," Brad cut in again. "You don't say things like that to our kids, Kate; it's mean. You've said yourself that you feel like Jess has pulled away from you, and then you say something like that?"

"It was a mistake, Brad, I'm sorry." But there was an edge of pride in her voice.

Brad shook his head. "Jess and I had a good talk, Kate, about a lot of things, and I told her she didn't have to take gymnastics anymore—she's really miserable in that class."

Kate's eyebrows went up. "Without even discussing it with me?"

"Did you talk to me about the dance?" Brad asked, waiting for an answer.

Kate ignored his rebuttal. "They are counting on her, Brad. She's part of a routine that involves a lot of people. We can't just pull her out, not to mention the fact that letting her quit tells her it's okay to just give up. When I was a kid, I never—"

"You never had a lot of things when you were a kid, Kate. But you can't try to live vicariously through our kids. They have their own talents, their own interests, and it's our job to support them in their own directions, not force them to do it our way. The studio has a month to make adjustments to the performance thing, and it's not worth hurting her, Kate. We should have just let her quit last summer when she wanted to. If I'd known she was this unhappy, I'd have pulled her out a long time ago."

Kate pinched her lips together. Brad couldn't remember a time he'd ever confronted his wife this way, so it didn't surprise him that she was at a loss about what to say. The discussion with Jess had brought everything to the forefront. "I've also made an appointment with Dr. Lyon. I'll meet with him next Thursday—before I go out of town. But in light of all this, I'm feeling more than ever that we can both use the energy that would go into another child to work harder on the kids we have. I obviously haven't been involved enough, and the last thing this family needs is another child."

"You can't mean that," Kate said slowly, and he looked away from the profound disappointment in her eyes. Why was it so hard for her to understand this? He understood she felt differently, but surely it wasn't *that* big of a deal. Seven kids was the dream of newlyweds, but life proved that it wasn't realistic.

"We seem to have more than we can handle well right now."

"That is so offensive," she said quietly, her eyes filling with tears. "I work hard to take care of this family, Brad. I do more than a lot of wives and mothers do, and I get very little gratitude for that. And now you're going to swoop in and start making decisions like this without any regard to my feelings?"

"No," Brad said. "I regard your feelings, Kate, but that doesn't mean you always win."

"Is it a contest?" she said, wiping at her eyes.

"Of course not," he said, exasperated by her obstinacy. "But I'm concerned. Jess has been miserable, and I didn't know. She asked you about the dance, and you didn't even tell me. That's not right, Kate, and no, it's not all your fault. We both have some changes to make. But I worry that if we don't get our priorities back on track, we're going to miss the opportunity to be there when our kids need us. We can do better than this."

18

From: coltinator_51@yahoo.com
To: jjk_hollywood@hotmail.com
Sent: Saturday, April 22, 11:08 PM
Subject: Hi

Jess,

It's me, Colt. Thanks for the get-to-know-you questions—we DO have a lot in common, even down to Red Cream Soda as our favorite drink. I really don't get why that's not the most popular soda in the world. Did my answers come through? It's almost scary how many answers were the same for you and me. Wow. Sorry it took me so long, it's been rough getting the house all set up.

I don't really like it here in Florida very much. All the girls look like Barbie dolls and all they care about is hair and makeup. I hate girls like that so school is pretty much lame but at least I only have a month or so to go. The guys are okay, except that all they care about are the stupid girls without a thought in their head. I just don't get how people can be so shallow. How about you? How is your school? What kind of guys do you like? Emily showed me your bored and between that and the answers, you seem like just the kind of girl I'd like to get to know—I'm taking Calculus this year, it's awesome! I'm so glad she hooked us up. She says you're an honor student—so am I. Anyway, write back.

Colt

Sunday was long and miserable. Kate woke up feeling sick again and desperately hoped she wasn't coming down with something. Even though it had been over a month, she still felt like she'd just gotten over the flu. In addition to that, she and Brad were still circling each other, the tension building up with every passing minute. After church Brad offered to make a pancake lunch once the kids were changed out of their Sunday clothes. Kate felt like her role had been suddenly extinguished—at least until it was time to do dishes. Then it was conveniently left up to her. She was up to her elbows in sticky plates when Brad asked if everyone wanted to go for a drive up Millcreek Canyon and then go over to Grandma's for a visit. The kids were beside themselves with excitement. Not only for the trip, but Kate suspected they were enthralled with their dad suddenly being so involved. Kate asked to stay home, and Brad just shrugged his shoulders and told her to do whatever she wanted. It made her feel horrible, but she waved to them as they drove away and hoped that in their absence she could get her head on straight and take a nap.

Brad's accusations from the night before cut to the quick. She didn't understand how he could see her that way—too busy to know her own kids. Like he should talk! But she knew she wasn't being fair. She did have room for improvement, especially with Jess, but he made her out to be a lot worse than she really was, and he completely discounted all the good things she did.

After trying several different positions in hopes of falling asleep, she gave up. Her stomach was rolling. What had she eaten? Was there something going around? April wasn't really flu season. She went to the pantry and pulled out a sleeve of crackers, that always helped calm her stomach when she was . . .

She froze and the crackers fell from her hands. The package was already open, and the individual crackers broke free and slid all over the floor.

"I can't be," she whispered, but ran into the bathroom anyway. She popped open her package of birth control pills. She was four days into the placebos, meaning her period was late. And she'd been feeling sick since—she calculated the days in her head—Thursday. How had she not noticed this? But she was on the pill—she couldn't be pregnant!

She sat down on the edge of the tub and put her head in her hands. *This isn't happening; this isn't happening; this isn't happening.* But she reflected on how tired she was and how the syrup on the pancakes had increased her queasiness—sweets always made her sick when she was pregnant.

With each piece of evidence her heart sunk deeper into her chest. She didn't know how much time passed before someone knocked on the front door. She lifted her head and blinked. She hadn't cried—it was still too new—but her reflection looked pale when she passed the mirror of the bathroom. *This isn't happening,* she told herself again, willing herself to believe it. *It can't happen. Not like this.*

"Hey," Julie said, smiling brightly when Kate pulled open the door. "I brought back your cheesecake pan; I appreciate the . . . are you okay?"

Kate nodded but felt her chin quiver. Julie stepped inside and took Kate by the shoulders. "What's going on?" she asked, her face showing her concern.

Kate remembered Brad being upset that she'd talked to Julie about the appointment with Dr. Lyon before she'd talked to him, but she couldn't help herself. Maybe saying it out loud would prove it to be ridiculous. "I think I'm pregnant."

Julie blinked. "No way!" she said in a breathy voice that well communicated that she knew what this meant.

Kate nodded. Seeing the shock on Julie's face was like confirmation. Rather than prove the idea impossible, Julie's reaction seemed to make it more real. Kate took a breath and burst into tears.

19

—Original Message——
From: jjk_hollywood@hotmail.com
To: coltinator_51@yahoo.com
Sent: Monday, April 24, 5:29 AM
Subject: Re: Hi

Colt,

Emily sent me an IM program and said you use the same one. I'm hoping to try it out tonight—right now I'm about to start my piano practice but had just enough time to squeeze in one last e-mail.

My school is having their last formal dance of the year, I so wish I was going. My best friend, Britney, gets to go, but not me. Have you gone to school dances? Were they fun? Did you have a girlfriend back in Pennsylvania? Where are you going to go for college in the fall?

Gotta go.
Jess

———

Monique held Harrison's hand tight, and he rubbed his rough thumb over the back of her hand. They still didn't talk much, but they were at least together on this, even if the words still wouldn't come. They'd been waiting in the police station for over half an hour, and

Monique felt sure she was going to completely lose her mind any minute now.

"Mr. and Mrs. Weatherford?"

Monique and Harrison looked up to see the owner of the voice—a stout white man in his fifties with a salt-and-pepper mustache and a bald head that gleamed under the fluorescent lights. They both stood. He introduced himself as Sergeant Morris and indicated for them to follow him into his office.

Once they were seated, he closed the door, moved around to the business side of the desk, and sat down. He may have smiled slightly, but it was hard to tell behind the mustache, and it certainly wasn't the kind of smile that reached his eyes.

"Well, Mr. and Mrs. Weatherford, in November when you reported your daughter missing, we did an initial check of your computer. But with her history, we didn't do much more than talk to some friends and put her into the national database." He opened a manila folder on his desk and moved a few papers around. "We have thousands of runaways reported every year in this county, and she seemed to be a typical case."

Monique nodded. She knew they had felt that way, even though she'd explained that Terrezza had changed, that she was no longer having the problems that had created so much turmoil the previous summer. To dwell on the police and their lack of interest only made her angry, however. She was anxious for him to get to the point.

"You already know that the file you found was instructions for installing an instant message program—but it's not the kind a kid downloads and gets access to millions of people through. This one was a type of homemade instant message that allows communication through only two people. It's hidden on a hard drive, but we haven't found the program. Your daughter may have deleted it."

"What does that mean?" Harrison asked. Monique squeezed his hand. Harrison had owned his own mechanic shop for over twenty years. He was as smart and handy as a man could be, but she doubted he'd ever even used the Internet. Like her, he was a hesitant immigrant to the technology that was so simple for the younger generations.

The sergeant didn't answer directly. "Your daughter also saved conversations, e-mails, her own thoughts that spanned a five-week period of time."

"Five weeks?" Monique repeated. How could Terrezza have been talking to some stranger for that long and Monique not notice?

"He told her not to say anything. He became her best friend."

"He?" Harrison said. "A boy?"

Sergeant Morris took a breath. "A man."

Monique and Harrison were completely still. A man? But Terrezza was only sixteen. "What kind of man?" Monique asked, but she answered the question in her mind. What kind of man communicates online with a teenage girl and tells her to keep it a secret? She felt the blood draining from her face and her grip on Harrison's hand tightened as if that would stave off the fear that was rising.

"That's what we're trying to figure out," Sergeant Morris continued. "The information she kept is invaluable to this investigation, and it takes us down a very different road. There was an e-mail that talked about the two of them meeting the night your daughter went missing. He said he loved her, that they would be together forever, and she should leave a note saying she was going to stay with Danyelle."

Monique froze for a moment, but found herself almost instantly encouraged by the news. If Terrezza had fallen in love with this man and gone to be with him, then she could still be out there. Maybe it wasn't as frightening as she'd initially thought when Sergeant Morris told them it was an adult Terrezza was talking to.

"Mr. and Mrs. Weatherford," the sergeant said as if reading the expression on their faces. "His e-mails are very . . . manipulative. Pointed. He seemed to always speak of you, her parents, as untrustworthy, controlling. He told her things to distance her from her friends—setting himself up to be her sole confidant, her only real friend." Sergeant Morris paused. "I'm sure you've heard about Internet predators."

Monique blinked. "Yes," she said slowly, "but they go after young kids. They want pictures and stuff."

"Your daughter sent pictures of herself at his request," the sergeant said. "And they don't only go after young kids—they go after all kinds of kids. All ages, all races, all family and social situations. The only thing most of them want is someone they can overpower through their computers, someone they can manipulate. He said he was a senior in high school, but the way he talked was far too advanced. His knowledge of computers indicates he was much older."

Monique looked down, her earlier thoughts of what kind of man communicates with a sixteen-year-old girl becoming very stark in her mind. But she shook it off. After all these months she had hope. She did not take that lightly. Terrezza was out there somewhere, too embarrassed to come home. Like every other teenager in America, she didn't know just how much love and forgiveness she had at home.

"Mr. and Mrs. Weatherford," he continued. "You haven't heard from your daughter in over five months—that's a very long time for her to be hiding out with a boyfriend somewhere and never calling home."

"Don't you say that," Harrison said suddenly. Monique looked up at him, surprised by both his words and his anger. "We've considered for too long that we might never see her again. She could be alive; she could come home. We won't be hearing anything different."

The sergeant nodded slightly. "I called you in so that I could update you on our progress. We are putting everything we can into finding your daughter. That she left so much information is very helpful, but it doesn't change the fact that she's been gone a very long time." He paused. "I suggest you inform your family members and at least consider that, regardless of the outcome, regardless of what has happened to your daughter since she left your home, there is peace in knowing. That's what we are hoping for."

Harrison's eyes narrowed, and his face went a shade darker than usual. Monique gave his hand another squeeze, and when he looked at her she hoped to communicate her thoughts without saying them out loud. *Let them believe what they want to believe,* she thought. *We'll keep our newfound hope alive.*

He seemed to understand, giving credit to their many years together. He turned back to face Morris. "We appreciate all you're doing," he said. "We'll be waiting to hear more."

——Original Message——
From: jjk_hollywood@hotmail.com
To: emjenkins000@yahoo.com
Sent: Monday, April 24, 8:46 PM
Subject: Gymnastics no more!!!!

Em—

You won't believe this but my dad is letting me drop gymnastics today. I
bet my mom totally freaked and I think they are like fighting now, but I
don't have to do another round off for as long as I live! I'm so excited.
Dad's been like home more often and we had this awesome talk and he
was so great. He said he's going to talk to my mom about the dance
too, but I doubt he'll win again. Still, I'm trying to be positive and focus
on the good things. No more gymnastics, is that not the coolest thing in
the whole world? Anyway—how's you? Colt finally wrote me and you're
right, we have a ton in common. It's so cool to be e-mailing with a guy!
Thanks for getting us together.

Laters,
Jess

————

K ate?"
       Kate turned and scanned the faces of other parents taking posi-
tion to watch the soccer game. It was drizzling a light rain, but not enough

to cancel the game. Kate had left Jess with the other kids, so she was alone, wrapped in a blanket but still shivering. She saw Julie and smiled as her stomach dropped. She'd been avoiding her since dropping the bombshell on Sunday.

"So?" Julie asked. She had her thick winter coat on and her hair braided in two braids, topped with a beanie. She looked like a teenager, and Kate wondered if Jess wished she were more like Julie, full of energy, young and . . . liberal was the only word that came to mind.

Kate just shrugged as a reply.

"Have you told him?" Julie asked, wrapping her arms around her chest and bouncing on her feet. "Dang, it's cold."

Kate nodded. "It's freezing, but no I haven't told him."

"Kate," Julie said with a laugh and a shake of her head. "Why not?"

"I'm scared?" she said, phrasing it as a question. "He's going to be so mad."

"He's going to be even more mad that you didn't tell him. It makes you look guilty."

"But I'm not guilty!" Kate retorted, looking Julie fully in the face. "I did not do this on purpose."

"Then tell him that," Julie said. "But the longer you wait the harder it's going to be, and if he figures it out before you tell him . . ." She whistled under her breath.

Kate looked at the wet grass. "I haven't even taken a test yet," she said, stalling. "I mean, I might not be pregnant."

"Right," Julie said in sarcastic disbelief. "Lots of women on the pill skip their periods and you've only been sick for a week without it getting better or getting worse—which if you had the flu one of those two things would have happened."

Kate said nothing, annoyed and yet penitent. She knew she was going about this all wrong, but she didn't know *what* to do and didn't want to do anything until she was sure of which approach was the right one.

It didn't help that she and Brad were still avoiding one another. A lot of the tension had worn itself out. They were talking again, and she knew he was working hard to help out more in the evenings, but they hadn't resolved the weekend's argument. Kate wished they could fix that before she blew everything up again.

The timing was just all wrong. Today was the first Wednesday of no gymnastics, and Jess had gloated about it to Caitlyn. Kate had wanted to scream. Then, Brad came home early and informed her that Jess had asked him to take her to the women's shelter to drop off the quilt she'd made for her Good Works project. Kate had been the one who had helped Jess on *all* her projects—but Brad got to go with her for her big moment with her final goal? It had stung—badly. Even the thought of adding to all that trouble by announcing a possible pregnancy Brad didn't want was more than Kate could think about.

"Tell you what," Julie said, reminding Kate that she was still there. "I'll bring over two tests in the morning, after the kids and husbands are gone."

Kate wanted to say no, she wasn't ready, but she knew it was ridiculous. She let out a breath of defeat. "Okay," she finally said, then braced herself. Taking the test meant she'd know for sure if she were pregnant. She'd have no choice but to tell Brad the truth. She really wished she had the flu.

21

Jess—

Britney's your best friend? I thought Emily was your best friend. Just kidding, I know what you meant but don't tell Emily that. She thinks you're her *very* best friend and I think it hurts her feelings that even after Britney has been so rude to you, you still talk about her like it's not important that she treats you like crap. Just a little FYI.

Congrats on gymnastics, bummer about the dance. I'm surprised you even talked to your dad though. Emily's told me all about your mom, aren't you worried she'll be mad you went behind her back? You haven't told them about Emily or me, have you?

Colt

———————

Kate was putting the last of the dishes in the dishwasher when Brad and Jess got home. They'd been gone forever. The kids were in bed, the house quiet, and yet Kate felt herself stiffen when they entered the kitchen. Her toes were still frozen from the soccer game, so she'd been nursing a mug of hot cocoa in hopes of warming herself up.

"Where have you guys been?" she asked casually.

"Well, we dropped off the quilt," Brad said. "And then I took Jess out for ice cream to celebrate."

Kate nodded, swallowing her jealousy. She was the one who needed these kinds of moments with Jess. Why didn't Brad help her make things better instead of trumping her? But she forced herself to act like an adult. She looked at Jess. "How was it?" she asked.

Jess smiled, looking more open than she had in a long time. "It was great," she said. "They had a lady there with three little kids. Her husband left her and she doesn't have anywhere to go, and when we got there they said they wanted me to give it to her. I was, like, totally nervous but I went in there and she was so thankful. She looked at all the squares and couldn't believe I did it myself—well, with Grandma's help. Anyway. It was awesome. She cried and everything."

"Really?" Kate said, smiling as she pictured the moment. "That's wonderful. I'm so proud of you for doing that, Jess. You worked so hard, and what a blessing that blanket must be for her."

Jess nodded, still smiling, and Kate felt her heart relax. Maybe she was overreacting about the relationship with her daughter. Maybe it wasn't so bad. "Yeah, it was really great," Jess said.

"And now you can get your Young Womanhood award," Kate added. "Do you want me to make you an appointment with the bishop for Sunday?"

Jess shrugged. "Sure, uh . . . I have a little more homework to do. Can I get on the computer for a minute?"

"I thought you finished it earlier," Kate said. She'd already been giving Jess more computer time because of the term projects that were coming due.

"I forgot something," Jess said in a challenging tone that set Kate's back up.

"Go ahead," Brad said, intercepting. Kate clenched her teeth together. Was he going to bowl over everything she did?

"Thanks, Dad," Jess said on her way to the study.

He waited until she was gone. "Jess asked about the dance again," he said.

Kate let out a breath. "She's not sixteen, Brad, and she already got her way with the gymnastics."

"That she shouldn't have been in, in the first place. And she turns sixteen three weeks after the dance."

Kate cringed at the insult. Did he really think she was so unfeeling? She decided to keep the conversation on task, however, and not get distracted by all their other issues. "Besides the fact that she's not sixteen, she's been a real pill lately, with all kinds of attitude. Did you know she told Sharla she hated her the other day because Sharla used her eye shadow?"

"Yeah, well, being one of a lot of kids can be annoying, Kate. I know you don't see that side, but I was always getting after my brothers for getting into my stuff. It's very frustrating when you feel inconsequential enough in your own home that no one respects that what's yours is yours."

"It sounds like pure selfishness to me," Kate said, trying to understand but unable to grasp it. "I'd have done anything to have a sister I could share my stuff with."

Brad shrugged. "Well, if you'd had one you'd probably feel differently."

"So it's okay for her to freak out at her sister and back talk me, and yet she still gets to go to a dance she isn't old enough to go to?"

Brad looked at her for a minute, his jaw working as if thinking hard. "Didn't you go to prom your sophomore year, when you were fifteen?"

Kate looked away and busied herself with wiping off the counter. "I had no limits—another thing I'm trying to repair with my own kids. My mom didn't care what I did or who I was with. It made *me* feel very inconsequential."

"And yet you turned out okay," Brad pointed out.

Kate let out a breath and stared into the sink. This was all so silly. He didn't get it at all. And yet, did she really want to fight about this when she knew an even bigger battle was looming? "Fine."

"What?" Brad said.

"I said, fine, let her go."

He eyed her suspiciously. "I'd rather you see my point and want her to go than just give in."

"I *don't* want her to go, and I think we're setting a bad example to go back on our own rule, but you're determined to be the hero so go for it. I don't have time to help her find a dress or anything, and since you're the one who wants this to happen, it's your gig."

He just stood there, looking at her. Then he shook his head, turned on his heel, and went downstairs. That was it. She threw the washcloth toward the sink, knocking over the dishwashing soap that hit a glass she had missed loading into the diswasher. The glass fell into the sink and broke. Perfect.

22

——Original Message——
From: emjenkins000@yahoo.com
To: jjk_hollywood@hotmail.com
Sent: Tuesday, April 25, 11:26 PM
Subject: Re: Gymnastics no more!!!!

Jess,

sorry it took me so long to rite back. my computer's been acting weird. wow, that is awesome that yr dad let u out of gymnastics, but it sounds like he's just trying to earn yr trust so u fit into that little mold they've created for u. i'd hate to see u change who u are because u feel u now owe yr dad for what he did. why did it take him so long to help u out? where was he four years ago?

it seems to me that they are far more interested in making u follow their rules than they are about u being happy. my parents are like that. so involved with their own lives that they barely notice I'm there. so lame.

i talked to colt today and he said yr like the most amazing girl he's ever met. i think he's totally into u. what do u think about him? u ought to send him some pictures of u—got any with u in a bikini!!

i'm glad u finally got the IM working—that's awesome—i can't get it up on my puter right now though. i'll let u know. i can't wait to chat with u.

Emily

How long?" Kate asked. She glanced into the bathroom where two pregnancy tests rested on top of the toilet. Just one result couldn't be trusted when the stakes were this high.

"Two minutes," Julie said, reading the box and pressing start on the kitchen timer. She put the timer down and leaned against the counter. Kate sat on the edge of the tub while their kids watched a movie in the living room. The two women were silent for several seconds. "It's going to be okay," Julie offered.

Kate looked up into her friend's face. "Is it? He'll think I did it on purpose."

"But you didn't," Julie said. "Did you figure out how it happened?"

"Other than sex with my husband?" Kate said, trying to lighten the mood. Julie smiled and Kate continued. "I think it was when I had that flu. I was throwing up everything—probably even my pills."

Kate headed for the bedroom. She needed to pace. Julie followed her and leaned against the door frame. "The timing is right."

"You were having sex when you were sick?"

Kate blushed. "It *was* tax season."

Julie laughed just as the timer dinged. She stopped laughing, and the women looked at each other.

"You go check," Kate said.

Julie looked as if she were going to protest, but she must have sensed the seriousness of Kate's suggestion. She nodded and Kate kept pacing, folding her arms and praying that it would be negative. How ironic that with how badly she wanted a baby, she desperately *desperately* didn't want to be pregnant right now. And yet, if she were pregnant, then Brad couldn't stop her. She felt horrible for thinking that but couldn't ignore it completely. In one way, she would win. But at what cost?

She turned when Julie came into the bedroom. Julie's face said it all, and Kate's eyes filled with tears.

"You could take another one," Julie said softly. "These home pregnancy tests can be less than reliable."

"They're both positive?" Kate said as the blood drained from her face. She took a step backward, hit the bed with the back of her legs, and was forced to sit.

Julie nodded. Kate looked at the floor and processed it. She was pregnant. She had exactly what she wanted, and yet it was all wrong. Julie came to sit next to her. She put a hand on Kate's arm. "It's really going to be okay," she said.

Kate nodded, needing to be strong now that it was official. "Oh yeah," she said. "Brad's a good man. He'll understand."

"Exactly," Julie said.

"It'll be fine," Kate said, wiping at the tears and standing up. She needed a distraction now; she needed a little time to put her words together.

"You okay with this?" Julie asked.

"Yeah, but I really need to bake something." She smiled in an attempt to lighten the mood. Julie smiled back, willing to play along. "Should I make cinnamon rolls or chocolate cookies?"

"Oh, chocolate cookies," Julie said with a decisive nod. "Chocolate helps everything. But I thought sweets made you sick."

Kate made a face. "But I need to *bake* something."

"How about butter-soaked, horribly fattening breadsticks?"

"It's not chocolate—but butter will do the trick, too."

23

——Original Message——
From: coltinator_51@yahoo.com
To: jjk_hollywood@hotmail.com
Sent: Thursday, April 27, 2:29 PM
Subject: checking in

Jess,

Emily just called me, her computer has fritzed on her. She'll be back
online in a week or two but until then it's just you and me. I hope you
can handle just chatting with me for awhile. I'm bummed that Emily's
not around but I have to admit that I like the idea of having you to
myself—looking forward to your e-mails is what gets me through the
days of school. I can't wait until I graduate. I'm glad you figured out the
IM program, let's try to chat tonight—okay. Emily said I should ask you
about some pictures—what's she talking about?

And I'm asking you on an official IM date—tomorrow night, 7:00 your
time. You up for it? I'll bring flowers :)

Colt

————

So," Dr. Lyon said after filling Brad in on the same details he had presumably given Kate last week. "Did that jibe with what she told you?"

Brad liked Dr. Lyon. He liked how up front he was, liked that he seemed to understand both sides of the coin. What bothered him was the way Kate had twisted the information—just as he'd accused her of doing.

"For the most part," Brad said with a nod, though he was still lost in thought. "But she didn't make things sound quite so serious."

"Well, it's a lot harder for women," Dr. Lyon said. "Especially someone like your wife who obviously wants another child so badly."

Brad nodded.

"You see, Mr. Thompson, for us men, it's a very logical decision. We weren't built for bearing children—physically or even emotionally. But women . . . ," he shrugged. "They are created to have children. Their bodies, their hearts, their spirits—if you believe in that—have a very different capacity than ours do. Thus for a woman, such as your wife, who has obviously counted on many children, it's—"

"We have six," Brad reminded him, though he smiled politely. The man's comments didn't sound very doctorish, and Brad regarded him carefully.

"And I'm certainly not trying to tell you that your family plans are any business of mine," Dr. Lyon continued. "I'm only saying that health concerns aren't the only issue to consider."

Brad had never heard a doctor talk this way. He wondered if it was even legal or ethical. And yet Dr. Lyon probably dealt with this kind of decision making every day.

"Health concerns certainly are not the only issue for me," Brad said. "Six kids feels like an awful lot, and adding the health complications makes me even more comfortable with our family the way it is now."

Dr. Lyon nodded. "I can completely understand that. I have four and can't imagine more than that—but neither can my wife." He smiled, but Brad couldn't ignore the pointed nature of the comment. "The number of children a couple can and should have is a very personal decision between themselves and the Man Upstairs."

God? Brad felt a tingling move down his spine and suddenly he saw the situation in a new light. Had he asked God? He'd prayed about this, of course, but he hadn't really sought a direct answer. The fact was that he knew what *he* wanted. But that wasn't enough. He hadn't humbled himself enough to ask for the Lord's opinion. Dr. Lyon interrupted Brad's thoughts. "I hope that my comments haven't come across as trying to interfere with any of that. I'm just a doctor."

Brad looked up and smiled. "No," he said, berating himself for the fact that he needed someone else, especially a stranger, to remind him of how these things were supposed to work. "I very much appreciate your comments. I think I need to ponder all this a little longer. But if my wife and I decide to pursue another pregnancy, you would watch her closely and do everything you could to help it come to term?"

"Absolutely," Dr. Lyon said. "I specialize in high-risk pregnancies, and I would take no chances with your wife."

Brad stood and put out his hand. Dr. Lyon stood as well and they shook on it. "Thank you," Brad said.

"You're welcome," Dr. Lyon answered. "If you and your wife wanted to discuss things further—together, perhaps . . . ," he smiled, and Brad nodded knowingly. It must seem a little strange that they had both come alone. "I'd be happy to make time for you both."

24

Journal entry, April 27

I don't really have much to write, except that I took the quilt into the women's shelter and gave it to this lady. It was so awesome, and so sad at the same time. She has 3 little kids and her husband was a creep and finally left her all alone. She loved the quilt and I was so glad I gave it to her. It was awesome.

AND I met this guy. His name is Colt, he's Emily's cousin, and he's like way cool. We have so much in common and even though he's not my boyfriend or anything, it's still really cool. He loves math, just like me, and loves to read, just like me, and loves shrimp, just like me—isn't that amazing. AND he's 18. I just wish I could tell Britney, she'd be so jealous. Anyhoo—I'm not going to the dance tomorrow, can you believe that? I even talked to dad and everything, but nothing's happened. So lame. But Colt and I have an IM date, so that will be really cool and it will keep my mind off of all the fun Britney and her friends are having. Anyway—off to bed.

me

———————

Kate did her best to avoid Brad on Thursday evening. He was late getting home, so that part was easy, and then there was another basketball game. She'd never appreciated the NBA so much. Jess wasn't jumping up and down, so she assumed he hadn't told her about the dance. She wondered why but wasn't about to ask. She managed to go to bed before he did, but was just turning off the lights when he startled her by opening the door. Shoot.

"You weren't going to try to go to bed without talking to me, were you?" He smiled at her, as if trying to let her know they were back on good terms.

"No, I'm just really tired." She still didn't know whether she was going to tell him before he left on his trip or not. With the dance, and the trip—it seemed so rushed, and she wasn't sure she liked the idea of him leaving right after she dropped that kind of bombshell. She was waiting for some kind of divine intervention to let her know which direction to go. It seemed like as good a plan as any.

"So I talked to Dr. Lyon," Brad said, sitting on the bed and looking at her. She remained standing, not daring to get too close. It was all so sad. It shouldn't be like this. She should be excited to tell him, like she'd been with all the other kids. This should be a celebration, not an apologetic admission.

"And?" she prodded after several seconds.

"And he didn't say much to change my mind."

Kate had expected as much, and she just nodded. Wouldn't it be perfect if he had just accepted this, been supportive? Then when she announced the pregnancy he'd be halfway to being okay with things.

Brad reached out and took Kate's hand, pulling her toward the bed and waiting for her to meet his eye. She was surprised by the intimacy of his actions and wasn't sure how to react. Brad continued. "But he also made another point." She furrowed her brow. What did he mean by that?

"Kate," he said, "this is a decision that you, me, and the Lord are supposed to make. It's not just about what either one of us wants, or are afraid of. It's an eternal choice, and one I think I've been trying to make on my own."

Tears started forming in her eyes as hope sprung up once more. "Kate," he said again, softly, gently. "I *do* know how much you want this, I do. And I'm sorry I was so hard on you Saturday—I wasn't really fair, and I apologize for losing my cool. You're an excellent mother, and I know you love our kids very much."

Kate appreciated the apology, but it was the first part of what he said that caught her attention. "Do you really understand how I feel about another baby?" she asked, just in case he was about to throw a "but" into the conversation. "Can you know?"

"I know *you*," he said, smiling softly and taking her other hand. He was still sitting on the bed, and she looked down at him. "I know your heart, and I know you take your role as a mother and wife very seriously."

She didn't know what to say, and so she said nothing. "But please try to understand my perspective." She looked away, and he waited until she met his eyes again. "I'm your husband. It's my job to protect you and provide for you. The helplessness I felt when you got sick with Chris was overwhelming, and the very idea of endangering you again is more frightening than I could possibly put into words." Brad wasn't one to express his feelings so directly, and she couldn't justify or ignore how seriously he felt about this. "Life is full of risk and unknowns—but to willingly step into such a scary situation is very hard for me to make sense of. Can you understand that?"

Kate pulled one of her hands away and touched his face, feeling so close to him, so sympathetic and yet knowing that it was too late. The die was cast, and there was no going back now. It didn't matter what he thought or how he felt. He was stuck. The guilt for not telling him before now pressed hard against her chest. "Brad, I need to tell you—"

"I know you feel as strong as I do about this," he interrupted. "So I have a proposal. I'm going to be gone for five days. Let's both take this time and really pray about this, really look for answers. If we can both truly consider the other person's perspective and then take *that* to the Lord, I think we can figure this out."

Kate was stunned . . . and touched . . . and realized this might be the divine intervention she'd been hoping for. He would go on his trip, he'd be prayerful, and the Lord would soften his heart because the Lord knew *exactly* what was going on. He'd prepare Brad for it—yet there was still a thread of deception on her part. She should tell him right now . . . and yet destroy this moment? Render null and void all the things he'd just said after the horrible week the two of them had endured? How could she do that?

"Thank you," she said, though she still felt guilty about it.

"You have to consider my position too," he reminded her. "We both need to be in this together. You have to be just as willing to accept the Lord's will on this and be open to the fact that perhaps he doesn't expect us to risk your health for another child. We might be done."

"Of course," she said with a nod. "Of course, I'll consider that, too."

25

--Original Message--
From: jjk_hollywood@hotmail.com
To: coltinator_51@yahoo.com
Sent: Friday, April 28, 1:34 PM
Subject: Pictures

Colt

I'm so sorry I wasn't online last night. My sister was trying to burn a CD and it took forever! I can't believe I'm risking a blocked computer to reply to you, but I can't seem to help myself.

I would love to go on an IM date with you!! It will make the evening so much more bearable since everyone else is going to Spring Fling. I didn't even get a baby-sitting job this weekend. I hate my mom for not letting me go—but at least I get to chat with you. Emily told you about the pictures? She is so funny. She wants me to send you a picture of me in a bikini—like I own one. I'm not a swimsuit kind of girl—trust me. But if I can help you with your dividends and statistics you just let me know.

Maybe I'll get Britney to take some pictures of me if you're sure you want them :). What about you—have you got pics? You don't even have a bored—how come?

Teacher's back
Jess

The school office told Brad where Jess's last class was, and he had been waiting in the hall for almost ten minutes. He really wished Kate had wanted to be a part of this, and yet he was loath to push things any more than he already had with the dance and gymnastics. She would come around and eventually she would understand why he'd done things this way. He was just glad the tension between them was somewhat lifted. It was nice to be friends again.

The bell rang, and he stepped out into the hallway so Jess would be able to see him.

"Dad?" Jess asked when she came out, clutching her books to her chest. "What are you doing? Is everything okay?"

Brad forced a smile. "Everything is great," he said. "We're going shopping."

"Shopping?" Jess said as the two of them got jostled by the other students filling the hallway.

"For a dress."

The furrow of Jess's brow sunk even lower.

"For the dance," he added.

Jess's eyes went wide. "What?" she said, a slight squeal in her voice.

"If you stick to some set parameters, you can go tonight. I'm here to help you find the perfect dress."

Brad had expected her to be excited, but when she dropped her books and jumped up to hug him, he was shocked. He hugged her back, and she started babbling and crying like a . . . well, like a teenage girl.

"I've got to tell Britney," she said, picking up her books. "Can she come?"

"Sure," Brad said, then hurried to add, "She can use my cell phone to call her mom. Julie's going to help you guys get fixed up."

Her expression faltered a little. "Did Mom say it was okay that I go?"

"Yeah," he said, forcing his smile a little bigger in hopes of giving Jess a little more confidence. "But she had a lot to do today so she couldn't do the shopping."

An hour and a half later Brad was beside himself with gratitude that Britney had come. If it had been up to him, Jess would have gotten a really nice Sunday dress—but Britney provided the female opinion so desperately needed. After trying on eighteen dresses—at three different stores—Brad was seriously reconsidering Kate's motives in suggesting he do this. It was torture.

But dress number nineteen changed everything. It was black, with a high waist that flattered Jess's figure, cap sleeves, and a gauzy top layer that gave movement to the skirt. It brought out the deep brown of her eyes and didn't clash with her hair. Seeing the smile on her face when she looked in the mirror was the final decider, though. It was as if she were seeing herself in a way she'd never imagined. She stood there for nearly a full minute, just looking at herself, with Brad and Britney behind her.

"Wow," Britney said with reverence. "You look awesome."

Brad nodded in agreement, but Jess didn't even respond. Brad imagined that she was saying to herself that she was as beautiful as he'd always told her. She turned and gave him another big hug, thanking him over and over again. It nearly brought tears to his eyes to think she'd almost been denied this opportunity. Sure, if not for this dance there may have been another. But seeing the light in her face now—when she was struggling with her own self-confidence and he was looking for evidence of his own importance with his family—it was a priceless moment he'd never forget.

It was just half an hour later that he dropped Britney and Jess off at Julie's house. Brad walked them up to the door and got another hug before the two girls dashed inside to get their hair and makeup done. Julie came to the door after they disappeared. "Great dress," Julie said, smiling, though there seemed to be some hesitation in her expression.

"Yeah, Britney's input made all the difference. Thanks for letting her come."

Julie waved it off. "Oh, sure, I'm just really glad everything worked out. Funny how that happens, you know, how things just seem to work out."

Brad wondered if he'd missed something, but then Julie smiled. "Yeah, it all came together," he said.

"You know," Julie said, watching him so closely that it made him uncomfortable. Did he have something on his face? She was acting kind of funny. "You're a great father, Brad."

Was she flirting with him? "Uh, thanks," he said, turning back to the car. "I appreciate all your help."

"Sure thing," Julie said. He didn't turn back. "I'll have Jess home by eleven."

He climbed in the car and reflected on Julie's strange comments. Then he shook his head. It didn't matter. What mattered was that he and Kate were on the same page again and his little girl was about to have the time of her life—because of him. Queen's song "We Are the Champions" was playing on the radio. He sang it at the top of his lungs all the way home.

"No time for losers cause we are the champions . . . of the world."

26

——Original Message——
From: jjk_hollywood@hotmail.com
To: coltinator_51@yahoo.com
Sent: Friday, April 28, 5:04 PM
Subject: Spring Fling!!!

Colt,

I'm going!! I can hardly believe it. Dad was waiting for me after school
and he took me shopping and everything! I'm at Britney's now and her
mom is helping us with our makeup. Can you believe it!! I'll tell you all
about it—I can't believe I'm going!! Dang, I wish I could tell Emily!! Will
you call her for me? She'll be shocked that my parents gave in on this.
I'm so excited!!!!!!!!!!!!!

Laters,
Jess

PS—I'm so sorry I won't be able to IM with you—but for sure tomorrow,
okay? I'll tell you all about the dance. I sure wish you guys were here
though. Wouldn't that be awesome?

———————

He read the e-mail and banged his fists on the computer desk, making
the laptop bounce and the pen container fall on its side.

No, no, no—this wasn't how it was supposed to happen, he thought to himself as he jumped to his feet and started pacing, raking his fingers through his thinning hair. "Jess can't go to the dance. She can't!" he screamed. His upstairs neighbor stomped on the floor and he swore at her.

For a moment he pictured his Jessie dressed up and dancing with a boy. It made his stomach tighten, and he clenched his eyes shut against the vision. She wouldn't dance with anyone, would she? Could she do that to him? He was such a fool to have taken things so slow. She wasn't dependent enough—she didn't need him the way he needed her. He ground his teeth and kept pacing back and forth, back and forth, trying to calm himself down but feeling the rage grow and boil inside him.

How could this happen? She'd been so certain her parents would never let her go—that's why he'd pushed it so hard, to help her feel angry and cheated. He was prepared to deepen that chasm tonight when she got online while her friends were having a good time. He'd already planned out the perfect things to say. It was going to be a defining moment, and *he* was the person she would have turned to. *He* was going to comfort her and make it all better.

His head began to throb, and he clenched his eyes closed. Janeece, the only other girl he was e-mailing, had become too aggressive, too much like Terrezza—demanding they meet or at least talk on the phone. As if it were up to her. He'd canceled the e-mail address he used for her just this afternoon, relieved that he'd figured her out before things had gone too far. Jess was his only one now—she was his destiny.

He couldn't allow anyone to come between them—not after all he'd done to gain her trust, to be everything she wanted and needed. He cursed and kept pacing, trying to calm himself while making plans to step things up. He'd been taking things slow—too slow. It was time to take this seriously. Time for her to see him as more than some boy online. He needed more, he needed her devotion.

But he had to do it right. He couldn't scare her away and waste all these months. He dropped back into his chair, his head in his hands, and groaned as he tried to figure out the right way to handle this new development. How could he use it to his benefit?

Jess, he thought, *don't do this to me.*

27

——Original Message——
From: jjk_hollywood@hotmail.com
To: coltinator_51@yahoo.com
Sent: Monday, May 1, 5:17 AM
Subject: Are you there?

Colt?

Are you there? You've never taken this long to get back to me—where've you been all weekend? It's Monday morning, everyone is still asleep and I'm waiting to chat with you but you're not online. Did you get my e-mail about the dance? It was so much fun. The girls from the track team that Britney introduced to me were awesome, and they invited me to come to the track meet this Friday. It's their final meet of the season and they'll all be going out to pizza afterward. It was so nice to get to know them—and I wasn't all tongue-tied either. I think you and Emily have helped me get so much more comfortable with myself. Did you see the new picture on my bored? I've never felt so pretty in my whole life.

Anyway—you're still not online. Is everything okay?

I really want to talk to you, I've missed you this weekend. Did you tell Emily I got to go?

Jess

Monday evening, Monique passed Jamie the plate of lemon chicken. She took a piece and passed it to Harrison, who then passed it to Karl. Next to go around was the broccoli and then the rolls. It had taken several minutes for Monique to decide whether to put a setting at Terrezza's place tonight or not, but in the end she couldn't imagine looking at the empty dishes. Not tonight. As Monique oversaw the rotation of the food, she wondered when was the last time they'd had a big dinner like this. Not since Terrezza left—she knew that. But she couldn't remember when they'd done it last before then.

Jamie had finished her finals last week and was able to take a few days off from work. Karl agreed to leave his skanky girlfriend at home and lay off the beer long enough for them to get together. The Weatherford family needed to talk.

"This is delicious, Mom," Jamie said a few silent minutes into the meal.

"Thank you, dear," Monique said, smiling slightly. Monique waited for Harrison to begin talking, and then finally realized he was waiting for her. She carefully laid her fork down on the edge of the plate and cleared her throat.

"There are some things we need to tell you," she said, looking at each of her family members in turn. "Some things concerning Terrezza."

The speaking of her name caused a heaviness to descend, and the forks stopped moving. After that first meeting with Sergeant Morris, their refusal to accept that Terrezza might be gone had dwindled. They'd been reading past cases, and they knew that no matter how hard they wanted it to be different, they needed to prepare for the very worst. That was why Harrison agreed to spring for a last-minute airline ticket for Jamie to come home, and why Monique insisted that Karl put his anger toward his father aside for one evening.

"Your father and I have been talking to the police for the last week or so—they've reopened Terrezza's case."

"They should never have closed it," Karl said with a snort, pushing his chair back from the table, but thankfully not standing up or storming off.

Monique continued. "One of the reasons the police didn't investigate very deeply was because it seemed as if Terrezza left of her own free will, and with her history. . . . Anyway, it turns out that Terrezza kept notes—lots of notes. E-mails, instant messaging chats—things like that. The police are putting together a time line, but they also created a profile of the person Terrezza was communicating with online."

She waited for someone to say something, but no one did, so she took a breath and continued. "He was pretending to be a teenage boy, but they think he was in his forties, from the northeast—maybe Boston or Chicago. He's likely white, very bright, but with limited social skills and—"

"I don't want to know who he is," Jamie said. "I just . . . I don't want to think about that. What about Terrezza? What did they say about her?"

Harrison broke in. "They don't know." He shared a look with his wife, and she understood in that moment that he wasn't going to tell their children the grim expectations the police had related to them. "But the investigation is moving forward—they're hopeful that if they can get some different people to cooperate, they can make some progress."

"People?" Karl asked, his jaw tight as he looked at his father. "Who?"

Monique answered. "Hotmail, Yahoo—online places that were used as means of communication. They guard their information pretty closely, and in the process they're protecting this creep. The police are trying to change their minds."

She paused and then continued, her voice heated as it had been when Sergeant Morris had explained it. "It makes me sick," she said. "They have what we need, and they won't release it."

"But we hope that will change," Harrison added. "She took

wonderful notes. That should convince them that this is more important than their privacy agreements."

"This is crap," Karl said suddenly, leaning back in his chair. "It took the cops five months to figure this out? They treated her like a freaking runaway even though we told them that wasn't what happened."

"Actually," Monique cut in, regretting her own heated emotions. She didn't want her children to think she wasn't backing up the police, no matter what her frustrations were. "That *is* what happened. She met up with this man of her own accord, and *we* had the program and the notes on our computer this whole time. It was right here."

They were all silent again, for nearly two more minutes. "What about Terrezza?" Jamie asked again, blinking her big dark eyes at her mother. "What are they doing to find her?"

"Well," Monique said, trying to keep her emotions at bay. "They are certainly looking for her, trying to put the pieces together. But it's time we—" She looked up into the faces of her grown children. They looked at her with such expectation, such longing for peace. It transported her back to the days when they were young, when she was their world. It seemed so long ago. She met Harrison's eyes, and that's when the emotion hit.

They needed to prepare their other children for what may happen— but it was so hard. The words stuck in her throat.

"Time we what?" Karl prodded, a hint of challenge in his voice.

"Time we pray," Harrison cut in. He reached his hands out to each of his children. His big brown hands were calloused and stained from years of working on engines and rear differentials, yet they looked tender, held out toward his children. After a few moments, Jamie took her father's hand. Religion hadn't been a focus of their family, though Harrison and Monique had both attended church growing up. Jamie reached her hand to her mother's, which Monique gladly took. She stretched her hand out to Karl, her palm facing up. They didn't speak, and somewhere from the back recesses of her mind came the phrase, "Be still and know that I am God." The thought tugged at her soul, making her anxious to connect with something bigger than herself, than Terrezza, than any of them.

Tears fell freely from her eyes as Karl finally lifted his hands, taking hers first and then, with hesitation, grasping his father's. Harrison immediately wrapped his thick fingers around those of his son and bowed his head. They all followed suit.

The prayer was not eloquent, and Harrison's voice was not booming. Rather it was soft and heartfelt. A strange calm descended upon Monique that, for the moment at least, relieved her mind. "Please let Terrezza know, wherever she is, that we love her," Harrison paused, and she heard him sniffle. Her own tears dripped onto her plate, forming little puddles along the edge. "We love her," he repeated, "and we miss her so much. Help us to be a family again, and help the police to catch this . . . man. Dear God, we pray, amen."

The silence that followed was almost sweet, confusing Monique. How could they feel comforted at such a time? Monique sensed the others felt it too and didn't want to be the first to break the moment. Maybe it was a sign from God that Terrezza was all right, that she would be coming home.

"I love you, Terrezza," Harrison finally said, his voice shaking.

"I love you too," Monique chimed in.

"Love you, sis," Jamie added.

Several seconds passed before Karl spoke. "Wherever you are, whatever has happened—I love you, too. Just come back home. Just . . . come back."

28

——Original Message——
From: coltinator_51@yahoo.com
To: jjk_hollywood@hotmail.com
Sent: Tuesday, May 2, 6:29 PM
Subject: Things I need to tell you . . .

Jess—

Sorry it took me so long to get back to you. I got your e-mail about the dance, but it took me a few days to gather my thoughts. I wish I could say the night was as enjoyable for me as it was for you. I have to tell you that when I read your e-mail I was hurt, not just because I was planning to chat with you but mostly because the idea of you dancing with other boys really brought home just how important you have become to me. I know we've only known each other a little while, but this dance made things very clear to me. You're the kind of girl I could fall in love with, Jess.

I hope I'm not being too forward, it's taken me hours to write this e-mail and I understand if you don't feel the same, but I couldn't keep my thoughts to myself. After hearing so much about you from Emily for so long, and getting to know you so well, I just can't help but feel this way. I hope you'll still talk to me again.

I can't believe I'm saying these things. Please don't tell anyone about

me, especially Britney or your parents, I know they won't understand.
The only feelings that matter are yours and mine.

Love,
Colt

———————

"Helloooooo?"

Kate looked up from the book she was reading to Justin, sitting on the living room floor stacking Cheerios, and Chris, asleep in her lap, and smiled. "Marilyn," she said, feeling instantly calmed by her mother-in-law's presence.

Marilyn came into view a moment later as the front door shut behind her. Her silver hair was nicely styled, as always, and her dentured smile was big and bright. Marilyn had always been a breath of fresh air—like the sweet old ladies in fairy tales.

"Gramma!" Justin yelled, jumping up and running into his grandmother, wrapping his arms around her legs.

Marilyn grunted at the impact, then mussed up Justin's hair. He looked up at her, and Kate shifted Chris from her lap so she could stand.

"What brings you out on a night like this?" Kate asked, embracing Brad's mother, then pulling back and smiling. It had been raining all day, and since Brad's father had passed away a few years ago, Marilyn didn't like driving by herself in "weather."

"Frankly, dear, I was worried about you," Marilyn said with a decisive nod. She had a cloth sack and shifted it from one arm to another while shrugging out of her jacket. Kate was too alarmed by the comment to help her. What did she mean? Why was she worried? Did she know something was wrong? Marilyn could be very insightful.

Justin let go of his Grandma's legs and went running downstairs yelling to the other kids that Grandma was there.

"Kate," Marilyn said, laying her jacket across the back of the couch and watching her closely. "Is something wrong?"

Kate smiled again, meeting her mother-in-law's eye. "Nothing," she said, perhaps too quickly.

Marilyn held Kate's eyes until Kate had to look away. She busied herself with returning to the living room and picking up the Cheerios now scattered across the carpet.

"Kate," Marilyn began again, but was cut off by the voices of two more grandchildren—Sharla and Keith—as they ran upstairs. Jess and Caitlyn were still at Mutual.

"Grandma!" they all yelled, and Kate was saved from whatever else Marilyn was going to say. It always amazed Kate how well Marilyn could give each child such individual attention. After a few minutes of listening to the chattering, Marilyn reached into her sack and pulled out a container of ice cream.

"How about dessert?" she announced. The kids screamed their agreement, waking Chris, whose blue eyes blinked a few times before he too scrambled off the couch. But he ran to Kate, not Grandma, likely in fear of the screams that interrupted his sleep.

"Oh, I'm sorry," Marilyn said, looking at the whimpering toddler as Kate hoisted him into her arms.

"No problem," Kate said, smiling. "Ice cream would be wonderful."

Marilyn nodded. "Good. I figured you were all likely missing Brad a great deal about now."

Kate smiled politely, but the reminder of her husband sharpened the unease that was growing by the day. He called every night, and they chatted about the conference, her day, and the kids—and she hung up each time with an "I love you" but no "I'm pregnant." She just couldn't bring herself to do it over the phone. But it was eating her alive. She wasn't one to keep secrets well—especially big secrets like this.

Together, Kate and Marilyn spooned up four dishes of ice cream.

"Don't you want some?" Marilyn asked. Kate smiled and shook her head. The very idea of something sweet made her stomach turn. The kids were nearly finished when Jess and Caitlyn came in. Marilyn hugged both girls, praised Jess's hair—which did look very nice—and complimented Caitlyn on her fashion sense. Caitlyn had matched her shirt to the brown stitching of her jeans and had used a chartreuse scarf as a belt. It was very trendy, and Kate wondered why she hadn't noticed that. Then Grandma dished up some more ice cream for the teenage girls.

"I think I'll put Chris down," Kate said when his whimpering turned to wails. He hadn't recovered from his wakening.

"I've got this covered," Marilyn said, removing the empty bowls from the table. "Take your time."

Kate thanked her and took Chris down the hall. It took several minutes in the rocking chair before he fell asleep, worked up from the late-night excitement. But even when his breath was tickling her shoulder, she kept rocking, enjoying the peace and solitude of the moment.

She was sure it was her fault, a reaction to her own tension, but the kids had been particularly difficult since Brad left. Especially Jess, who wouldn't say two words to her. On Sunday, Kate had asked for Jess's help with dinner and Jess had refused, insisting Caitlyn was old enough to help. It had led to a heated argument, and finally Kate had enough. She sent Jess to her room but hated that it meant Jess had gotten her way. Caitlyn helped with dinner, and Jess wouldn't even come up to eat it. Since then they had been pretending one another didn't exist. As if keeping the pregnancy from Brad weren't enough stress. She closed her eyes and allowed herself to do something she hadn't done for a very long time—relax. The muscles in her back and shoulders slowly softened, melting into the chair. Her head nodded, jolting her awake, once . . . twice. Well, maybe she could rest her eyes for just a minute.

She wasn't sure how long she'd been asleep but woke up with a jolt, causing Chris to startle as well. Luckily he didn't wake up. She blinked a few times, orienting herself to where she was. Then she stood and placed the baby in his crib. She pulled the blanket over him and hurried from his room. The house was dark except for the kitchen. How long had she been sleeping? Were the kids still up? Was Marilyn still here?

"Marilyn?" Kate asked as she rounded the corner into the kitchen. Her mother-in-law looked up from the book she was reading and smiled. Kate looked at the clock on the microwave. It was after eleven o'clock. "I'm so sorry," she said, embarrassed. "I guess I fell asleep."

Marilyn nodded, marked her place and pulled out one of the kitchen chairs, patting the seat of it. Kate accepted the invitation, but on the way to the table she noticed the kitchen was clean. She peeked into the living room and noticed it was clean as well. No shoes or backpacks in sight. She was even more embarrassed.

"I'm really sorry," Kate said, and she felt tears come to her eyes. *Oh, get a grip,* she commanded herself, blinking quickly.

Marilyn didn't respond verbally; instead she leaned over and put a hand on Kate's arm. "What's wrong?" she asked, kindly, gently. Her tone invited even more emotion, and Kate wondered if she'd ever be able to talk that way to her daughters. She hoped so, but based on her recent history with Jess it seemed impossible.

Kate shook her head. "Nothing," she said, staring at marker streaks from years of little kids' coloring projects on the kitchen table. They were now a part of the wood grain.

"When are you due?"

Kate snapped her head up and stared at her mother-in-law. She opened her mouth to refute it, but couldn't. Marilyn knew—of course she knew. She'd guessed it on four of the other six pregnancies. Kate looked back down and shook her head. She didn't know what to say.

"Congratulations," Marilyn said, sitting back in her chair as if Kate had just confirmed all the details. "Lucky number seven—that's what I said when it snuck up on me."

Kate tried to smile, but she felt her chin tremble. "Brad doesn't want it," she blurted out, then looked up to see Marilyn's reaction. She was visibly shocked.

"What?" Marilyn said.

"I mean, he doesn't know, but he doesn't want any more." Kate felt the tears overflow, and she wiped at her cheeks with the back of her hand. "We've been discussing it . . . and he doesn't want another baby . . . and I do . . . and I met with a doctor . . . and then he did . . . and then I found out I'm pregnant . . . and then he left and now . . . oh, Marilyn, I don't know what to do." She dropped her chin and gave in to the tears, feeling safe with Marilyn and yet still anxious about talking about it with anyone.

It was some time later that Kate's eyes finally dried. Marilyn, as always, was a great listener. "These things happen, Kate," she said. "In my day we didn't even have birth control—so they happened much more often." She smiled at her attempt for humor. Kate tried to smile too but couldn't quite pull it off.

"It would be easier if we didn't now," Kate said. "Then he wouldn't think I'd done it on purpose."

"Well, there is that," Marilyn said, and Kate wondered if she was making an accusation. "But it will turn out. You'll see. Brad's a good man, you've made him into a better man, and he'll show up for you in this. I think you know that."

"It's not just this," Kate said. "It's so many things. We just don't seem to see eye to eye about anything, and Jess is acting so weird, and he's going over my head with her, and it's just all so . . . miserable."

"What's wrong with Jess?" Marilyn asked, and Kate launched into her other topic of woe.

"I just don't speak 'teenager,'" Kate said with a shrug. "And I know it's a cliché, but it's like we're on two different planets."

Marilyn nodded. "I did notice she seems a little distracted," she said. "And she was on the computer for quite a little while. Is that safe?"

Kate nodded. "We have really good virus protection. And she uses the computer for homework—but I can't seem to do anything right. How did you do it, with your kids? How did you make it work?"

"Well," Marilyn said with a laugh. "I didn't always. I mean, Brad was a piece of cake—but Devon?" she shook her head. "If we'd had eBay back then I'd have sold him off for a quarter."

"They don't let you sell living things," Kate said. "I checked."

Marilyn laughed and Kate laughed too. "Oh, there are hard years as a parent, aren't there?"

Kate nodded. "I really thought by now that I'd know her well enough that we wouldn't have this kind of tension, ya know? As stupid as it sounds, I didn't see it coming."

"Of course not," Marilyn said. "That's the way God intends it—if we knew how bad it would get, we'd reconsider the whole thing and miss out on the good stuff. But seriously, Kate, you just have to learn her currency and then open up the trade markets."

"Currency?" Kate asked, looking at her mother-in-law for clarification.

"Yes," Marilyn said. "What does she value? Then give it to her in trade for what you need from her."

Kate furrowed her brow. What did Jess value? She didn't even know her daughter enough to figure it out.

Marilyn continued. "Devon, for example, loved to move. So as a family we played soccer every Saturday. He was one of the older ones, so it was easy to get the little ones out there—but I hated every minute of it."

Kate smiled at the image of Marilyn, with all her poise and elegance, head butting a soccer ball. "But it kept us clued in," Marilyn continued. "And then he was on a competition team, so I dragged my row of ducklings to every game. He also highly valued his friends, weird and obnoxious as they were, so we made the house a place he wanted to bring the kids to. Then with Capri, well, she was dramatic and just plain rude, but she valued stuff. Lots of stuff—the pinker the better. So I helped her redo her room and made new curtains. When I found a shirt on sale I'd buy it for her and slip it to her on the sly. By playing the game their way, I was the winner because they would talk to me, and they trusted me because I made a point to know them."

"Currency," Kate repeated, things becoming more clear in her head. She looked over and met her mother-in-law's eyes again. "Bribery."

Marilyn smiled. "A parenting tool highly underrated."

29

Journal entry, May 2

I think I'm falling in love. Me! I've wondered if I would ever find a boy who would see me as anything other than a good partner in science class, but Colt . . . he thinks I'm pretty and smart. All those things I said about him before are more true than ever. He makes me feel like I can do anything. No one has ever made me feel so good about myself. I just wish I could tell someone!! But Colt made me promise.

It's just all so incredible—I don't have enough words in my heart to truly explain it. But just know that I have never been so happy in all my life. I haven't written him back yet—but wow. It's like a fairy tale.

Anyway—I gotta get ready for bed. Maybe I'll dream about Colt tonight.

me

———

Jess, you're acting weird," Britney said, watching her closely at lunch on Wednesday. "What's going on?"

Jess shrugged, but she couldn't wipe the smile from her face. All her life she'd believed that there was one special person made for everyone in the world, and at fifteen Jess had found her special someone. It was an amazing feeling.

"What's going on?" Britney pushed again.

Again, Jess shrugged, wondering what Colt was doing right now. Was he thinking of her like she was thinking of him? Jess stirred ketchup with a french fry while she imagined his picture on the body of a man—a senior even. It sent a thrill down her spine. Wow. It was all just so incredible. She nearly forgot Britney was there.

"Jess," Britney said loudly, causing Jess to startle and several other students to look their way. Jess met her eye, and Britney's cheeks turned pink as she looked at the people now looking at her. She cleared her throat. "You're acting really weird, why?"

Jess took a breath. Britney could never understand. So even if Jess could tell her, which she couldn't, it wouldn't make sense. Britney had never been in love before. She had nothing to base this on, and she'd likely be so jealous that she'd say something horrible about it—about Colt. "Brit, don't worry about it. I'm fine." She stood up and picked up her tray. "Good luck at your meet today," she added before going to dump her tray. She could feel Britney watching her, wondering, and it made her smile even bigger. Today she felt invincible, powerful, as if no one could touch her. She had a secret, yes, and she wanted to share it, but not being able to made her feel somewhat superior. What did Britney have in her life that was as precious as this?

For the first time in a very long time she didn't question herself, what she said, how she acted. It didn't matter if her clothes weren't right, or if she was too quiet. She had Colt, and that's all that mattered now. It was just so . . . amazing.

30

——Original Message——
From: jjk_hollywood@hotmail.com
To: coltinator_51@yahoo.com
Sent: Wednesday, May 3, 1:49 PM
Subject: Wow . . .

Colt,

I've got a few minutes of free time in computer class, so I'm writing you back even though my thoughts are going a hundred miles a minute.

I've always been told that it's impossible to really fall in love when I'm so young, but I have to admit that I think about you all the time. At the dance I only danced two times and I know this will sound silly but I closed my eyes on the slow dance and pretended it was you. I just feel so close to you—especially now that we're e-mailing so often. I have friends, and I have a lot of boys in my ward, but I've never felt like this and I missed you—even though we've never met. I'm so sorry I stood you up on the IM. I feel really bad about that. So now what? Where do we go from here? I've waited to IM you every morning this week and during my computer time, but you didn't show up—maybe you've been waiting for my answer. I can understand that. I've never known a boy so easy to talk to and get to know.

The bell's about to ring—but I'll write again when I get home.

Love, Jess

Kate peeked out the front window Wednesday afternoon, saw Jess heading up the driveway, and felt her heart rate increase. She'd thought hard on Marilyn's words long after she'd left last night, and by morning Kate had come up with a plan. Not only did she hope to repair things with Jess, but she liked to think Brad would be pleased with the reparations she'd made in his absence.

"I'm glad you're home," Kate said with a big smile when Jess walked in the door. Chris had awakened early from his nap, so she'd sent both boys outside in order to give her and Jess a little one-on-one time. Thank goodness it wasn't raining today. She needed the quiet for a minute. Jess looked longingly into the computer room, and Kate wondered if Marilyn was right; maybe Jess was online too much. But she pushed that away, anxious to get to the heart of this moment she'd worked so hard to create. "I got you something."

Jess furrowed her brow suspiciously and took off her backpack. She'd been putting more into how she looked since the dance. She was wearing a little makeup, and her hair was pinned up. It looked really nice, and Kate made a note to compliment her on it later. "What?" Jess asked.

"Well, I'm so proud of you for finishing your Young Women's Award, so I got the medallion from the Young Women's president today and had something special done with it." She pulled the box out of the silverware drawer and held it out to Jess. "It's still not officially yours yet, 'cause the bishop needs to give it to you on Sunday, but you get a sneak peek."

Jess opened the box, looked at the medallion for a minute, and then looked up with a confused look on her face.

"I don't get it," she said. "I mean, I'm glad it's silver."

"Turn it over," Kate said, almost unable to hide her excitement.

Jess reached in, and Kate came to stand next to her as she turned over the medallion. Into the silver back was etched in tiny letters:

Love you

Jess

**

Dad

&

Mom

"Wow," Jess said in just the reverent tone Kate had been hoping for. "That's really cool."

Kate fairly beamed. "I got you something else as well," Kate said, really on a roll. She took the velvet case back from Jess and put it away in the drawer again so it wouldn't get lost before Sunday. Then she picked up the Dillard's bag from the floor and handed it over. Jess took it and looked inside. Her face didn't show the same level of excitement as it had when she opened the jewelry box.

"It's a new dress," Kate said in case Jess couldn't tell. "I thought you could wear it on Sunday when you get your medallion."

"It's yellow."

"You love yellow."

Jess pulled a handful of the yellow fabric out of the bag and looked up at Kate. "When I was, like, eight."

Kate's smile faded. Could she do nothing right? And when did Jess's favorite color change? "You look beautiful in yellow."

"No, I don't," Jess said, shoving the fabric back in the bag. "It totally washes me out. I haven't liked yellow for, like, ever."

Kate let out a breath. Was it so hard for Jess to say thank you? Kate had wrestled both boys at the mall, of all places, in order to get the medallion engraved and buy the dress. She took the bag back. "Fine, I'll go exchange it. They also had it in green and light blue."

"Can I take it back myself and find something *I'll* like?"

Kate took a breath and reminded herself that just because she was ready to make things better didn't mean it would be easy. "Okay," Kate said, turning away. "Maybe we can go on Saturday."

"Or maybe Julie could take Britney and me tomorrow. Britney doesn't have practice tomorrow and was going to get some new jeans. I bet I can just go with them."

Kate swallowed and tried to keep her cool. Jess dropped the bag on the counter and headed for the study. "Thanks anyway," she said. Kate bit the inside of her lip to keep from screaming at Jess or crying—either option sounded good right now. Why was it that the harder she tried to make things better, the worse she felt? Was it worth the effort if the effort gave no reward?

31

——Original Message——

From: coltinator_51@yahoo.com

To: jjk_hollywood@hotmail.com

Sent: Wednesday, May 3, 7:09 PM

Subject: Re: Wow . . .

Jessie—

I can't tell you what a relief it was to get your e-mail. I was worried you would think I was such an idiot and never want to talk to me again. I should have known you wouldn't do anything like that. I feel like we've known each other forever. After I got your e-mail I closed my eyes and pretended it was me you were dancing with too. It still makes me sick to think of you in another boy's arms though. I want you to be with me, Jess, and only me. I'm so happy I feel like I could fly. Tonight, I want you to look at the sunset, knowing I'm doing the same thing. Dang, I wish I could meet you in person. I wish I could just hold you and tell you with my own lips how much I love you. Maybe someday—though it will never be soon enough for me.

I also wanted to ask a favor. I know Britney invited you to go to the meet on Friday and then to pizza and everything, but I wonder if you would consider staying home. Maybe I can call you and we can talk or something, but I'd like to be with you on Friday—somehow. Can you do that for me?

Love
Colt

P.S. Do you believe in soul mates?

—————————

Despite the frustration of the dress incident, Kate kept working on her plan. Jess was on the computer for a long time, but Kate didn't interrupt her. At one point, Jess went outside and watched the sun set. Kate thought that was weird but didn't want to be overbearing, so she didn't say anything. She didn't even ask for Jess's help with dinner—though with Brad having been gone for four days now she was hammered and could have used an extra set of hands. Still, she hoped that it would work—that Jess wouldn't see her as such an enemy. After the dishes were done and the kids were in bed, she took a breath and went downstairs. Time for the second part of her plan. She'd done her part; now it was time for Jess to reciprocate—fair trade.

"Jess?" Kate said as she opened the door to her daughter's room only to catch her half dressed as she was getting ready for bed.

"Mom!"

Kate quickly apologized and pulled the door shut. After several seconds Jess came to the door and opened it a couple of inches—as if Kate were a vacuum salesman or something equally annoying.

"I'm really sorry," Kate said, embarrassed for having walked in on her daughter.

"Why can't you just knock?" Jess asked, her arms wrapped protectively around herself as if still trying to hide her body.

"I just wanted to talk to you for a minute," Kate said, hating the awkwardness and not knowing how to behave.

"I'm really tired," Jess said.

"Please?" Kate asked.

Jess shrugged and opened the door. She went and sat on her bed, pulling her legs beneath her and tugging at the hem of her oversized T-shirt.

"So," Kate said, searching for something to say. "How's school?"

"Fine."

"Good! What's your favorite class?"

Jess eyed her strangely. "Math."

"You must get that from your dad. I hated math."

Jess said nothing and went back to looking at the bedspread. The seconds ticked by. Kate watched Jess smile to herself, and it made Kate uncomfortable. Was she enjoying how awkward this was for Kate? The idea made Kate squirm.

"Is everything okay?" she finally asked.

Jess looked up as if she'd forgotten Kate was there. "Uh, yeah," she said, but the distraction was obvious.

"What's wrong?" Kate asked.

"Not a thing," Jess said, smiling even wider, deepening Kate's concern.

"You're acting really . . . odd, Jess."

"What do you care?" Jess mumbled, her smile fading.

Kate raised her eyebrows. "Excuse me?"

Jess looked up and met her eye. "You don't really care about my life, so why do you pretend you do?"

Kate blinked, completely deflated by the comment. "I do care about your life, Jess. I'm your mom. I love you."

Jess just shrugged, and Kate was out of words. After several moments, she stood up—suddenly anxious to be done with this. It wasn't fair for Jess to treat her this way, and she'd run out of patience. "Well, I guess I'll let you get to bed. Can I get a goodnight hug?" Kate asked, hoping they could at least end things on a positive note.

"Uh, I'm really tired," Jess said and she quickly pulled back the covers and slipped underneath.

Kate clenched her teeth and took a breath to calm herself down, but it didn't work. All the hurt and anger and frustration exploded in her mind.

"What is wrong with you?" she demanded, her voice shaking as tears filled her eyes. Jess looked at her over her blanket, startled by the tone. "Do you even care how hard I work to take care of you? How much I do every day to keep this family going? I have bent over backwards to support you, to love you, to make your life good, and you act as if you're some prisoner of war!"

She stopped to take a breath, ashamed to be gratified by the almost scared look on Jess's face. "I'm sick of all the attitude, do you understand that? And I'm not going to put up with it anymore. Starting tomorrow your computer time is determined by your attitude. If you keep playing this poor-Jess role, then you get no computer time at all—I don't care about your homework. But I can't do this anymore, do you understand?"

Jess said nothing, just stared, and Kate's anger began to fade enough that she now felt like a fool standing in the middle of Jess's room pontificating like an idiot. Yet part of her thought, *I've tried everything else.*

"I love you, Jess," she said, still yelling, "but I'm sick of this. I'm your mother and I deserve your respect." She slammed the door on her way out and stomped up the stairs. Currency—shmurrency. She just wanted Jess to act human again. She did not have the time or the energy to try to figure out the jigsaw puzzle of adolescent arrogance. Jess knew how to behave—she'd been taught all her life what was right—and it was simply time for her to step up. Kate needed compliance right now. Was that so much to ask?

32

From: jjk_hollywood@hotmail.com

To: coltinator_51@yahoo.com

Sent: Wednesday, May 3, 10:53 PM

Subject: Re: Wow . . .

Colt,

I had to wait until my mom was in bed to write you back—she totally wigged on me tonight—kinda freaked me out. She said if I don't start respecting her she's going to take away my computer time—even for homework. I wish she'd either leave me alone or really care about me. The in between fake stuff makes me crazy.

But I did get to see the sunset. I closed my eyes and imagined I was with you. It was awesome. I wish you lived closer. Have you thought more about going to the U of U? Then we'd be really close to each other—though my parents would still totally freak out about you cause you're so much older than me.

Wow, Colt, I just don't know what else to say except thank you so much for making me feel so good about who I am. No one treats me like you do, no one cares about me like you do. It's amazing to feel this way, isn't it? I hope Emily gets back online soon. Not telling anyone is torture!

As for Friday, it's a date! I'll tell Britney I can't go—I owe you that much
for standing you up last week, right?

Will you be IMing in the morning? I hope so.

Love, Jess

————

"Why can't you come?" Britney said, whining just a little. It was cold
that morning, and their breath clouded in front of their faces as
they walked to school. "You said you could."

Jess made an apologetic face. "I'm really sorry," she said, and she was.
She hated letting Britney down. And she really wanted to go to the meet
and the pizza party. Hanging out with Britney's friends would be so fun.
But she couldn't do that to Colt, and part of her didn't want anyone else to
become important to her. If she got too close to Britney's friends, would
she have time for Colt? Would there be room? If only she could tell
Britney!

"So why can't you come?" Britney asked again.

"I . . . have to baby-sit," she lied.

"For who?" Britney asked.

"My mom," Jess said. "Dad's been out of town all week, and I think
they're going to go to dinner tomorrow."

"You think?"

Jess let out a breath. "I just . . . I have to help out, Britney, you know
that. I'm real sorry."

Britney turned her head and looked at Jess again. "You know what,"
she said as if making an official pronouncement. "Sometimes you need to
stand up for yourself. You never get to do anything, and now you're staying
home because your mom needs you to baby-sit? My mom would watch
the kids, or even Caitlyn. This is a big deal, Jess. Everyone really liked you

143

at the dance, and you said yourself it's hard for you to make friends and things. This is your chance and it's like you're wimping out."

Jess knew she was right—based on the story Jess had told her. But what choice did she have?

"I'm really sorry," Jess said again, feeling horrible but not knowing what else to do. They had reached the school now and hurried toward the front doors to get out of the cold.

"Whatever," Britney said, but she was mad. "I'll see you later." She hurried ahead and through the doors. Jess took a deep breath and shook her head. If only she could tell Britney; if only she could explain.

33

——Original Message——
From: coltinator_51@yahoo.com
To: jjk_hollywood@hotmail.com
Sent: Thursday, May 4, 2:09 PM
Subject: computer time

Jessie—

You need to be so careful right now. Your mom is picking up on the fact
that you have something powerful going on in your life, but we both
know that she would freak if she knew the truth. I know this will be
hard with how badly she's been treating you, but you need to play nice.
Just do whatever she says, don't argue, don't give her any reason to
worry about you right now. If you were to lose your computer privileges
I just don't know what I would do. She'd love to ruin this for you, Jess—
both of your parents would. So please, be careful, okay. Don't take any
chances.

Love you,
Colt

———

Kate heard Brad pull into the garage Thursday night and she closed
her eyes, saying a little prayer about the evening they were about to
have. She was sure everything would be fine, that Brad's heart would be

softened—which made her wonder why she was still *this* nervous about his reaction.

"Mom, are you okay?"

She opened her eyes to look at Caitlyn, who was setting the table. "Fine," she said with a smile. "Your dad's home. Call all the kids up for dinner."

Caitlyn's face lit up. "He's home?" Instead of running downstairs where the other children were, she ran for the garage. Kate picked up the abandoned silverware and finished setting the table, her stomach churning and rolling with far more than just the pregnancy hormones.

Despite Caitlyn's lack of announcement, the kids came upstairs immediately, even Jess, who had been closeted in the study most of the afternoon. Since last night Kate had divided most of her time between dreading Brad's homecoming and being ashamed of yelling at Jess. Everything seemed to be falling apart instead of getting better.

Brad came in, Caitlyn attached to his arm, and the kids plied him with questions about his trip.

It was a few minutes before he was able to make his way to Kate and give her a homecoming kiss. She smiled but found it difficult to look him in the eye. Marilyn had said he would understand, and she was banking on that, but how long would it take for him to get to that point? It had taken her several days, and she'd *wanted* another baby.

"How are you?" he asked sweetly, the kids still clamoring for his attention.

"Good," she said. "And you?"

"I'm wonderful now that I'm with you," he said with a wink.

Kate looked away. Would he feel the same way when she told him the truth?

"Mom made fishies for dinner!" Justin yelled out, making a face.

"Salmon," Jess said, rolling her eyes at her little brother.

"I hate fish!" Keith shouted.

"Daddy loves salmon, and so I made some for him and me, and you guys get fish sticks," Kate said—though she felt "fish" was an exaggerated term to describe whatever meat substance was hidden beneath the breading. The theory was further proven in her mind when she noted that even though all the kids hated fish, they loved fish sticks.

"Do I get salmon?" Jess asked.

Kate looked up in surprise. "You like salmon?"

Jess nodded, but didn't meet her eye. The tension between them was dreadful.

"I didn't know you liked salmon," Kate said, frustrated that she hadn't even considered making her some. This could have been an opportunity to make things better. Add that to last night and she felt like the worst mother on the planet. What would Brad think of her losing it? Would Jess tell him?

"Remember I had some at Britney's awhile ago and said I liked it."

Oh, yeah. Kate remembered. It had been several months and apparently it hadn't "stuck" in her head. "You can have my salmon," she offered, wondering if something as simple as that could make a difference.

"Okay," Jess said as if she were doing them a favor. Kate and Brad shared a look as they took their seats, but at least Jess hadn't freaked out.

"Why don't we each give you some of ours?" Brad said.

They had a blessing on the food; then the kids' incessant chatter helped put Kate's nerves on relax mode. This was normal; this she could handle. She and Brad both gave Jess a portion of their salmon, which she was surprisingly gracious about. Brad asked all the kids about their day, then listened to their excited responses, commenting as needed. When he got to Jess she just shrugged.

"Come on," Brad said. "You have a life that's far more exciting than any of the rest of us. Surely something exciting happened today."

She mumbled something.

"What was that?" Brad asked.

"Nothing," Jess answered, glancing quickly at Kate. "My day was very *pleasant*. Thanks for asking."

Kate furrowed her brow, wondering about the sarcasm in Jess's tone. But she didn't get much time to dwell on Jess's comment because Brad turned his attention to Kate.

"And how was your day, Mommy? Anything new happen while I was gone?"

34

——Original Message——
From: coltinator_51@yahoo.com
To: jjk_hollywood@hotmail.com
Sent: Thursday, May 4, 7:12 PM
Subject: You won't believe this!

Jessie,

You are not going to believe this! My uncle has a business meeting in
Nevada next week. Since I'm already cleared to graduate, my parents
said I can go with him so that we can check out the University of Utah
campus.

Isn't that amazing! Maybe you and I could meet for dinner somewhere.
Would that be okay? I can't believe the fate of how this has worked out.
I have been dying to meet you and now I'm coming to Salt Lake! wow!

We'll be there Wednesday the 10th—can you make this work? I don't
know what I'll do if you say no.

Love you,
Colt

———

Jess stared at the screen, not sure how to make sense of this. Seeing
Colt seemed amazing, but . . . wrong. *How could it be wrong?* she

asked herself. They were in love, he made her feel so good, but . . . meeting him in person?

She bit her lip, and got up from the computer. She was too stunned to reply right then, and she'd been on the computer a lot today. Colt had told her to play nice, so she'd been working on it, and she knew she shouldn't push the computer time much farther.

On her way to her room she heard her mom reading a book to Chris in his bedroom, getting him ready for bed. Instantly she thought she should go in there and tell her what had just happened. It surprised her how badly she wanted to do that, but then she remembered mom's freak-out last night. *She wouldn't understand,* Jess reminded herself, and she'd get mad.

The consideration was quickly booted out by the reminder as she descended the stairs that Colt was actually coming to Salt Lake. Her stomach was instantly full of butterflies. What should she do? But quick on the heels of that thought was what *could* she do? He and Emily had become such important parts of her life; they helped her to feel accepted and appreciated and so comfortable and confident. Not seeing him would be an insult. And she did want to see him, didn't she?

"Hey, Jess."

Jess looked up to see Caitlyn standing in the hall. Caitlyn had Mom's light skin and blue eyes but Dad's dark, straight hair. She was always getting dressed up and playing with her hair. Tonight she'd put her hair up with a bunch of bobby pins so it stuck out all over the place. "Do you like my hair?" she asked. "I'm thinking of wearing it like this to school tomorrow—should I?"

It was punkish looking, but it didn't look bad, and Caitlyn could get away with stuff like that. "It looks great," Jess said, wondering what Caitlyn would think if she knew the secrets Jess was keeping. For a minute Jess wished she were a little girl again, playing in the yard until dark, sneaking cookies when Mom wasn't looking. Life felt heavy all of a sudden.

35

Journal entry, May 4

I can hardly believe this, but Colt is coming to Salt Lake and he wants me to meet him. I'm so excited but I'm so scared. I feel like I've known him forever, but it's really only been a couple of weeks. Emily is still not back online so I can't talk to her about it and I can't talk to anyone else. I just know Britney would tell her mom. I feel weird about it, but how can I not go see him? He's so in love with me and I love him too. I can't help but think this is fate and destiny—but what if I get caught?

I just never imagined this, but it's such a thrill too, ya know? Oh, I wish I could talk to Britney, or somebody. I guess this journal will have to do. No one else would understand.

me

Kate took a deep breath when Brad walked into the bedroom after saying goodnight to each of the kids. She was trying to read, but the words were blurring on the page. She put the book on her nightstand.

"How was the conference?" Kate asked, watching him unbutton his dress shirt, her heart pounding. Every minute that ticked by was one minute closer to her having to tell him.

"Fine," Brad shrugged. "I caught up on a lot of work in the evenings, but I'm glad I'm home."

"Me too," Kate said.

"I spent a lot of time thinking about the baby," he said.

"And?" she asked evenly.

"And I think I was dismissing it too quickly."

Kate closed her eyes as the relief washed over her. Thank goodness, but then Brad continued. "But I also think we need to wait a little longer. I need to be home more, help out more than I have been, and with you needing to get ready for this—I think we ought to plan on waiting at least a year."

"A year?" Kate repeated.

Brad nodded. "You can lose some weight like the doctor said, and in another year Chris will be a lot more independent; Jess will be driving. It will be a much easier time for the family should the same complications arise. We'll be better prepared to work together as a team on this." He sat down on the bed and smiled at her. "But I think we just might have room for one more Thompson-terror."

Kate stared at him and didn't know what to say. This wasn't what she'd expected, and suddenly she understood why she had still been so anxious.

Brad's smile fell as the silent seconds ticked by. "What's the matter?" he asked. "I thought you'd be happy about this."

"I'm pregnant," she blurted, then clamped her mouth shut. Hardly the easing-him-into-it she'd been hoping for.

Brad pulled back. "What?"

"I didn't mean to . . . it was when I had the flu; I must have vomited the birth control . . . and then last week I started feeling sick . . . and then I took a test . . . and then—"

"You're pregnant?" Brad interrupted, as if she hadn't made herself clear enough.

"I'm sorry, Brad. I didn't mean for it to happen like this."

"But you meant for it to happen," he snapped, standing up and pushing his hands through his hair. His shirt was unbuttoned, the tails hanging at his sides.

"Not like this," Kate said, looking up at him, desperate for him to understand. "I wouldn't do this without your okay, you know that."

He turned to look at her, his eyes narrowed, cutting through her and causing a lump to form in her throat. "Do I?" he said. Then he broke eye contact and stepped back into his shoes, buttoning his shirt back up.

Kate threw back the covers and got out of bed. "What are you doing?" she asked, panicking. He wasn't leaving, was he?

He looked up at her again, that same look of anger on his face. He said nothing. Just held her eyes, then opened the door and slammed it behind him. It took a few seconds for Kate to follow, and by then he was pulling out of the garage. She stood in the hallway, and tears filled her eyes again. She didn't know what to do. Could she have said it better? Should she have told him as soon as she found out? But it was too late now. She'd deceived him and just like Julie said that had made it harder. With nothing else to do, she covered her face with her hands and started to cry.

36

——Original Message——
From: jjk_hollywood@hotmail.com
To: coltinator_51@yahoo.com
Sent: Thursday, May 4, 11:19 PM
Subject: Re: You won't believe this!

Colt,

You're coming through Salt Lake??????? I can't imagine having you so close and not seeing you but I don't know how to make it work. I've never done anything like this and if my parents found out, they'd kill me. I can't date until I'm sixteen—remember how freaked out my mom was about me going to the dance?

My parents had a fight tonight, I could hear them from my room and my dad left. I snuck up to write you back but I can't write for long. I don't know when my dad's going to come home.

I don't know how to do this, Colt. I don't know if I can, but I want to. I'll be on IM in the morning, okay.

Love
Your Jessie

———

Brad rolled over to find a better position on the terribly uncomfortable couch. After the bomb Kate dropped last night he'd gone to the ward meetinghouse and played basketball against himself for over an hour, until he was so tired he couldn't think about anything but sleep. When he got home, he just couldn't make himself go into their bedroom and settle things between them. He'd already learned that she'd manipulated the information Dr. Lyon had given her. And yet, even then he was willing to ponder this, pray about it, make sure his heart was in the right place. And now this? What was he supposed to think?

It was still dark outside the living room windows, but he could tell it was early morning by the sound of birds twittering. He dreaded the day before him, knowing he needed to patch things up with Kate but unable to dispel the doubt in his mind. Had she done this on purpose? Was his opinion of no worth to her?

A movement in the darkness caught his eye, and his heart increased with instant fear until he recognized the shape of the body heading into the study. "Jess?"

She whipped around, and he heard her suck in a lungful of air. Apparently she was as surprised to see him as he was to see her. "Dad?" she asked in a panicked voice. "What are you doing on the couch?"

"I . . . uh, was snoring, and I didn't want to keep your mother awake." He sat up and flipped on the lamp. They both blinked against the sudden light.

"Oh."

"What are you doing?" he asked, sitting up. He looked at his watch. It was 5:15 in the morning.

"I . . . couldn't sleep so I thought . . . I'd work on my report before I did my piano."

Brad swung his legs over the side of the couch and stretched his arms over his head. "It's not even five-thirty in morning."

"It's due Monday and I'm behind."

"What's your report on?" he asked, rubbing his eyes.

"Um . . . appendicitis."

"Sounds like fun."

Jess glanced into the study. "But I think I'll wait after all. I've got lots of time today. Sorry I woke you."

"That's okay," Dad said. "I was thinking of going running for the first time in five or six years. I can't sleep either."

"Okay," Jess said in a rush. "Have fun. I think I'll just take a shower before piano."

"Sounds good," Brad said while listening to her footsteps retreat. He shook his head again. What fifteen-year-old takes school so seriously that she gets up at 5:15 in the morning? That just wasn't normal.

He crept into the bedroom and closed the door to the master closet behind him before turning on the light. The brightness hurt his eyes, but he blinked it away and eventually dug out running shoes of dubious age and arch support. The basketball had been a great release last night; now he was hoping for another one since the anger had built back up.

Brad was less than two blocks away when he turned around. Apparently the basketball had taken more out of him than he'd thought. He considered going for a nice, easy walk, but he wasn't in the mood. He wanted a run—a hard, gut-wrenching run. But his knees wouldn't allow it, and his enthusiasm was quickly squelched. *And* it was cold outside— colder than he'd expected it to be in early May.

He walked up the driveway, anticipating just how uncomfortable the day was going to be. As he crossed the lawn, a blue glow from the window of the study caught his eye. The study was located at the front of the house and had three long, skinny windows with Roman shades on each one. Two of the shades were down, but the third was halfway up. He took a few steps into the flower bed to get a better look and shook his head when he realized Jess was at the computer after all.

But she wasn't working on a report. He crept out of the flower bed as slowly as possible and quietly let himself into the house, glad he'd oiled the hinges of the front door last month.

"What are you doing?" he asked from the doorway of the study.

Jess nearly jumped out of her skin, typed a few letters, clicked the mouse once, and then tried to smile. Brad was not dissuaded by her attempt at casualness. He walked to where he could see the front of the computer, and there on the screen was a website about appendicitis.

"Jess, what's going on?"

"Nothing," she said. "I just changed my mind about the report."

"I saw what you were doing through the window. Who are you instant messaging with at this time of day? Get up." He gestured for her to stand, and she did, her face pale and her eyes wide. He sat down and began clicking on things, looking for the IM program.

"Where is it?" he said, trying to control his anger but frustrated by the situation.

"I wasn't instant messaging, Dad," Jess said from behind him.

He turned in his chair. "Jess," he said as evenly as possible. "Don't insult my intelligence. I use an IM program at work—I know what it is. I've always trusted you, but if you choose to lie to me right now, that's going to be a serious problem. Do I need to take the computer to work and have the IT guys pull it apart until they find the program?"

Jess's chin started to quiver, and her shoulders slumped. "I . . . I wasn't doing anything bad."

"Then why do you look so guilty? And when did we get instant messsaging?"

"Everyone IMs, Dad."

"Did your mother give you permission to have a program?"

Jess was quiet. "No, but I'm like the last loser on the planet because I'm the only kid that doesn't IM. I knew if I asked she would say no—she always says no."

Brad took a deep breath. Dang, he wished he and Kate were speaking right now so he could confer with her. He wasn't sure what to do other than try to make this make sense to Jess.

"The problem with instant messaging is that it's so easy for people to feel close to one another when they're chatting that way, and both people forget that they are still essentially strangers. Who were you chatting with just now?"

Jess hesitated and wouldn't meet his eye. "Britney," she finally said. "I was working on my report—I swear—but I saw she was online so we started chatting."

"So if I asked Julie, she could verify it?"

Jess seemed to stop breathing, but he couldn't help but give Jess the benefit of the doubt. She was such a good kid.

"Well," she said, "she's online because her mom won't let her . . . uh, go to this one end-of-year party if she, uh, misses any assignments, and she missed this one, but the teacher is letting her make it up. If her mom finds out, she'll be, like, totally grounded from the party."

"Are you telling me the truth?" Brad asked after he processed the plausibility and it came up short.

Jess looked up at him then, her expression determined. "Why would I lie, Dad?" Her tone was sad and angry. She folded her arms across her chest, shifting her weight from one foot to the other. "I do everything you guys say, all the time. I clean my room, watch the kids, and now because I didn't do *one* thing just right you assume I'm a liar?" She started to cry and wiped at her eyes. She had a point, but so did he.

"It's not okay to go behind our backs. I really stood up for you last week so you could stop gymnastics and go to the dance, and then to have you do something like this is disappointing. Do you understand that?"

She nodded slightly. "Can I keep the IM program?"

Here he was again, put in a position of overriding Kate. Yet, he couldn't help himself. "If you'll promise me that you will only chat with friends—no strangers—and that you'll tell me if anyone ever contacts you that you don't know, or if anyone you know says anything that's inappropriate, then you can keep the IM account."

"I can?" Jess said, barely breathing.

"I need your word to follow my rule."

"Yeah, I promise."

"Just friends."

"Of course," she said with a sharp nod.

Brad stood up and pulled her into a hug. "I love you, Jess, and I trust you—okay?"

"Okay," Jess said, remaining stiff in his embrace. She pulled away after a few seconds and wouldn't meet his eye. "Are you going to tell Mom?"

"Yes, eventually. That's why it's so important that you promise to do it right, so I can prove to her it's been okay."

Jess nodded, but again she didn't meet his eye.

"Don't you need to get started on your piano?"

Jess nodded.

"I'm going to get in the shower. I'm glad we worked this out."

"Me too," Jess said, and she finally smiled, though it was tense. "Thanks, Dad."

He put an arm around her shoulder and gave her a squeeze. "You're my best Jess," he said, kissing her red curls.

"And you're my best dad," she said back, just like she used to do when she was little.

37

——Original Message——
From: coltinator_51@yahoo.com
To: jjk_hollywood@hotmail.com
Sent: Friday, May 5, 5:45 AM
Subject: Logging off

Jess,

I wondered what happened when you logged off so fast. It's a good thing I didn't reply or the instant message would have popped back on your screen again. Your mom will totally freak when he tells her. Even though he said it's okay, I think you should delete the program and never use it again—just in case.

I love you, Jessie. Be sure you do everything I told you in the IM before we meet on Wednesday, okay. Don't take any chances. And don't be scared. Find a way you can get out of the house after they go to sleep—through a window or an unlocked back door. You'll want to get it ready beforehand. Wait until they're asleep and then be really quiet. I know it seems scary but it's not that big a deal. Emily and I used to sneak out together all the time when I still lived in Pennsylvania, then just go for walks or get a drink from the soda machine. You'll be fine, Jess. Perfectly fine. Trust me. This is fate.

And I know you're dying to tell someone, so after we meet you can tell Britney, okay? You only have to keep this secret for a few more days.

Love always,
Colt

I've just got to check this one thing online," Jess said after putting her cereal bowl in the sink. Dad had left for work already, but she didn't think he'd told Mom about the IM. She was pretty sure they were still fighting.

Mom looked at her skeptically, and Jess worried—almost hoped—she'd say Jess couldn't get online. But she finally nodded and Jess hurried into the study. She needed to see if Colt had written her back after her problem with her dad. She felt like a schizophrenic the way she had such conflicting thoughts—scared to death one minute and completely excited another. Then she thought of her mom and felt so mad. How could so many exciting things be happening to her and her mom didn't even know? Sometimes Jess felt invisible.

She sat down and logged onto a homework-help website, in case Mom tried to check up on her; then she opened her e-mail account. She read Colt's e-mail two times. She could tell Britney! The relief was incredible. And it would be so much easier to explain when she'd actually met him. She didn't take the time to reply just then, not wanting Mom to get suspicious, but she felt so much better to know that Colt understood how hard this was for her.

"Did you find what you needed?" Mom asked when Jess entered the kitchen a minute later. She was pouring Justin a bowl of Cheerios and didn't look up.

"Yep," Jess said with confidence, feeling arrogant in her secrecy. "Exactly what I needed."

38

——Original Message——
From: jjk_hollywood@hotmail.com
To: coltinator_51@yahoo.com
Sent: Friday, May 5, 1:24 PM
Subject: We meet

Colt

I can't believe this is happening. I'm trying hard to be brave and I am excited to see you. I just need to get used to this idea, it's something I never expected to have happen—at least not so soon.

It's so hard not to tell Britney right now. I won't, but it's hard.

The bell's about to ring, love you.

Jess

———

Kate survived Friday by getting lost in housework. She made an elaborate dinner, organized the master bedroom closet, and cleaned like she hadn't in weeks. She'd waited for Brad to come home last night, eager to explain herself. Instead, she listened to him prepare a bed for himself on the couch. He didn't even come into the bedroom to change. She'd wondered if she should go talk to him, but if he wasn't ready to talk, did she want to force it?

Marilyn called during lunch, asking Kate how things were. She didn't come out and ask directly about Brad's reaction, but Kate felt her own tone and attitude reflected it pretty well anyway. After lunch was over, Kate sat down to read Chris some stories before putting him down for a nap. Justin was going to play with a neighbor in about ten minutes, and she felt guilty for being so grateful for the break. Once Chris was down, she'd have an hour or two to herself. She needed it.

"Kigs, kigs," Chris shouted, clapping as she moved to their second book—the three little pigs. After all the new, interesting, and creative children's books she'd bought over the years, he loved *The Three Little Pigs* the best.

Kate positioned Chris on her lap, and Justin settled in beside her.

"Once upon a time, there were three little pigs . . ."

When she got to the part about the first pig hiding from the big bad wolf in his house of straw, she paused, staring at the illustration. One very frightened pig stood in the window while the wolf blew. Pieces of straw were flying through the air, and half of the house was already stripped down to its stick frame. Kate felt her eyes fill. That's what all this felt like—a house of straw.

But she hadn't been like that first little pig. She hadn't played and wasted her time. She'd worked and toiled over this family, over this home. Somehow it had transformed from the sturdy brick she'd chosen, to straw, easily destroyed. First Jess, who was behaving better but still withdrawn, and now Brad. How had it happened? Would it get worse? How could bricks be straw without her realizing it? Brad's words came back, "But you meant for it to happen." She didn't know what to do about his accusations, how to convince him she hadn't planned this.

"Mommy sad?" Justin said. She looked away from the book and quickly wiped her eyes.

"I'm fine," she said with a false smile. "Now where were we? . . . Oh, yeah, right here. Now, what does the wolf say?"

Chris mimicked the words as Justin said them along with her. "I'll huff and I'll puff and I'll blow your house down."

39

——Original Message——
From: coltinator_51@yahoo.com
To: jjk_hollywood@hotmail.com
Sent: Friday, May 5, 2:04 PM
Subject: Re: We meet

Jessie,

I know this is so hard for you, keeping secrets. It's not something you're used to doing and I know you want to talk to a girlfriend about this, like all girls do. But you just can't—not yet. I'm so sorry. I wish it didn't have to be this way, but just for a few more days, okay. Trust me on this, Jessie. Come Thursday you can tell anyone you want, okay, but keep it to yourself for just a few more days. Besides, Britney wouldn't under-stand. Has she ever been in love like this? Just hang on, Jess, you can do this.

Love always,
Colt

———

B rad knocked on the front door of his childhood home with one hand, while opening it with the other. "Knock, Knock," he said. "You home, Mom?"

"I'm right here," Marilyn called from somewhere down the hall. "In the main bathroom—I'm afraid I've made quite a mess of things."

Brad shook his head as he turned down the hallway. Dad had always taken care of household repairs, and his mom had struggled to take over after his unexpected passing a few years ago. She always tried to fix things herself, then ended up calling one of her sons when the situation got desperate. No matter how many times he said he'd be happy to come out for any reason, she continued to try to be her own handyman. Tonight, having to help his mom was a blessing, however, since he didn't know what to say to Kate yet.

Dad, Brad found himself thinking as he passed a row of old family photos in the hallway. What Brad wouldn't do to discuss things with his dad right now. He wondered if Dad had ever felt tricked into so many kids. Had Brad's mom been like Kate?

Then he felt guilty for thinking such things. His dad had been very involved with his family, more than Brad was. There was no reason to doubt that his father had wanted so many children.

Brad reached the threshold of the bathroom and stopped. Water had started seeping into the carpet, wet magenta slowly overtaking the usual pink.

"What happened?" Brad asked, stepping into the bathroom. The floor was covered with half an inch of water—clean water, he was pleased to see. There was a huge chunk of porcelain on the floor and Brad followed it with his eyes, matching it to a hole in the bowl of the toilet. A huge monkey wrench was sticking out of the hole—a wrench far too big and heavy for Mom to use.

Mom was sitting on the edge of the tub and looked up with a regretful smile.

"Well," Mom said, repositioning a curl so that it was no longer hanging over her forehead. "After I fiddled with the u-joint of the sink, I accidentally dropped that big monkey wrench in the toilet. And next thing I know—bam—the wrench had popped a hole in the toilet and water went everywhere. So I called you."

Brad bent down to look at the hole. He'd never seen anything like it.

"Wow," he said, with a laugh. "Impressive work."

His mom shrugged as Brad lifted the lid off the back of the toilet and undid the chain, so the toilet would stop running. Then he turned his attention to the U-joint of the sink—where the whole fiasco had started.

"So why were you fiddling with the U-joint?"

"So I'd have a reason to get you over here."

He looked up at her confused. Did he hear her right? She smiled innocently and shrugged. "I thought I could play dumb about a leaky sink and get you here—silly me. I underestimate my own ineptness at times."

Brad looked at her strangely, not wanting to ask what it was she wanted to talk about this much—even though he knew she must have picked up on something.

"How are you and Kate?" Mom asked, putting his wonderings to rest. He turned his attention to the u-joint, making it so tight he was sure his mother wouldn't be able to undo it should she get an equally brilliant idea sometime in the future. His mother was usually the first one to stay *out* of other people's business. "We're fine, Mom," he said.

"Good! I told her you'd be okay with the baby—I told her you were a good man and you'd rise to the occasion."

"You know?" he asked, though he wasn't surprised. It seemed that Kate was always talking to someone else before she bothered to tell him. He'd been dwelling on his wife's faults all day, so this was only one more to add to the list.

"I brought ice cream over while you were away. Kate said she didn't want any."

"Ah," Brad said. Kate had a notorious sweet tooth, except when she was pregnant. He was almost disappointed to realize Kate wasn't guilty of blabbering about their personal business. He *wanted* to be mad.

He finished the sink and decided to start sopping up the water.

"You're mad, aren't you," Mom stated as he pulled towels off the rack and put them on the floor. He even grabbed the nice towels he'd been raised never to use, and Mom didn't stop him. She *was* serious.

"I'm . . . frustrated," he said simply, wishing Kate had told him his mother knew so he'd have been prepared.

"You know she didn't do this on purpose, though, right? You know she wouldn't do that?"

"Wouldn't she?" Brad asked, shooting his mother a look. "She just happens to bring up the idea of having another baby at the exact time that she gets pregnant. It's just a little too convenient. And she's going to get sick again, Mom. She's never taken that seriously, and now there is no time to prepare for it. I'd accepted the idea of having one more child, but not for another year. I wanted to get things on track."

"What things?"

"I'd like to work less, be home more, get to know my wife again—take a family vacation."

"You can still do all these things," Mom said. "Just do them sooner. Why do you need a year for any of that?"

Brad let out a breath. "So you're on Kate's side, huh?"

"No," Mom said, looking at him hard. "I'm on the baby's side, and that's the side you and Kate should be on as well. And if you are, even if she gets sick, even if things get really hard, you'll be a team. And that's what matters. You can blame work, you can blame Kate, you can even blame God for creating the distance you're feeling, but you can't blame the baby, and you're the only one that can fix it."

Brad put his hands on his hips and looked at the towels now sopping up the water. "I just need a little more time to set my head straight on this," he said, though her words had hit their target.

"You need time?" she echoed. "Since when did time make it any easier to do the right thing? Use this opportunity to get closer to Kate, not farther from her, Brad, and the longer you wait, the harder it will be for her to forgive you for this."

"Forgive *me?*" he asked, incredulously looking up at his mom with surprise. "I'm not the one that—"

"She was scared to tell you, Brad, terrified. And you're now proving all those fears to be true. What good can that possibly bring to either one of you, let alone your family? You've taken enough time to make things right in your head; now just get back home and tell her you're sorry, that things will be okay."

"How do you know I haven't already told her that?" Brad asked, not liking the fact that he was thirty-eight years old and being reprimanded by his mother.

"'Cause I talked to Kate today. She didn't say anything, but I could tell something wasn't right. And you're my son. I know you. You tend to pull away when things aren't going the direction you think they should be going. If there's distance between you and your wife, you need to look at yourself first. Even if some of the responsibility is hers, you are only in control of your actions, not hers."

40

—Original Message——
From: jjk_hollywood@hotmail.com
To: coltinator_51@yahoo.com
Sent: Friday, May 5, 6:49 PM
Subject: Nerves

Colt—I got the rest of those instructions and I'm getting scared, Colt. Leaving the note is scary. I mean, I get that if they realize I'm gone they'll freak whether there's a note or not, but if I leave a note it feels so different. Gosh this is scary. I don't know what to do. I really want to see you, but they will kill me if they find out! I'm scared! I hate not being able to IM—I really need to talk to you about this. Are you there? Please e-mail me back.

Jess

———

Kate?"

Kate started and turned quickly, dripping glue from the Popsicle stick she was using to help Sharla with the English castle model for her term project. She was surprised to hear Brad's voice. They had given each other only twenty-four hours of the silent treatment, but it felt like days.

"Can I talk to you for a minute?" he asked.

Kate swallowed and nodded before turning back to Sharla. "I'll be back in a minute."

"But, Mo-om," Sharla said. "I can't do this alone."

She'd been able to choose between marshmallows or sugar cubes to use as the bricks of her castle. She chose the pastel-colored marshmallows, which was a mistake since she also wanted them perfectly patterned. They'd been at it for over an hour and had only three rows of foundational pink marshmallows completed. Kate let out a breath. "Jess," she called as she stood. Jess was working on an assignment for biology.

"Yeah?" Jess answered in a flat voice.

"Can you please come help Sharla with her project for a minute?"

There was silence for a second or two while Kate washed her hands, Sharla pouted and poked at her marshmallow castle, and Brad waited on the sidelines. Finally Jess replied. "Yeah," she grumbled. Kate nodded. Okay, one fire put out for a minute. Then she looked up at Brad and felt her stomach flip. Was he still mad?

She followed Brad into the bedroom and shut the door softly behind her. He stood awkwardly on one side of the bed while she stood awkwardly on the other. "I'm not mad at you," he said.

"You're not?" she asked, relief washing over her even as she wondered why he'd been acting like he was mad if he wasn't.

"I am disappointed," he said. "But I know you didn't do this on purpose, and I know it's going to be okay." He looked down and took a breath. "I love our kids, Kate, all of them. And this will be great." He looked up and smiled, almost shyly. Kate felt the tears come to her eyes. He really was a good man.

"But," he added and she braced herself. "I want more of you in my life." He walked around the bed that had been serving as a buffer between them and reached up to tuck a lock of curly auburn hair behind her ear. "I love you, Kate, but sometimes I feel like I've lost you to the kids. I want time with you again."

"Like date nights?" Kate said, humbled by his words, wondering how true that was. Had she lost herself in motherhood?

"And *just us* time—putting the kids to bed at the same time every night, talking about our days. I love our family, but I loved you first and I want there to be an *us* again."

The first tear spilled over. "I love you too, Brad, and I'm sorry things happened this way."

He nodded once. "But don't be sorry any more, okay? I felt good about having another baby when I prayed about it—I just didn't expect it this soon."

"Neither did I," she said, hoping he really believed that. They looked at one another for several seconds, and then he pulled her into his arms. She held on tight, thanking the Lord for that softening she'd been praying for. They stood that way for what felt like a long time—in parent years. Until Justin's shrieking broke into the moment. She resisted the impulse to pull away completely and run to his aid. Instead she smiled and forced herself to move slower. "Why don't we go out tonight," she said.

Brad looked surprised. "Tonight?"

Kate smiled wider and nodded. "Jess is home. We can get the little kids in their PJs, and then they'll be ready for bed. Maybe we can even catch a late movie." She couldn't remember the last time they'd seen a movie in a movie theatre.

Brad smiled. "You don't think Jess will mind?"

Kate shook her head. "Of course not," she said, reflecting on how much better Jess had been since she'd gone on her rant Wednesday night. Apparently, Jess had simply needed a reminder of who was boss. "I'll just let her have a little more time on the computer after the kids are in bed. Everything will be fine and you're right—we need to find us again, and why not start today?"

41

Hey Jess,

i just talked to colt on the phone and he said he's coming through salt lake! so i drove all the way to the library to check in with u. i have missed you sooooooo much. maybe u ought to give me yr phone number so i can call u. i'm going through Jess withdrawals and my puter is totally fritzed. mom says she's gunna buy a new one—yeah right. i'm the only one that uses it at home and she's not gunna spend all that money just for me.

anyway, how are u feeling about meeting colt? he said he thinks yr nervous—i don't blame u. u guys have only known each other a little while. but anyway, if u need someone to talk to, i'll b here for another half an hour and i'll come back tomorrow—okay? i'm here for u girl!

Em

Jess read the e-mail and felt tears come to her eyes. Finally, someone she could talk to. Thank goodness!

Jess had been playing nice, like the good-old-Jess Mom wanted her to be, and Mom was totally taking advantage of her. It was so not fair. Jess had already watched the kids all afternoon. Mom did get the little ones ready for bed before she left, like that was so helpful.

But now the kids were in bed, she was alone and could have all the computer time she could possibly want. And Emily had written her. It was feeling more like fate and destiny all the time, even if she was still scared out of her mind.

She put her fingers on the keyboard and started typing. Having Emily contact her was like an answer to a prayer.

42

——Original Message——
From: jjk_hollywood@hotmail.com
To: emjenkins000@yahoo.com
Sent: Friday, May 5, 9:08 PM
Subject: Re: I'm back!

Em,

It's so weird you wrote to me. I am so nervous about meeting Colt. I mean, I'm excited too, but I never expected this—and especially not so soon. It's so hard to believe this is happening. How could a guy like him be in love with a girl like me? Oh, I'm dying to meet him in person and he's such a great guy, but I've never done anything like this and I'm really scared. What if I get caught? What if he thinks I'm totally lame? But the fact that he's coming at all is so amazing—like fate or something. But I don't know. I get sick to my stomach when I think of writing the note he told me to write or sneaking out of my house. I'm so confused.

Write soon! Or yeah, you can totally call. My number is 801–555–9436. But since you have to use the library computer you won't get this tonight. Dang!

Jess

Monique clenched Harrison's hand tightly—perhaps too tight. He didn't complain. After several days of intense investigation, including multiple interviews with all different kinds of detectives and experts, Sergeant Morris had called them into his office that morning—Monday. He'd also asked them to bring their other children if they could. Jamie was still in town, having chosen not to fly back to New York after the dinner last week. In fact, she had since asked about moving back home and finishing her degree at Ann Arbor. Monique was glad. She needed her children around her right now. They were all trying to remain calm, but the staggering level of tension made it difficult.

"Thank you for coming," Sergeant Morris said after opening the door to his office. "I'd like to speak with Mr. and Mrs. Weatherford alone first, please."

Monique nodded, smiled at her children, and entered the room, taking a seat across from the desk. Her heart was racing, and even though the sergeant hadn't said anything, she felt tears fill her eyes. He'd been so official on the phone, but she'd been trying to ignore it. She told herself she was prepared for anything, but she didn't know if she could handle bad news.

"As you know, we reopened this investigation and hit it hard. We sent Terrezza's picture nationwide and even to a few Canadian provinces, hoping that someone had seen her."

Monique didn't like the careful, calculated tone of Sergeant Morris's voice. She looked at the glass top of his desk. It needed to be dusted. She wanted to run from the room in search of a dust rag. Her throat was tight.

"When we spoke last week, I told you to be prepared for anything, that six months was a long time for a young woman to be gone."

The room went silent, and Monique didn't even try to brush away the tears as they dripped into her lap.

"I'm so sorry," he said after several heavy seconds. Monique felt as if her lungs had collapsed. Harrison wrapped his arms around her and pulled her into his shoulder, his own chest shaking as Monique began to sob.

43

From: emjenkins000@yahoo.com

To: jjk_hollywood@hotmail.com

Sent: Saturday, May 6, 2:29 PM

Subject: Re: I'm back!

Jess,

if yr this nervous about seeing colt, maybe u shouldn't. i mean, he wouldn't want u to do something like this if u can't trust him. but i really think u would regret it. i think yr right that this is fate bringing u guys together. he's never had a reason to go to utah before and may never have a reason to come again—how often do u get to florida to see him? how would u feel if u made all those arrangements but then he was too scared. remember when we talked about being free to make our choices and live our own life? this is one of those moments. i know colt would be heartbroken if u were too scared to see him, but he loves u Jess. i'm totally biased :) but he really is great.

the choice is yrs, Jess, but don't make it lightly. colt said he's helping u cover yr tracks—that's important and yr parents won't find out—they barely notice yr there at all and maybe u need to ask yourself which one of them makes u feel better about u, do yr parents understand u more than colt does? i know he told u that he's coming along to check out that college, the real reason is because of u :) i'm out of time so i gotta go, but i'll try and call okay. i don't know if i can, but i'll do my best.

Em

_____

He hit send and bit the inside of his lip so hard it started to bleed. This was the ultimate test. How devoted was she?

After a few minutes he had to get up and start pacing, his head pounding as the fear rose in his chest. What if she didn't follow through? What if he'd done all this for nothing? He walked to the wall, where he'd put up the pictures of Jess he'd taken off her board. He reached out and touched her face. He was so close. What would he do if she said she wouldn't meet him?

But he knew right where she was. She'd given enough clues that he'd been able to track down her home address. If she did back out, maybe he'd go find her anyway.

44

Jessie,

I can't wait to see you

I can't wait to hold you

I can't wait to tell you how much I love you

I can't wait to take moonlight walks with you

I can't wait to gaze into your eyes

I can't wait to hold your hand

I can't wait to promise myself to you forever

I can't wait to make all your dreams come true

I can't wait to caress your face

I can't wait to tell you how beautiful you are with my own voice

I can't wait to kiss you in a way that makes you realize that you are the only girl in the world that could ever make me feel this way.

I love you Jessie—just hold on to that, okay. I promise all this will be worth it. Please write me back as soon as you get this, I need to know you'll be waiting for me.

Love you,
Colt

———————

It wasn't quite 5:30 Monday morning; the house was dark. Jess hadn't gotten much time on the computer over the weekend, but she didn't try very hard. Yesterday she'd received her Young Womanhood award. It had been a great moment, and Mom and Dad had been so proud of her. She could still hear Mom's voice whispering, "I love you, Jess," when Mom had hugged her. Jess had felt so good right then, but it didn't take long for everything to come back to her. She woke up with the knowledge that Colt was leaving Florida that morning. He'd told her that he'd use his uncle's laptop to check in with her.

She read the e-mail twice, then once more. This should be so exciting, shouldn't it? She reached up and fingered the Young Womanhood medallion hanging around her neck. Wasn't it every girl's dream, her dream, to have someone feel this way about her? It was, and yet it felt so wrong.

Why?

Was it because she'd been raised not to keep secrets? Was it because he was so much older? Maybe it was normal to feel this way. Maybe everyone that fell in love felt scared like this. She'd heard people talk about cold feet before; maybe this is what it was.

She had to give him an answer, and after e-mailing with Emily she knew she couldn't say no. For the last few weeks she'd felt so . . . trapped. At home, at school, everywhere. She would look at the faces of people she thought knew her and wonder how Emily and Colt could know her so much better than they did. Did anyone really care about her? Did anyone notice anything other than her report card? And then she wondered if she really knew the people around her either. If she could hide so much, could other people hide it, too? Her parents had been acting strange; and Britney, the person who was supposed to know Jess better than anyone, hadn't figured it out. It was like no one in the whole world even cared about her. No one but Emily and Colt.

She'd really hoped Emily would call, but she didn't. Jess had lain awake for hours, thinking things through, trying to make sense of everything. She'd listened to her parents' footsteps upstairs and wanted so badly to go talk to them. And then she felt horrible for thinking that. Poor Colt. After everything he'd done for her, should she really be this confused? It wasn't fair to him for her to feel this way. She needed to trust him. She needed to trust someone.

"Jess?"

Jess jumped and looked up. Caitlyn was standing in the doorway in her robe, blinking into the room. "What are you doing?" Caitlyn asked in a sleepy voice.

Jess quickly closed her e-mail program, feeling horrible for being so relieved at the interruption. "What?" she asked, her voice sounding scared.

"I asked what you were doing."

Jess froze. What was she doing? Such a simple question that Jess couldn't answer. In fact, she was taken so off guard that she couldn't even think up a good lie like she had with Dad. "What are *you* doing?" Jess finally countered.

Caitlyn blinked her big blue eyes, like Dad's, and looked embarrassed. "I'm supposed to have a current-events article for world studies today and I forgot. I didn't want Mom to know, so I got up when I heard your alarm go off. You won't tell her, will you?"

Jess let out a breath. Keeping Caitlyn's secret would be payment for Caitlyn keeping hers. "No," Jess said, double-checking that she hadn't left anything open. "'Cause I had to look something up, too." She stood up and smiled at her sister, wondering what Caitlyn would say if Jess suddenly blurted out that she had an online boyfriend who wanted to meet her in person. Actually, Caitlyn was totally boy crazy—she'd probably think it was cool.

She passed Caitlyn in the doorway. "I'll wait five more minutes to start my piano so Mom doesn't wake up early—but you better hurry."

Caitlyn smiled at her. "Thank you, Jess."

Jess smiled back, thinking maybe with Caitlyn getting older they would have more in common now. She'd always been so much younger than Jess, but she was in Young Women's now. Maybe she wasn't so annoying.

Jess shrugged like it was no big deal. "You're welcome," she said. "But get going."

Caitlyn nodded and hurried to sit down at the computer. Jess watched her for a minute, surprised to be feeling a little bit jealous of how uncomplicated her life was. Should she warn her? Jess wondered. Should she tell her that one day she might feel split in two with having to make a choice that felt wrong either way? If she didn't see Colt, she'd feel horrible for breaking his heart. He might never talk to her again. But going felt just as wrong. After a few seconds she turned around, deciding to take a quick shower before piano, giving Caitlyn a little more time to get her homework done without getting caught. At least Jess wasn't the only one with secrets now.

45

——Original Message——
From: coltinator_51@yahoo.com
To: jjk_hollywood@hotmail.com
Sent: Tuesday, May 9, 1:37 PM
Subject: Minor change in plans

Jessie,

I haven't heard back from you yet, but I'm assuming no news is good news. However, I have some good news and bad news about my visit too. The good news is that my uncle is totally cool with us getting together for a late dinner, and 11:30 Wednesday works just fine. He totally understands what it's like to be young and in love. He's really an awesome guy. You'll love him. The bad news is that we stopped for lunch and were playing basketball since we've been in the car so much and I sprained my ankle. I had to go to the emergency room and everything. They gave me crutches but my uncle said that when we get into town he's going to drop me off at the hotel so I can lay down and elevate my foot for awhile. He'll come pick you up and bring you to the hotel restaurant where I will meet you guys.

Did you get ALL the files deleted at home? I can't wait to see you, to hold you. Wow. Thinking of you is the only way I've been able to deal with the pain in my foot. Be sure and leave that note. You're such a beautiful and amazing girl, Jess. I can't believe how lucky I am to have found you.

We need a meeting place—where would be a good spot?

Your mom takes your little brother to karate today, right? While she's gone double check everything—make sure the computer is totally clean.

I'm saying all of this with the assumption that you aren't going to let me down. I have to know that you are real. Is there anyone in your life that makes you feel as good about yourself as I do? Is there anyone that loves you the way I love you, Jessie? Cause no one has ever made me feel the way you make me feel.

Your love,
Colt

———————

Morgan Sanford finished putting the paper plates in the Young Women's closet and locked the door. She picked up the box full of items she'd brought from home for tonight's activity and turned out the lights on her way out of the Mutual room. Jess Thompson stood in the foyer, staring out the window.

"Hey, Jess," she said. "Do you need a ride home?" Morgan had thought all the Mia Maids had left already, and Jess only lived a short way from the ward meetinghouse. But it *was* raining, so maybe she had a ride coming. Jess turned sixteen in just over a week. Morgan would miss having her in her class when she moved up to Laurels. Jess was such a good girl.

Jess didn't turn to look at her. "Mom said she'd pick me up after Sharla's dance thing. I guess she had some other stuff to do first."

Morgan shifted the box in her arms and looked at her watch. It was almost nine. Their class activity had been over for half an hour, and the building was empty. "It's getting late," she said. "Why don't you come with me?"

Jess shook her head. "My mom will be mad if she comes and I'm not here."

Morgan furrowed her brow. Something wasn't right in the tone of Jess's voice. She put the box down on the couch. "Jess," she asked, taking a step closer. "Are you okay?"

Jess started to nod, but then she sniffed and hurried to wipe her eyes. Morgan raised her eyebrows. She'd never seen Jess get emotional—in fact, Jess was one of the most level girls in the ward. She was always quick to comply, eager to help out, and wasn't one who continually drew attention to herself. She'd received her Young Womanhood award last Sunday—the youngest girl in the ward ever to have completed it.

"Jess?" Morgan asked, placing a hand on Jess's shoulder. "What's the matter?"

"Nothing," Jess said quickly, wiping at her eyes.

"It's got to be *something* for you to be upset about it," Morgan said.

Jess turned away and took a step so that she was out of range of Morgan's hand. "I'm fine. It's just some . . . stuff."

"Do you want to talk about it?"

"No."

Morgan took a breath. It wasn't really her place to pry, so she needed to be careful. But she was worried about this girl—someone she had never worried about before. "Jess, if something is bothering you, then you need to talk to someone—maybe your parents."

She couldn't be sure but she thought Jess snorted. "No," Jess said quickly. "I can't talk to them."

Then there is *something bothering her,* Morgan thought. "Jess, your parents love you. They'll help you any way they can." Kate Thompson was the ward's model mother. Morgan herself looked up to Kate as much as she looked up to her own mom. Though Morgan only had one child, she marveled at Kate. She was so . . . together. And her children always looked and acted their best. She had no doubt that Kate and Brad would do everything in their power to help their daughter. The trick was convincing Jess—or any fifteen-year-old—that her parents were trustworthy.

"I can't talk to them," Jess repeated.

"They love you, Jess—they would do anything to help you, I know it."

Jess shook her head. "Dad's never home."

"Well, your mom is, and—"

"Mom's too busy." There was a chill in Jess's voice that surprised Morgan. Her own daughter was only two—but she was suddenly dreading those teenage years. If Jess Thompson could see her parents as unavailable, there was no hope that Morgan would be any more effective. Morgan's own adolescence wasn't that long ago. She remembered feeling the same way—she wished she'd given her parents a little more credit.

"Your Father in Heaven isn't too busy," Morgan said, hoping it wouldn't sound trite. Helping these girls understand just how important they were was a continual struggle. Sometimes it seemed that because they heard of their Heavenly Father's love so often, they didn't seek to find out for themselves as much as they should. If Morgan had any agenda in her leadership of the Young Women of this ward, it was to convince them of how much they were loved. Sometimes it was an uphill battle, but Jess was one of the girls Morgan would have assumed was secure. Now she wondered if that was the case. She opened her mouth to say something else, but right then the Thompson's minivan pulled up to the curb. Without a word, Jess pushed the door open and headed out into the rain. Morgan felt a powerful impression not to let things end that way.

"Jess!" she called as she pushed out the door and hurried down the sidewalk after her. Jess was almost to the van and turned to look at Morgan for the first time. Her eyes were anxious, and Morgan wondered if she was afraid Morgan might say something to Kate. "Uh . . ." Morgan said, trying to find the words. The rain, though not cold, was coming down hard, dripping down her face. "You're a wonderful girl, Jess."

Jess looked down. "I know," she said, almost with a sigh of disappointment.

"I'll, uh, see you Sunday," Morgan added. Maybe by then she'd have figured out a better way to approach Jess. She'd make it a matter of prayer and see if she could come up with any ideas.

Jess shrugged, not meeting Morgan's eyes as she turned back to the van. "I guess."

46

Journal entry, May 9

I don't know what to do. We're soul mates, so why do I feel this way? Mom forgot to pick me up from Mutual and I got myself all freaked out thinking about how I would be meeting Colt in just 30 hours—Sister Sanford caught me crying about it, I'm so embarrassed. I hope she doesn't tell my mom.

I have to see Colt, I know I do. Emily was so great, she totally understood and that made me feel so much better. I'm still scared though, but I feel stupid for it. I don't want to be some dumb loser girl about it. Emily would meet him if she were me, I think Britney would too. And if I don't go I might lose him forever.

He's sent me all these instructions on cleaning off my hard drive and canceling my e-mail account. It seems really weird to do all this—but he makes it sound so important. I don't want him to be mad at me for not doing it and I can't lie, but it makes me even more nervous. Still, this is Colt. I love him and I need to trust him.

I guess I've made my decision. I need to let Colt know, but then he doesn't want me using the home computer and I'm trying not to. I'll have to e-mail him from school.

me

I want cabin thirty-seven for the next nine days," he said to the desk clerk late Tuesday afternoon, not meeting her eyes. "Is it available?" He'd let his beard grow out the last few weeks, but he didn't want to take any chances of being recognized. Yesterday he'd left the office he'd worked at for the past few months without saying good-bye. He was probably replaced already. He didn't care. He had more important things to do.

The clerk whistled, her eyes stuck on the computer screen. "Are you sure you want number thirty-seven?" she asked. "It's the farthest away from our main lodge."

That had been the selling factor. "That's the one I want."

"Well, okay. That will be ninety-nine dollars a night. Can I have a credit card number?"

"I'd prefer to pay in cash."

"That's fine, but we need a credit card number for any incidental charges."

"Like what?"

"Oh, uh, the phone, damages, things like that."

"What if I pay cash up front, with an additional deposit? That will cover things, won't it?"

"Let me ask my manager." She looked up and smiled at him. She was very pretty, but far too old. By the time a girl was twenty, she had her mind made up about things. Youth made all the difference.

The clerk walked back to the office, and he tried not to look nervous. By the time she returned, he was tapping his fingers and shifting his weight from one foot to another.

"The manager said that if you're willing to leave a four hundred dollar deposit, he would waive the credit card number. With the deposit, your total comes to thirteen hundred forty-seven dollars and fifty cents. That includes tax."

He nodded and removed the wad of hundred dollar bills from his pocket. He'd been saving up for months.

"Okay," she said, still tapping away at the computer. "For extended stays like yours, housekeeping comes every other day, unless you prefer to—"

"I prefer my privacy," he said, laying his money on the counter. "No housekeeping."

"It's included in your room charges. They can call in advance to schedule a time."

"No housekeeping," he said again, shaking his head. "I'll take some extra towels. That's all we need."

"O-kay," she said in a suspicious tone. "Is there anything else we can do for you?"

"No," he said, taking his change and shoving it in his pocket. "You've been very accommodating."

Once back in his car, he headed south toward Highway 89. He had an appointment with a very pretty girl in Salt Lake City, Utah—a girl who was young enough to be trained to love him the way he wanted her to. Everything was going according to plan—except for Jessie's hesitation. But he refused to give in to the panic. Surely she'd go along with things.

He slept in the car at some rest stop in Idaho; then, early the next morning, he drove past her house for the first time. There were lights on and he imagined Jess getting ready for school. His palms got sweaty just thinking about their meeting tonight.

Thirty minutes before her school started, he parked on a side road that afforded a clear view of the route she would take to school. He watched every student as they walked toward him, scanning every face until he saw his Jess. His heart began beating hard in his chest as he watched her talk to a pretty blonde girl, probably Britney. Jess was so beautiful, so perfect. The girls passed his car without looking at him, and he furrowed his brow. He didn't like that Jess was still so close to Britney.

He'd tried hard to fracture that relationship. Jess wouldn't tell her, would she? He refused to entertain the idea. She wouldn't betray him, not now. She had to be as excited as he was. He watched her in the rearview mirror until she entered the school; then he took a deep breath. He was going to have a long wait, but all his efforts were about to pay off. And if for some reason she didn't show up tonight, he knew right where to find her.

47

——Original Message——
From: jjk_hollywood@hotmail.com
To: coltinator_51@yahoo.com
Sent: Wednesday, May 10, 7:36 AM
Subject: I'll be there

Colt

I'll be there, I promise. I won't let you down. You're right that there is no one in my life like you. I'm sorry I worried you. I made sure the computer at home is clean and I'll go over it one last time before tonight. I'm writing this from a school computer and I'll delete the entire account as soon as I finish. I love you so much. See you in a few hours. Meet me at the Allied insurance building 1894 E. Stag Street. I'll wait in the front alcove.

Love
Your Jessie

For Kate, Wednesday was all about getting back on track. She and Brad were working things out, and she didn't even feel as sick as she had been. The truth was out, all of it, and she felt free in that respect but still burdened by all that had happened.

The doorbell rang and she looked at the clock. She hadn't forgotten about her visiting teachers or something, had she? She hoped not, because she didn't feel up to visitors.

When she opened the door, she froze.

"Mom?" Kate said.

Her mother's bright red lips broke into a wide smile, showing gleaming white teeth. Her face was, as always, tan and smooth, though it had a softness that hinted at her age. "Katie!" she said, taking two steps forward and pulling Kate into a hug. Kate kept her arms at her side. Of all the people she was not up to dealing with right now, her mom was at the top of her list.

"What are you doing here?" Kate asked, still standing in the doorway.

Her mom pushed a lock of bleached-blonde hair behind her ear. "Gary has his final interview for the job in Ogden. I had him drop me off here." Without invitation, she squeezed past Kate and entered the house. She was dressed in a red knit top, which stretched tight across her implanted breasts. Her white shorts also fit snug against her legs, and she wore nylons to cover her varicose veins. Kate shook her head as she closed the door. Even at fifty-eight years old, her mom still tried to look young. It had embarrassed Kate as a child to have her mom look like a teenager.

Joy kept talking. "It's a great opportunity for Gary. I hope it works out."

Just then the thunder of little feet exploded up the stairs. Justin ran a few more steps, saw the strange lady in the hall, and stopped.

"Jordan?" Joy said, smiling.

"Justin," Kate corrected.

"Wow," Joy said, as if getting his name wrong was no big deal. "He's so big. What is he, six years old now?"

"Four, Mom, Justin is four." Didn't she even bother to read the Christmas letter Kate sent every year? She walked past her mother and picked up Justin on her way back to the kitchen. "Would you like a snack?" she asked the toddler as she deposited him onto a barstool. He nodded, still looking at his grandmother with trepidation. Kate went about getting him a banana while wondering just how long her mom was going to stay.

"I hope it's all right that I stay with you for a few hours," her mom said, as if answering Kate's unasked question.

"Sure," Kate said, though her tone was flat.

"I thought maybe we could go shopping. I heard the Gateway Mall downtown has all the best shops. I absolutely love American Eagle—their jeans fit me perfectly."

Kate glanced at her mother's figure, dismayed to realize that Joy had Kate's college body—the body Kate had traded for her kids. A moment of envy passed through her, but she quickly turned her attention back to Justin. "I can't go shopping. It's the middle of the day. Chris just went down for a nap, and the kids are coming home from school."

"Just for a little while," her mother said. "An hour, maybe two."

"I can't," Kate said.

Her mom laughed. "You won't," she reiterated, and began tapping her bright red fingernails on the countertop. "You never take a moment for yourself. How good of a mother can you be if you never fill your bucket?"

Kate felt the rage build inside, but she said nothing. "Can I get you something?"

"Diet Coke?"

"We don't have Diet Coke," Kate said. "I have milk, water, or apple juice."

Joy scowled, then shrugged. "Apple juice would be wonderful, dear."

For the next hour Kate listened to her mother prattle on about nothing of substance. Eventually her mother wandered into the living room. Kate looked at the clock and furrowed her brow. It was 3:12. Jess should have been home ten minutes ago. Just then the phone rang. She fairly ran to answer it.

"Hi, Mom," Jess said when Kate picked up the phone.

"Where are you?" Kate asked. "I've been worried."

"I'm at Britney's—is it okay if I stay?"

"No, you better come home."

Jess was quiet. "Why?"

"Because I said so," Kate said, trying to turn away so her mother couldn't hear her. "You've got chores, and I have to take Keith to practice and Caitlyn to her last soccer game in an hour."

"Is that Jess?" Joy asked.

Kate turned, the phone still against her ear, and looked at her mother just a couple of feet away. "I need you to watch the kids," she said into the receiver.

"I can watch the kids," Joy said. Kate turned again and clenched her eyes shut, taking a deep breath and trying to ignore her mother.

"Who is that?" Jess asked.

"Grandma Joy," Kate said reluctantly.

"Grandma's there?" Jess said as if in shock. Kate completely understood. The kids hadn't seen her mother for over a year.

"Yes, but I need you to come home."

"But Grandma said she'd watch the kids—can't I please stay?"

The last thing Kate was going to do was leave her kids with her mother.

"Let her stay there," Joy said again. "I can watch the kids."

Kate covered the receiver and turned to her mom. "No," she hissed, unable to keep her annoyance at bay. Her mom pulled back slightly, her eyes wide with surprise. Kate went back to the phone. "Home. Now," she said with finality.

"Fine," Jess spat back, and the line was suddenly dead. Kate took a deep breath and hung up the phone. Then she turned to face her mother, who was staring at her.

"What was that all about?" Joy asked, her tone guarded.

"Jess has responsibilities," Kate said, moving past her mother to busy herself with the few dishes in the sink.

"Let her be a kid," Joy said. "I'd love to watch the children."

Kate whirled, and all the annoyance spilled over, thanks to a generous amount of stress and pregnancy hormones. "You don't even know my children, Mom."

Joy pulled back again. "You really do need a break," she said.

Her mother's flippant response set her off, and Kate felt her face get hot at the insulting nature of her mother's comment. "You know what, Mom? I think you take enough breaks for the both of us. I have responsibilities. I know you don't *get* that, but it's my life."

Her mom was quiet, and Kate dared herself to feel guilty. But she didn't. She wondered how many years she'd been waiting to let this out on her mother. Unfortunately, even though she didn't feel guilty, she didn't feel great about it either.

"Is that how it is between us?" Joy asked after several seconds, her expression changing from shock to sorrow.

"Yes, Mom," Kate said, turning away, not wanting to feel sympathetic. "It is, and it always has been."

"Well, I guess I better go then." But no sooner had she said the words than the front door burst open. The kids came into the kitchen, all of them freezing in place for just a moment.

"Grandma?" Caitlyn said, her face breaking into a wide smile. Both Kate and Joy looked at the kids. Finally Joy smiled.

"My goodness," she said. "You guys are so big."

Caitlyn ran forward, and Joy pulled her into a hug. Caitlyn was always sending Grandma pictures and letters. In fact, sometimes Caitlyn reminded Kate of her mother.

"Homework, kids," Kate said, ushering them to the table. A minute later Jess walked in the door, scowling. Chris woke up, and Kate busied herself with getting him a snack. For the next fifteen minutes Kate ignored her mother, who sat at the table with the kids and asked them questions while they all ate the cookies Kate had baked that afternoon.

Sharla and Keith, who had been more hesitant at first, soon opened up and began chatting with this new person they had mostly seen only in pictures. Kate looked at the clock. Her mother had only been there for an hour and a half—but it felt like an eternity. When the kids finally finished their homework, they disappeared downstairs, leaving Kate and Joy alone again.

"Katie, I know I wasn't a perfect parent."

Kate didn't want this to turn into a "poor Joy" moment, so she looked up and held her mother's eyes. "I know that too."

Joy pursed her lips and stood up. "But I took care of you. I gave you the freedom to be yourself."

"It's called neglect," Kate said. "You left me alone to figure things out."

"That's not fair. I think I had a little to do with how you turned out," Joy said, looking at the tabletop and tracing a pattern with her fingernail. "You're independent and hardworking and—"

"The reason I turned out the way I did is because I made sure every choice I made was the exact opposite of what you'd have done."

Joy jolted and looked up at her daughter. Kate held her eyes. "I don't know why you came here, Mom."

Joy nodded and stood. "I came to see my daughter—someone I'm very proud of. But I guess I overstayed my imagined welcome. Tell the kids good-bye. I'll have Gary pick me up at that café I saw on the corner." She didn't say another word, and the door shut behind her a few seconds later.

Kate just stood there. After all these years she'd finally told her mother how she felt. Why didn't she feel victorious? Why did it feel like she'd just swallowed a stone? Hot tears filled her eyes, but she didn't know why. Was she embarrassed to have lost her cool? Was she mourning her childhood all over again? If only her mother were someone she could talk to, someone who understood Kate's life. Was that so much to ask for?

Thank goodness she had other things to distract herself with. "Keith! Caitlyn!" she called out. "It's time to go."

She turned to find Jess standing in the doorway of the study. How long had she been there?

"Why are you so mean?" Jess asked calmly. The question caused Kate to raise her eyebrows in surprise.

"What?" she asked.

"You told Grandma to leave. You told her that you hated her."

"I didn't tell her I hated her," Kate said, but her heart was hammering. It had never crossed her mind that someone might have overheard what she said.

"I don't think she's so bad," Jess said, surprising Kate with her candor.

"You didn't grow up with her," Kate said. "She wasn't a good mother to me."

Jess held her eyes for a moment, making Kate feel vulnerable and judged. The anger in Jess's eyes, the sorrow and the . . . fear? . . . confused her. What was going on with her daughter? she wondered. She knew it wasn't simply the way she'd spoken to her mother. But just as she opened her mouth to ask, Keith came bursting upstairs.

"I'm ready," he announced.

Kate looked down at him, then looked back up at Jess, but she'd already disappeared into the study. She let out a breath, and for the first time in her life she wondered if she was making mistakes in her own motherhood that would one day alienate her own children the way her mother's choices had alienated her. The idea seemed impossible—and yet, as the events of the last couple of weeks marched through her head, the thought wouldn't go away.

48

——Original Message——

From: coltinator_51@yahoo.com

To: jjk_hollywood@hotmail.com

Sent: Wednesday, May 10, 3:29 PM

Subject: Love you

Jessie,

I'm sending this to test whether or not you canceled your account—make sure you do. Like I told you before—everything will be different tomorrow. We'll start all over again. I'm glad you understand how important it is for us to meet, how important you are to me. It will be worth it, Jessie, I promise. Today is the first step in the rest of our lives together. No one could ever love you like I do.

See you in a few hours. If you get this message, make sure you delete the entire e-mail account.

Your soul mate

Colt

———

He scanned the Internet café and waited five minutes, then smiled when he got the failure notice. The e-mail hadn't gone through.

Perfect. He quickly cancelled his own account, shut down his laptop, and returned to his car. It was time to go shopping. They'd need food, movies, maybe some games. Only time and distance separated them now.

49

From: jjk_hollywood@hotmail.com
To: emjenkins000@yahoo.com
Sent: Wednesday, May 10, 7:39 AM
Subject: I'm so nervous!

Emily,

Sorry it took me so long to write back—but anyway, I decided to meet Colt. I don't think I was ever not going to, but it was just so BIG, ya know? Anyway, thank you for letting me talk to you about it. It was just what I needed. I'll let you know how it goes. He told me to clean off my computer as a symbol of the new beginning we'll be making tomorrow. Isn't that sweet?

Don't be a stranger and wish me luck. I'm still really nervous, but he's almost here now and I know I need to follow through. I think I've got it all figured out.

Jess

————

Jess, are you okay?" Brad asked at dinner. She seemed tense. He looked over at Kate but she just shrugged—but it was a guilty shrug. Brad wondered what had happened.

"Yeah," Jess said, pushing her noodles around her plate. "I'm fine."

"Grandma came over today," Sharla said.

"Oh? I ordered her a new toilet, but need to put it in. I better do that tomorrow."

The kids started laughing, confusing him.

"Not that grandma—the other one."

Brad lifted his eyebrows and looked quickly at Kate, whose face darkened enough to confirm what the kids had said. "Oh really," he said slowly. "Why was she here?"

"I don't know," Caitlyn said matter-of-factly. "But she is so pretty." They went on to discuss this exciting new development for several minutes. Kate never said a word. Jess said very little but kept looking at her mother with an expression Brad couldn't quite read.

Brad tried to get Jess engaged in the conversation, but she wouldn't give in. After a few more attempts to get her to open up, he gave up. Fifteen was so hard. He wouldn't go back for all the season tickets in the world. Well, maybe New England Patriots season tickets . . . and complimentary airfare to get him to the games. He started asking Caitlyn about her day, and she didn't disappoint him. Caitlyn was always interested in talking. After several minutes, and talking to each of the kids in turn, they seemed to run out of things to talk about.

"I have something exciting to tell you guys," he said. Kate looked at him and caught his eye. "Your mom's going to have another baby."

"Really?" Caitlyn said, dropping her spoon and bringing her hands together as if she were in a Hallmark commercial.

"Ohhh, I hope it's a girl," Sharla added. They all started talking at once, asking questions. Brad smiled, relieved at their acceptance. Jess's response brought silence, though.

"You're kidding, right?"

Brad looked at Jess, who was looking at Kate with an anger that surprised him. Kate looked between Jess and Brad as if unsure what to say.

He cleared his throat. "Jess," he said, "your mother and I are excited about this new baby, and—"

"Is that why you were sleeping on the couch last week? Why you guys have been acting so weird?" Jess suddenly spat out, glaring at him for just a moment. "Because you're so excited about this?" She looked at Kate again. "You can't even wait up for me after the dance? You tell Grandma to leave? But you'll have another baby? All you care about are babies. Why don't you just sell us off when we grow up!" She pushed her chair out, threw her napkin on the table, and stormed out of the room.

The rest of the family was silent. Emotional outbursts just didn't happen in the Thompson house very often. The silence was strangulating, and Brad tried to sift through what he ought to do or say. Jess's reaction had taken him totally off guard.

"Am I a baby?" Justin finally asked in a quiet voice.

Kate's chin started to quiver, and she shook her head. "I love all of you guys," she said. She opened her mouth to continue, but finally stood. "I'll be back in a minute." Brad thought maybe she was going to go talk to Jess, but she headed for her own room.

"Why is Jess mad?" Keith asked, returning to his green beans as if having his mom and sister run from the table was a daily event. "Is the baby going to share a room with her?"

Jess, as the oldest girl, and Chris, as the youngest boy, were the only kids with their own rooms. The others shared. And now they were going to have another baby. Where would they put it? They would need a bigger car too. Brad hadn't resolved those issues, but he ignored them for now.

"I'm not sure why Jess is mad," Brad said. "But she'll be okay. I think she's just surprised."

"And she's a teenager," Keith added, with his mouth full. "Teenagers are crazy."

"I'm almost a teenager, and I'm not crazy," Caitlyn said, glaring at her brother.

Keith just snorted as if he'd made his point.

50

Journal entry, May 10

I can't believe it—Mom's having another baby! But I guess she's got plenty of time since all she does is ignore me anyway. She doesn't even know me but she wants another kid? Grandma came over today and Mom kicked her out. She hates Grandma—I bet she'll be surprised when she realizes how much I hate her too.

I'm glad I agreed to meet Colt tonight and you know what, I don't even care if I get caught. I feel like such an idiot for being worried about it. This perfect little life she's created for all of us stinks!! Colt really is the only person who cares about me. Even Dad seemed fine with another baby. Neither one of them thought for a minute about how I might feel. They don't even care about me. I turn sixteen in a week—that means I only have two more years until I can leave this place. Colt says he wants to marry me—then we can move far away and forget about my stupid family. I leave to go see him in less than two hours and I'm too mad to be scared now. I hate it here.
me

———

Kate stopped in front of Jess's door and took a breath. Kate had stayed in her room until after the house had gone quiet, leaving Brad in charge of bedtime. Now she had to confront this. She put her hand on

Jess's doorknob, then remembered the last time she'd walked in. She knocked lightly.

"What?" Jess called. Her voice was angry. Kate had hoped for sadness.

"Can I come in?" Kate asked.

"Do I have a choice?"

Kate flinched. "I won't come in if you don't want me to."

"I don't want you to."

Kate felt her chin begin to quiver, and she rested her forehead against the door. The house of straw analogy came to mind, and she took a deep breath. "Jess, I'm sorry."

"For what, having another baby? I don't care. Have all the kids you want. Why should it even matter to me? Maybe this kid will be skinny and perfect so you can be happy."

The level of rage took Kate off guard. "I'm sorry for not making you feel important," she continued. "I love you just the way you are."

"Yeah, right," Jess responded.

Kate blinked. Where was all this hostility coming from? "Can I please come in so we can really talk about this?"

Jess was silent for a few seconds. "I don't want to talk to you right now." The sadness was in her voice now, and Kate longed to hold her, to convince her of how much she was loved. Had she really made Jess feel that she had to be perfect?

"Please," Kate asked one more time.

"You still don't care what I think," Jess replied. Her voice grew closer, and Kate imagined that she stood on the opposite side of the door. She placed a hand on the door, overwhelmed to consider that she'd created this distance between her daughter and herself—so much like her own relationship with her mother. The thought made her nausea increase. It might only be a door between them, but she realized there was far more than a slab of wood that kept them apart.

"I do care," Kate said, wiping at her eyes. "Are you sure you don't want to talk?"

"Yes."

Kate closed her eyes and shook her head. "Just . . . know that I'd like to talk if you feel like it. I love you, Jess. So much. I'm sorry I haven't told you that more often."

Jess said nothing, and Kate stood there for almost a full minute, hoping Jess would change her mind.

"Good night, Mom," Jess finally said.

"Good night," Kate said in surrender. "I love you."

More than an hour later, unable to sleep, Kate thought she heard something. She held her breath and concentrated, but she didn't hear anything further. She placed a hand on her stomach and breathed deeply enough that it raised beneath her hand. There was a baby in there, and she hated that it was such a burden on her family. But it wasn't the baby's fault. It was Kate's. She hadn't been there for Jess the way she should have been, and now Jess seemed too far away to reach out to.

"I'm sorry," she whispered into the darkness, imagining the words slithering through the vents into Jess's room and repeating themselves into her subconscious. But the words weren't for Jess alone. Maybe Brad could take a piece of them—and her baby. She pressed her hand on her belly again, hoping the baby understood. Rolling onto her side, she looked at Brad, reaching out to touch his face. *It's going to be all right,* she reminded herself. Maybe they could talk this out tomorrow. *It's going to be all right,* she said in her mind again.

So then why did she still have that unsettled feeling in the base of her chest?

51

Jess stared at the ceiling, waiting for the footsteps upstairs to stop. It seemed to take forever, and by the time she realized the house was silent, she had nearly talked herself out of going. Not only had she never done anything like this, but she'd never imagined it before. Not until now. She was still scared, and her heart was beating so fast that she felt a little light-headed.

She pushed one foot out from under the covers, then pulled back the blankets, sat up, and took a deep breath. Tomorrow the sun would come up just like it did today. She'd practice the piano, eat her Cheerios, and go to school. No one would know what she'd done, but she could tell Britney if she wanted to. The idea was hard to really believe.

Jess pulled the note she'd written earlier out from under her pillow and laid it on top of her bed. The note and deleting all the computer stuff still scared her, but she trusted Colt and didn't want to disappoint him. She liked the symbolism of starting all over tomorrow. A new Jess, a new Colt, a new relationship in every way. Unable to leave it out in plain sight like that, she tucked it under her pillow, just one corner of the pink stationery peeking out from under the blue pillowcase. It made her feel better somehow. She was still doing what Colt had asked her to do, but it wasn't so obvious.

She quietly slid the window open, and, having already removed the screen earlier in the day, it was easy to slip out and close the window behind her. As she did so, she told herself that if she didn't do this, it would be one more way in which she had become who her mother wanted her to be, instead of who she really was. She thought of the conversation they'd had through the door and felt her anger rise again.

There was more to Jessica Catherine Thompson than red hair, big thighs, baby-sitting, and Gershwin. There had to be. Colt seemed like the only person in the world who saw it. She needed to be with him. And like he said, it seemed that God knew it. Despite her breaking all the rules, going against her parents, and taking such a risk, He understood that she needed this—that she needed someone she was special to.

She was out of breath by the time she pulled herself out of the window well. It had been raining off and on for the last few days, but she was glad it had stopped. She took it as another sign. She hurried down the driveway toward the corner.

The night had definitely become chilly by the time she reached the office building where she would be picked up. She stepped into the shadows and rested her back against the stucco wall. She couldn't seem to catch her breath. The cold, the anticipation, and the sheer fear compounded to create a feeling of such intensity it didn't seem real.

Five minutes before midnight, a red Pontiac drove into the parking lot, and any control she'd managed to pull together went right out the window. He was here.

But he hadn't seen her, and she pulled farther into the shadows. *What am I doing?* she asked herself, without being sure whether the question was posed for having left home or for staying hidden. Her heart hammered.

After a few more seconds, she took a deep breath and stepped out when the car pulled up to the curb. She knew she'd never forgive herself if she let this opportunity to meet Colt pass her by. And she couldn't risk his disappointment if she didn't follow through. She needed him so much, more than ever before. If she stood him up now, she might lose him forever. He would understand why her parents' announcement was so hard for her. He'd know why she was so upset.

There was a click—unlocking the door, she assumed—and she took a deep breath. The door handle was cold to the touch as she pulled it open.

"Colt told you I would be picking you up, right?"

She had hoped Colt would come anyway, but knew she would see him soon enough—and considering how much he talked about his uncle, she felt as if she knew him too. So she slid into the passenger seat without looking too hard at the driver. She felt awkward and embarrassed—sure that Colt's uncle was appraising her and wondering what Colt possibly saw in such a fat redhead.

"Yeah, he told me," she said, hating how young her voice sounded. She did not want to sound like a child. "How's his ankle?" she asked.

"Feeling better," his uncle said.

Jess nodded. She was glad.

"He said to give you this." He held out a bottle of red cream soda.

She smiled and took the bottle, staring at the label. The anxiousness to see Colt built even more.

"That's your favorite?" the uncle asked, and she looked at him for the first time. His giving her a gift seemed to be permission somehow. He was old—older than Dad. He had a beard, and his hair was shaved really short, like a soldier. She glanced away, feeling bad for looking too close. He wasn't at all like she'd expected. She'd assumed Colt's uncle from Florida would be a surfer type—young and hip. This guy was nothing like that. It was disconcerting to be wrong.

"Yes," she said, unscrewing the lid and taking a long swallow, hoping it would calm her nerves—and wishing Colt was here to enjoy it with her. She wondered how far away the hotel was. She thought of her parents at home asleep, and the guilt began to rise up. She quickly squelched it. She couldn't feel bad about that. Her parents had created this—they had put her in this position.

"Mine, too," she heard him say. She swallowed and leaned against the back of the seat, feeling herself relax. Her body was almost instantly warmed, and she took it as a sign that everything was okay.

"That's so funny. It's Colt's favorite too," she said, noticing that her tongue felt funny—like she'd sucked on too many jawbreakers and rubbed some of the roughness off. She licked her lips and then took another long drink. "Where's the hotel?" she asked as they pulled onto I-15.

"Not too far," he said. His voice was soft like kitten fur, and she felt a melting sensation in her muscles. That was weird. "Go ahead and close your eyes. I'll let you know when we get there."

She opened her mouth to say that she was too excited to see Colt, but her words came out garbled and hushed. It felt as if her brain were slowing down. Maybe she did need to rest, just for a little while. It was nearly midnight, after all.

"Sleep tight, Jessie," he said as she drifted off. She was confused. Only Colt called her Jessie.

52

Kate blinked her eyes a few times before she could focus. The nausea hit hard as soon as she sat up. She winced, bowing her head and taking a deep breath. With each pregnancy she hoped the morning sickness would be more bearable—but that hadn't been the case yet. If anything, it felt worse.

The clock read 6:19. Why wasn't Jess practicing her piano? Did she sleep in?

Kate shook her head. No doubt this was further rebellion on Jess's part. Quietly she slipped out of bed, but the movement woke up Brad.

"Hey," he said.

"Hey," she said back as she slipped her feet into her slippers.

"Wha—what time is it?" he asked, rubbing his eyes as he rolled onto his side.

"Jess didn't get up. It's almost six-thirty."

Brad ran his hand through his already bedraggled hair. "I think we might have a teenager on our hands, Kate."

Kate nodded. It sure looked that way. "I'll go get her up."

"I'll do it. I wanted to talk to her about last night anyway," Brad said as he swung his feet over the side of the bed and stretched his arms over his head.

"Oh, okay. Maybe that would be better," Kate said, relieved to have his help.

The early morning was still gray, so she turned on lights as she headed toward the kitchen. Brad exited the bedroom after she did and soon disappeared downstairs. Kate opened the pantry and pulled out boxes of cereal while nibbling on saltine crackers, hoping they would settle her stomach.

"Kate!" Brad called a moment later. She turned to look at a concerned Brad standing in the doorway. "Jess isn't here."

Kate furrowed her brow. "What?"

"She's not in her room."

Kate put the box of Mini-Wheats on the countertop and headed toward him. He moved aside to let her pass. "Maybe she's in the shower."

"I checked. I'll look around up here," Brad said. "You can look downstairs."

Kate hurried to Jess's room. The light was off, and she wondered if Brad had even lit the room before he looked. She flipped on the light as soon as she reached the doorway.

"Jess?" she called. Silence. She scanned the room. The blinds were open, and the bed was messed up. But when she stepped in and placed her hand on the sheets, they were cold.

She ran to the bathroom. "Jess?" she called, turning on the lights and then falling silent. The only answer was the slow drip-drip of the shower faucet. She checked the tub and found it dry—Jess hadn't showered today. Her heart began to speed up, even though she was telling herself to stay calm.

She turned on the light in Caitlyn and Sharla's room, and the bodies cocooned on the beds shrank from the light. "Is Jess in here?"

"Wha . . . what?"

"Is Jess in here?" she asked. Her words were clipped and fast. She crossed the room and looked in the closet. What would Jess be doing in her sisters' closet?

"No," Caitlyn finally said in a voice still heavy with sleep.

She said something else, but Kate was already moving on to Keith's room . . . and then to the storage room. As she ran back to the stairs, she scanned the living room again. Kate hurried up the stairs and met Brad in the hallway. They held each other's eyes, speaking volumes without words.

"Oh, my gosh," Kate breathed, and had to reach out for the wall to steady herself as the room seemed to spin just a little bit. Her heart was beating hard. Jess was gone.

Brad was breathing fast too, his eyes panicked. Kate started reliving their argument last night. Jess had been so mad, so hurt. *Hurt enough to leave?* The idea seemed impossible.

"Let's check the house one more time," Brad said. "Look everywhere."

Kate nodded, and Brad ran past her while she headed toward the rooms he'd already checked. They met up at the top of the basement stairs just a couple of minutes later. Brad was holding a pink piece of paper in his hand. He held it out to Kate, and she took it with a shaky hand.

I need a time-out. I'm at Terrezza's and I'll be home soon.

Jess

"Who's Terrezza?" Brad asked, taking the note back, his voice flat. Kate had a hard time concentrating.

"She ran away," she said, not believing this had really happened. How could *this* happen?

"Who's Terrezza?" Brad asked again.

Kate shook her head. "I don't know any Terrezza," she said.

They both stood there then, not knowing what to do, staring at the note in Kate's hand. "I've never heard her even talk about a Terrezza," she added. How could Jess have a friend she didn't know about? Was that why Jess was acting so strangely? Had she made some bad friends at school? How would Kate not know? Kate knew everything her kids were involved in—every friend, every teacher. Everything.

A few more seconds passed before Brad sprang into action. "I'll go drive around the neighborhood to see if she's on her way home. You start calling her friends." He turned toward the kitchen and fumbled in the basket for his keys. Kate watched him, but she didn't move.

"Mommy?" a timid voice called up from the bottom of the stairs, causing both Brad and Kate to turn and look at the frightened faces of their other children. "What's the matter?"

"Nothing," Kate said, but she shared a quick glance with Brad, and seventeen years of marriage allowed her to speak without words. She would take care of the kids. He would find Jess.

53

Jess tried to open her eyes, but her eyelids were too heavy. So were her arms, her legs, everything. It was the strangest feeling, one she'd never experienced. She didn't understand what was happening. Maybe she was dreaming, but had she been asleep? She couldn't think fast enough to figure out anything. She'd been going somewhere, but had she arrived? She was going to see someone, wasn't she? Her mind reached back, strained to hold on to a solid thought, something she could build on, but her thoughts were as vaporous as her body was unresponsive.

Colt!

She forced her eyes open as simply thinking his name cleared her head, but the sun was too bright and she had to close them again. She took a deep breath. Even inflating her lungs was difficult. The vibrations beneath her told her she was in a car, but why? And where? She felt her heart rate increase as her thoughts cleared enough to let fear in. Something was wrong; that much she knew. After several seconds, she opened her eyes again, squinting this time, but all she could see was the upholstery of the car's seats. She was lying down on a back seat. A bump in the road jolted her and the road became rough. *Colt,* she thought again, trying to hold on to that thought, trying to figure out what was happening.

"You're awake," a voice said, startling her. She squinted toward the voice and saw two dark eyes beneath grey eyebrows looking at her in the rearview mirror.

"What's . . ." She meant to ask what was happening, but the effort it to took to form just one word seemed to drain her of energy.

"We're going to see Colt," the man said.

Colt. That name gave her comfort, and she let her head fall back against the seat again. "Why . . . is . . . it . . ." She couldn't finish that question either. What was wrong with her? Her mouth was dry, and she tried to work up enough saliva to ask again while looking at the window positioned above her. She saw sky and trees and sun. With a jolt she realized it was morning. Daytime! Her breath caught in her throat, and she looked up at the eyes still watching her in the mirror, which was bouncing up and down in rhythm with the road beneath them.

"It was the only way you and Colt could be together," he said, and she felt a chill run through her body.

"You'll understand, Jessie," Colt's uncle said. "When Colt explains everything you'll understand that this was the only way it could work. It's destiny, Jessie. It's fate."

It's daytime, Jess thought in her mind as her heart hammered. She felt sick to her stomach. Tears leaked from her eyes and panic consumed her. She was supposed to be at school, shocking Britney with the story about sneaking out to dinner with Colt. It was supposed to be a normal day. Her whole chest was tight, her stomach spasmed, and her head was spinning. What was going on?

I'm supposed to be home.

54

I t's seven-fifteen," Kate called out half an hour after Brad left, her stomach still in knots. "Backpack check." Brad hadn't called. She hoped that meant he had found Jess and was reading her the riot act in the driveway. How would Kate act toward her daughter when she got home?

The kids weren't even dressed yet, let alone ready for her to do the final inspection to be sure they had all their homework and books. She ran from here to there, finding shoes, matching shirts to pants. Despite her worry, she felt the anger build up toward her oldest daughter. Had she any idea what her little tantrum was doing to her family?

The phone rang and she ran for it, tripping over Keith in the middle of the floor putting on his shoes. She almost did a face plant but managed to catch herself with the wall.

"Hello?" she said breathlessly, hoping—praying—begging—it was Jess. Just as she picked it up, she saw the number on the caller ID. Julie. Maybe she had news.

"Did you guys find her?" Julie asked.

Kate felt tears rise at the realization that Julie didn't have anything that was going to make things better. She also realized another feeling—embarrassment. She hadn't thought about it before now, but if Brad was calling people, everyone knew Jess had run away. "No, Brad called you?"

"Yeah, half an hour ago. He hasn't found her?"

Kate wiped at her eyes and turned so the kids couldn't see that she was crying. But they knew something was wrong. As Caitlyn and Sharla had gone about getting ready, they kept glancing at her, their expressions worried and scared. "No, did you ask Britney?"

"Yeah. She was as surprised as I was."

"Does she know a Terrezza?"

"She said she knows a couple of Theresas at school, but she's never seen Jess hang out with any of them, and she's not familiar with the odd spelling. She doesn't have any idea where Jess would go, other than coming here—and she didn't."

Keith began yelling about someone hiding his other shoe, and it woke Chris up, who started wailing. Kate moved the phone away from her ear and hollered at Caitlyn to get Chris and Sharla to help Keith find his shoe. They did it without grumbling. "I'd better go," Kate said into the phone as she glanced up at the clock. She hadn't even done the girls' hair yet . . . how ridiculous was she to be worried about their hair?

"I'm coming over," Julie said. "Clay's going to go to work late so he can handle things here. I'll be right there."

"No, it's okay," Kate said quickly, automatically falling back on her ability to take care of everything. "The kids will be off to school in just a minute and—"

"I'll be right there," Julie repeated. The line went dead.

Kate hung up the phone and wiped at the residual tears. She didn't want Julie here. It would be easier to deal with this without thinking about other people and their reactions. The very idea made her stomach tighten. No matter how relieved she would be when Jess got back, she was going to tell her in no uncertain terms that this was not the way to handle an argument.

"Mom, where's Jess?" Caitlyn asked.

Kate looked at her twelve-year-old daughter. What could she say? Tell her Jess ran away? That Kate didn't know where her own child was? What would people think when they learned what had happened? The humiliation caused Kate's neck to get hot.

"I think she just had something to do at school." She forced a smile but had a hard time meeting her daughter's eyes. It was paramount that she pretend nothing was wrong. She had to be strong for her children right now. Jess would be home soon; Kate was sure of it. She would not make things worse by getting hysterical. "Everything's fine."

55

Monique stayed in bed for five days. Harrison bought a casket online and arranged with a mortuary close by the morgue in Canada to have Terrezza sealed within it and shipped home as soon as possible. They had a simple funeral service Wednesday. Monique could hardly stand it; she was consumed with anger and unfiltered sorrow. Seventeen years old and gone forever. As soon as she got home she went back to bed. Karl and Jamie stepped in to greet the numerous acquaintances dropping in with flowers or food. Monique did nothing but mourn.

Thursday morning Harrison came into the bedroom and sat on the edge of the bed, reaching over to place a hand on her arm. He didn't ask how she was doing. She knew he didn't need to.

"I've been thinking," Harrison said.

Monique didn't respond.

"Remember that insurance policy we had on the kids? If any of them died before eighteen, there was a fifteen thousand dollar benefit to help with expenses."

Monique winced inside. She never wanted to make money off of her children. "I don't want to talk about this," she said, and her voice sounded weak. She pulled the blankets farther up to her chin.

"I know you don't," Harrison said with tenderness. "But I need your permission for something."

Monique opened her eyes. "My permission?"

"The police are investigating this on their end, but we all know that the chances of solving this are slim. Just getting her information listed on their databases takes several days. It's been six months. It involves two countries. And Karl, Jamie, and I are having a hard time sitting here doing nothing. We've used up all our waiting." Monique kept it to herself that she had no problem doing nothing. She was becoming quite comfortable with it.

Harrison continued, "After the funeral yesterday Karl started designing a website of some kind—a website about finding Terrezza's killer. He suggested an idea where we buy space on certain Internet listing sites—search engines, I think he called them. We also buy advertising on other websites and send e-mails all over the Internet. I don't really know if it will do any good, and if Karl weren't so excited I'd just tell him no. But he's been working on it all night, and Jamie is on fire about it too. It's almost like a tribute to their sister."

His voice went quiet, and she knew he was remembering all over again. She wished she could forget so that she *could* remember, instead of marinating in it the way she was.

Monique said nothing, unable to find an answer. Harrison continued, "But what they want to do isn't cheap. So I thought maybe we could charge it to our credit cards and then pay it off when we get the insurance."

Monique let out a breath and rolled onto her back. "What's the point? It's not going to change anything. It's not going to make this better."

Harrison's eyes filled up, and he looked at his roughened hands. "She was talking to this guy in our own home, Monique. He lured her away from us and killed her. We didn't know." He looked at his wife. "We never thought something like that would happen to our kids—in our house."

"Please don't say this is my fault," Monique whispered, clenching her eyes closed. The tears leaked out anyway. Without knowing it, he'd pierced her deepest fear, the thing that had sent her spiraling so fast. It was one thing when she thought Terrezza had just left. It was quite another to realize she'd been seduced while Monique watched Dr. Phil or washed dishes. She should have known what was happening—especially after the problems Terrezza had had. Monique should have paid more attention. "Don't you think I've thought of that? Don't you think I could just die for not knowing?"

Harrison turned and placed his hands on either side of her face. She tried to avoid his eyes, not wanting to connect with him that way, but she couldn't help it. His face was soft, his furrowed brows creasing his forehead. His eyes were like melted chocolate and she felt captured by them—like she'd always been. For all his hardness, his quiet presence, he was soft as butter on the inside and she knew this was tearing him up just like her—even if he could push through it and still be functional. "It's not our fault," he said in slow, calculated tones. "You are a wonderful mother, and Terrezza loved you."

Monique closed her eyes and shook her head. "Not good enough," she whimpered. "I should have known."

"This man knew what he was doing, Monique. We were all blindsided—even Terrezza. But someone out there has to know something, and if we start asking questions, maybe we'll find answers. Maybe we can find a little peace."

Monique started to sob, unable to think about any of it. Harrison reached out and gathered her into his arms, rocking back and forth for what felt like hours. She clung to him like she never had before and gave into the full heartbreak of her loss. Even when she'd considered Terrezza never coming home—even when she'd thought that something horrible may have happened—she'd had no idea it would hurt this much. How could she possibly know? And how could she be expected to move on?

56

By the time they pulled up outside the cabin, Jess had managed to work herself into a sitting position, though her muscles were still slow in responding to her commands. Inside she felt panicked, but outside she showed very little. She didn't know what was happening, but she was scared and didn't want to make Colt's uncle mad. As they drove he'd talked about how Colt hadn't been able to travel after spraining his ankle, so they'd changed the plan. He said he'd talked to her parents this morning and that they said it was okay. She knew that wasn't true, but she desperately wanted to talk to Colt. He would help this make sense, she would make him take her home, and then . . . then she didn't know what would happen. But Colt would help her. It was all the hope she had.

As soon as the car stopped she opened the door and moved toward the cabin as fast as her heavy legs would allow. The door was locked, and she banged on it. "Colt!" she shouted, her voice cracking. Colt's uncle came up behind her. He placed a hand on her shoulder, and she pulled away, shrinking from him and wiping at her eyes. Her parents knew she was gone. They had probably found the note. Was that why Colt had told her to write it? Was that why he was so insistent? But he hadn't hurt his ankle until Monday, and he had told her to leave the note days before that. Nothing made sense. She had to talk to him.

Her breathing was fast and shallow, and she looked around while Colt's uncle unlocked the door. They were in the mountains, surrounded by tall trees and low-growing grasses. It was cold despite the sunshine, and she was shivering. She wrapped her arms around herself and began shaking.

Run, a voice said in her mind. *Don't go inside.* She looked at the door. Colt's uncle opened it, looked at her with an expectant expression, and stepped inside, leaving her outside alone.

Run, the voice said again, just as Colt's uncle said, "We're back, Colt, you need to explain things to her."

Jess looked at the road one last time; then she looked at the door of the cabin. Colt was in there. He'd explain everything, and she didn't know what else to do. If she ran, where would she go? And could she run? Was her body up to it? Colt's uncle hadn't explained that, why she felt so weird, and she hadn't dared ask questions. But Colt loved her, and even though things were so messed up, she couldn't figure it out on her own.

She made an instant decision to talk to Colt first, to convince him that she couldn't do this. She couldn't stay in a cabin in the mountains. She had to go home. He would help her. She knew he would.

When she stepped into the cabin, it was dark—all the blinds were pulled shut. She peered into the darkness and took two steps inside. "Colt," she said, her voice shaking, "you have to take me home."

Silence.

The door slammed behind her and she jumped, turning around to see the shape of Colt's uncle in the darkness. She heard him latch the chain on the door. She scanned the room again, her heart thundering in her chest, her stomach feeling like she was going to throw up. "Colt?" she asked again as tears again overflowed. But there was no one else in the cabin. No Colt.

A sob broke from her chest as she wildly tried to make sense of this. She stepped away from the man by the door just as he took a step toward her. A slice of light from the side of a window crossed his face as he moved forward.

"Jessie," he said again, and in that instant she knew. She took a step back and was hit with such intense fear and panic that she felt completely frozen.

There was no Colt.

57

ook, Daddy!" Justin announced after Brad came in from yet another drive-by scan of the neighborhood, school, and mall. "It's a flower."

Brad looked down at the black and brown mottled picture and managed a small smile. "It's very nice," Brad said, ruffling his son's hair and leaning in to kiss his head. When he stood again, he turned to look out the window. His thoughts seemed far away.

Kate's heart ached, but she didn't give into it. She knew that the best thing to do was keep life as normal as possible for the other kids. Showing her own panic would undo everyone else. She couldn't take the risk. What good could she do if she was a basket case?

"You're making dinner?" Brad asked as he watched her put together the enchilada filling.

"We have to eat," Kate said. And she needed to stay busy. Kate continued what she was doing while he paced, stopping to look out one window then walking to the next and stopping before moving on to another.

"I think I'm going to call the police again."

"Again?" Kate asked, looking up from her task of spooning enchilada filling into tortillas. "You already called them?" The chill of embarrassment seized her again. Wasn't Brad the least bit hesitant to share this?

"I called them once, and they said they don't come out for runaways until the second day. I should never have told them about the note. I think that's why they won't take it serious."

"So why call them again?"

Brad shrugged in a helpless way. "I don't know," he finally admitted. "I just . . . need to do something. Maybe if I make a big enough deal about it they'll come out."

Kate just nodded. She didn't know what the right thing to do was, but she couldn't get over the idea that kids ran away from screwed up homes with screwed up parents.

"What time is school out?" Brad asked.

"Three."

"Okay," Brad said with a sharp nod. "I'll go drive around again, and then I'll pick up the kids." Kate watched him leave and felt the tears building up. What she really wanted was for him to hold her, tell her it would be okay and that he'd bring Jess home. But he hadn't said those things, he hadn't touched her and Kate didn't know how to ask.

The phone rang as soon as the door shut and Kate took a breath and wiped her eyes. It was her mother. Brad had tracked her down at the hotel she and Gary were staying at earlier in the day. Kate hadn't talked to her yet, but all the fire she'd felt yesterday had disappeared. She didn't feel . . . anything anymore.

"No, she's not back . . . yes . . . no, I don't need anything . . . please don't bring dinner . . . I'm okay . . . yeah, I'm sorry about yesterday too . . . okay, I'll let you know . . . no, I'm fine, really . . . thanks." She hung up and looked around the house. Everything looked so normal. This was her home, her family—and yet everything was different now. A certain innocence was gone. The house of straw analogy came back and she shuddered. How did this happen?

She stood there for several seconds, but as soon as she noticed the tears rising again, she shook herself out of her dismal thoughts. She couldn't break down. The kids needed her strength. *Jess*, she thought, *please come home. Let us talk about this.*

58

Brad came through the front door at nearly ten. He'd expanded his search area to include much of the west side of the Salt Lake valley and had been gone for nearly two hours. Kate stood up from where she'd been spot-cleaning the carpet and tried to hide what she'd been doing, knowing that Brad was aggravated by her determination to do such mundane things.

"Anything?" she asked.

He shook his head and went into their bedroom. Kate returned to her knees and kept scrubbing at the carpet. She was exhausted but knew she couldn't sleep. She'd fielded phone calls all day from friends and ward members wondering if Jess was home yet. The bishop had come over that evening, then the Relief Society presidency. She'd wanted to scream. Yes, their intentions were good, but it was awfully hard to pretend everything was fine when so many people were so intent to remind her that it wasn't.

She'd used everything possible to get the kids to bed—bribery, threats of no TV the next day, ignoring the growing fear taking over her chest cavity, and eventually yelling at them until they gave in. Then she felt horrible for it. She never yelled and hated scaring the kids into obeying her. Marilyn had been doing dishes and took Kate's place at bedtime without saying a word. Kate wanted to explain herself, but she just went into the living room, wishing the numbness wouldn't wear off so quickly. Then she saw the spots in the carpet she'd been meaning to get to, so she grabbed a rag and started scrubbing. Now instead of dark spots on the carpet, she had light ones from overdoing it. Marilyn had left half an hour ago, after Kate promised she'd call if they needed anything.

Brad returned from the bedroom and looked at the carpet. Kate tried to ignore his judgments and sat down on the couch, folding the rag into a tiny square and fantasizing about him pulling her into his arms and forcing her to feel something other than this gnawing fear and compulsion to deny everything. He didn't.

"The kids are getting scared," Kate said, lining up the corners of the fabric, trying to keep her panic in check. She looked up and noticed a nick in the wall, next to the TV. It had been there for months, and she thought maybe if she scooted the TV over it would be hidden. Or should she fill it and repaint?

"The kids?" Brad asked, looking at her strangely. "What about you?"

Kate felt tears come to her eyes but continued looking at the wall, trying to lose herself in something trite and passing. The only other option was obsessing over what had happened, where Jess was, what Kate had missed. "I passed scared a long time ago."

Brad came to sit beside her, but they weren't touching. She kept her hands in her lap, not knowing how to reach out to him. If she sought his affection, his physical comfort, would he judge her for that too? "It's my fault, isn't it?" she finally said, daring to shatter the hastily built wall she'd been hiding behind all day. "I thought all this was typical teenage stuff, and now she's gone." She sniffed and wiped her eyes. "I can't believe she did this, Brad." She looked up at him, begging for some help. He made no reaction. *Does that mean he agrees with me?* she wondered. He was staring at the wall, maybe thinking the same thing about the nick. He didn't answer.

"I'm not so sure *she* did this," he said. "It's something bigger."

"Bigger than running away?" Kate asked incredulously, feeling her emotions rise. "Bigger than throwing away everything we've done for her, all we've taught her her whole life? How can anything be bigger than that, Brad?"

Brad looked at the floor as if trying to decide whether to argue with her. Evidently he decided against it. "I'm going to go drive around again."

He'd been driving all day, but Kate wasn't about to stop him. It was one thing to blame herself, but quite another to bear the weight of his silent accusation.

"Are you going to go to bed?" he asked on his way to the door. "You probably should."

Kate agreed, she *should* sleep; but she knew she wouldn't, couldn't. Not with so many questions in her mind. "I'll wait up a little longer."

Brad just nodded. "Let me know if she calls."

Kate nodded. She could do that. She didn't watch him leave, just listened to the shutting of the door and tried to keep breathing. In and out, in and out. How had she missed this? What would she do when Jess walked through the door?

59

And you have no idea where she could have gone? She wasn't behaving strangely? Was she angry about anything?"

It was almost one in the afternoon, and the three of them—Brad and two police officers—stood in the middle of the living room.

"Jess and her mother argued the night she left."

"About what?"

Brad relayed the details—the pregnancy, Jess's reaction, Kate's attempts to make amends.

"And where is your wife?"

"She had some errands to run," he said, hating how horrible it sounded, as if this kind of thing happened all the time. Kate was certain Jess would be home any time; she felt calling the police was overreacting. But Brad knew something was wrong. He could feel it. Jess didn't just run away—there was more—and yet he'd searched her room, talked to everyone he could think of, and could find nothing.

The officer made some notes. "And you've called all your daughter's friends?"

Brad nodded. "And neighbors and the school. No one knows who Terrezza is. I also drove around the neighborhood, over and over. Jess's church leader said Jess was upset about something Tuesday night—but she didn't know what. I can give you her name."

"How about the computer? Has she been on more than usual?"

"Maybe a little," Brad said. Then he thought about Friday morning.

He'd taken Jess's word about the report she was working on. His stomach sank. "I caught her using an instant-message account on Friday. Is that important?"

"She wasn't supposed to IM?"

Brad nodded. "She downloaded it without our permission. But after I caught her, we talked about it, and she promised it was just for friends."

"How about e-mail?"

Brad shook his head, then realized that he would have said no to the instant-message question just last week. "I don't know," he finally admitted. If she was instant messaging behind his back, maybe there was even more going on. He closed his eyes and took a breath he hoped would stave off his panic. Why hadn't he paid more attention? Especially with the computer. Kate stayed far away from it, but he used a computer all the time. Why hadn't he installed protective software?

The officer made some notes. "Can I look at the computer?" He turned to his partner, who so far had remained silent. "Why don't you go check out the bedroom?"

"It's downstairs—last room on the right," Brad said to the second officer before leading the way into the study, anxious to see what might be hiding on the computer.

"Do you know what the IM program was? MSN, AOL, something else?" the officer asked after almost a minute of doing the same things Brad had done trying to find the program on Friday. "It's not on the desktop."

"I don't know," he said. "It was really early in the morning, around five-thirty, and I didn't get a good look. She'd exited the program by the time I figured out what she was doing."

"Five-thirty on a Friday morning?"

"Yeah, she said she was chatting with her friend down the road—and she promised me she never chatted with strangers."

"But if she'd already met someone online, they wouldn't be

considered a stranger to her." He let out a breath and stopped searching; then he stood up and opened his notebook again. "I'd like the name of the person she claimed to be chatting with. And if you don't mind, I'd like to call in a computer forensics team to see what they can find."

Brad nodded, relieved that they were doing something—anything. "Britney. Britney Peterson. She's a sophomore, same as Jess, at the high school. Jess said Britney had an assignment she was trying to get done, and that's why she was online too."

"And what was your daughter working on?"

"She said she was working on a report of her own—on appendicitis." It was sounding more and more ridiculous to Brad every minute.

The officer nodded and wrote some more.

After another minute, the officer stood, flipped his notebook closed, and looked at Brad with compassion. "Look, I know this is scary, but teenage girls get angry with their parents all the time. Chances are she'll be on her way home by the time school is over." Exactly what Kate thought.

"Jess isn't just some teenager," Brad said, though he sensed the officer was attempting to offer some comfort. "She's a good girl. I mean, she's never done anything like this. It's hard to imagine she'd run away."

The officer just nodded.

The second officer returned upstairs. "Who went through her room?" he asked.

"Well, I did. I wanted to know what she'd taken with her, if she'd left anything else."

"If there was any evidence there, it's gone now—but it looks like she went out the window. The screen is out of place."

Brad looked at the ground. He hadn't thought of messing up any evidence.

"Did she have a diary?"

"Yes," Brad said. "But I haven't seen her write in it for years. Not that that means she didn't."

"I didn't find one in the room," the second officer said.

"If you find it, call us," the first officer said. "What was she wearing?"

"Uh," Brad said. "I'm not sure. But she had a necklace—a silver medallion on a chain with her name engraved on the back. I didn't find it in her room and I know she was wearing it last night."

"Did she take any extra clothes?"

"Uh, I don't know. But her jacket is gone."

"The grey backpack down there—is that hers? Did she have any other type of bag she'd use to pack clothes in?"

"I don't know," Brad answered and wished Kate was home. He wished she was taking this as seriously as he was. "My wife would know that."

"Well, have her check on that," he said almost casually. "And let us know." The officers turned toward the door.

"What about an Amber Alert?" Brad suggested.

"We don't have a vehicle description, and there is no sign of forced removal. Amber Alert is for emergency situations."

That was it? "There has to be something more we can do. My daughter is gone. You treat it as if it happens every day."

"It does happen every day," the officer said, turning to face Brad in the hallway. "Chances are she's going to turn up."

"Is that what you people said about Elizabeth Smart?" Brad said as calmly as possible, though he didn't feel calm.

"She was taken. Your daughter, by all accounts, left. I will, however, stop at the high school and talk to her friend, Britney. And I'm getting the computer checked. That's more than a lot of jurisdictions would do with a missing teenager that left a note following a fight with her parents. I suggest you continue doing what you can do on your end."

Brad nodded and tried to keep his frustration from showing further. Was he the only person who knew something very wrong had happened?

This wasn't normal; it wasn't typical. He was certain of it, but everyone else seemed to be taking it all in stride.

"The IT crew will be by sometime today or tomorrow."

"Tomorrow?" Brad said.

The officer shrugged as if to say that was the best he could do, as if daring Brad to say it wasn't enough. Brad walked to the door and held it open, unable to trust himself enough to open his mouth for fear he'd say something he'd regret later. That anyone would treat this as one more thing on their to-do list was inconceivable. The officer nodded on his way out the door.

Brad slammed the door and stood rooted in the foyer of his home. It was so quiet—oppressively quiet. He didn't know what to do, where to turn. How important was the computer in all of this? What was he supposed to do?

Did you think to pray? a voice asked in his head, and he paused. He'd been bartering with the Lord all along: Just bring Jess home and I'll do better, or give me strength for this, and I'll be sure it doesn't happen again. But he knew that wasn't enough, and he hadn't really *let* himself pray. He finally gave in, having trusted in his arm of flesh as long as he could and having gotten nowhere. He fell to his knees, bowed his head, and pleaded with his Father in Heaven to please help him know what to do next. The tears came and soon he was crying, begging for Jess to come home safe. *What can I do?* he pleaded. *What is my part in this? Where do I go from here?* And then he thought of the journal. His mother had given it to Jess when she was baptized. Maybe it would be useless, but maybe it wasn't. Jess hadn't been talking to anyone else in her life; maybe she was using the journal as her only confidant. What's more, finding it was something he could do. Scrambling to his feet, he ran to her room as if every second counted. If it was in the house, he would find it.

60

Kate bent her head over Chris as she hurried into the house, Justin trailing after them. It had started to rain about an hour ago and didn't seem to be stopping any time soon. She reached the front door and opened it, shooing Justin inside.

"I need medicine!" Justin cried, still traumatized by the immunizations he'd had to get at the doctor's office. Kate had held him tight, but he'd howled, reminding her of how little she could do for her children sometimes.

"In a minute," Kate said, putting Chris down and shutting the door. She helped both boys out of their jackets and turned toward the kitchen, only to find Brad sitting on the couch. He was looking at the floor and held a book—Jess's journal—in his hands.

"Brad?" she asked.

"I need medicine!" Justin wailed again. Kate looked at Brad one more time, but then hurried into the kitchen to get Justin some children's Tylenol. As soon as she finished she sent the boys downstairs and went into the living room.

"Brad?" she asked again, her heart pounding. Had something happened? Maybe Jess had called.

"I found Jess's journal," he finally said, looking at the book. "It was wedged in between her bed and the wall." Kate stared at the book and swallowed. Did Jess even write in her journal anymore?

She sat down on the love seat across from him. "Did you read it?"

Brad looked at her, a hesitant expression on his face. "We should take it to the police."

"Without reading it?"

"I read it," he said.

"What did it say?"

Brad shrugged. "Too much. Will you go check her room and see if there are any clothes or bags missing? The police wanted us to check."

Kate stood, her eyes still on the book in his hands and finally nodded, suddenly afraid to know what he was afraid to tell her. "Yeah," she said on her way to the stairs. Several seconds later she stood frozen in the doorway of Jess's room.

It was a mess. She knew Brad had gone through it earlier that morning while she'd been getting the boys ready, but now she stared at the evidence of his panic. He really thought something was wrong, didn't he.

She didn't dare go inside, but after nearly a minute she forced herself to do so. She opened Jess's drawers almost reverently, fingering through her pants to see what was missing. Then she went to the closet. She was well aware of the clothing Jess owned, especially her favorite items, and the only things missing seemed to be her new Gap jeans they'd bought a couple months ago, Jess's favorite black T-shirt, and her coat.

As soon as Kate determined those were the only things missing, she fled the room, overwhelmed by the emptiness of it. *But she's coming back, right?* she asked herself. If she weren't coming back, Kate would be panicked, right? She'd know, wouldn't she?

"She didn't take any extra clothes as far as I can tell," she said upon entering the living room. Brad was still sitting in the same place, gripping the journal so hard his knuckles were white. "What?" Kate asked. "What is it?"

"I need to get this to the police," he said with a nod. He suddenly stood and hurried past her, into the kitchen. "Have you seen my keys?" he asked.

Kate followed him. "What does it say?" she asked.

He shook his head. "I just had 'em," he said. "I did a neighborhood drive-by, then I came into the kitchen and . . . no, I went into the study first." He passed her again and she turned dumbly, watching him.

"What did it say!" she shouted, surprising herself with the force of her own voice.

Brad was silent for a second. "She met someone, Kate."

"Someone?" Kate asked. "Someone, who?" Had she sneaked out to see a boy from school? Overnight? Kate's head began to spin.

"Someone online," he said, looking at her with fear in his eyes. "She was meeting him late Wednesday night, but planned to come home."

Kate inhaled sharply and took a step back, encountering the wall behind her. The edges of her vision were going dark. Brad hurried over to her. "Kate?" he asked.

"I'm okay," she said, but was feeling dizzy. "Online?" she asked, looking into his face, wishing the room would go still again. "How?" It was too much. Brad helped her to the couch, where she leaned back and closed her eyes, not wanting to fall apart.

She took deep breaths, but they weren't helping. Jess had met someone—a stranger? She'd left to meet him? Jess? She listened to Brad go into the kitchen. He dialed a number and filled up a glass of water.

"There were some officers at my house a short time ago taking a missing person's report on my daughter," she heard Brad say. Then suddenly he was in front of her, offering her the water glass he'd just filled, the phone held to his ear. She took it but didn't drink. Brad continued. "I found her journal—should I bring it to the police station?"

He was quiet for a moment. "Yes, it was an Officer Jensen and Malkov. . . . Yes, they were sending someone to check the computer . . . bring it in too? . . . Okay."

He hung up, but didn't move from his spot directly in front of Kate.

She had tears coursing down her cheeks, but she opened her eyes, trying to get a grip.

"I need to take the journal and computer in," he said, looking worried. "Uh, maybe you're right, maybe the best thing to do is keep things as normal as possible."

Kate's chin trembled even more. He was protecting her. There were things in the journal he didn't want her to see. She took a deep breath and lifted her chin. "It's fine," she said. "I have laundry and floors to do—I'll be better here."

She reached out and took his hand. He responded by holding hers tightly. It was the most touching they'd had since all this started. She wanted more but refused to ask for it. There was a twisted kind of safety in the distance between them. She needed the insulation.

61

"M r. Thompson?"

Brad jumped to his feet. He'd been waiting almost half an hour just to hand over the journal, and he'd taken the opportunity to read more. Every page made his heart get heavier. He'd had no idea what was going on in his little girl's head, in his own home.

He reached out and shook the hand of the portly man standing before him.

"I'm Detective Smithton," the man said.

"Brad Thompson."

"You found your daughter's journal?"

"Yes," Brad said. He gestured toward the computer tower. "I brought the computer too."

"Excellent," Detective Smithton said. "We appreciate it, and we'll get right on it." He pulled a small notebook from his breast pocket. "What number can you be reached at?"

"I'll wait," Brad said, handing over the journal, both anxious to not have the temptation of reading more and hesitant to let go of this shred of his daughter's life—the secret parts. The parts he didn't dare let Kate read. It was shocking to know the depth of Jess's life he'd never imagined existed.

"Uh, it may be several hours," Detective Smithton said, furrowing his thick eyebrows. "It would be best if—"

"I'll wait," Brad said again, sitting back down to prove his point. Kate was at home, and he didn't know how to be around her with the secrets he now felt he was keeping. He had nowhere else to be but here. Waiting.

62

Julie looked up from scrubbing the grout in the kitchen tile when Britney came in from school. She sat back on her heels and forced a smile. All the worry and fear for Jess had given her a nervous energy that she was using to deep-clean her kitchen. When she'd talked to Kate this afternoon it sounded like she was doing the same thing. She was worried about her friend, worried about Britney, and scared to death for Jess. Sheila lay on a blanket in the living room, grabbing her toes, and filling the air with baby sounds.

"How was school?" Julie asked, but the question sounded lame considering the situation with Jess. She'd actually wondered if Britney should stay home, but in the end they both decided she'd try it out and call if she couldn't handle it.

"A policeman came and talked to me," Britney said, pulling out a kitchen chair and sitting down. Julie got to her feet and pulled out another chair, her heart pounding. The police were involved?

"What did he want?" she asked, aching for her daughter and yet suddenly on edge. She couldn't help but wonder if Britney knew anything and had been keeping it from them.

Britney shrugged. "Just wanted to know if I knew where Jess was, that kinda thing."

Julie nodded. She had a hundred questions of her own, but hesitated to take on that role. Britney fidgeted with the strap of her backpack. "Jess told her dad that she and I were instant messaging on Friday."

"And you weren't?"

"At five o'clock in the morning?"

Julie nodded her understanding. No one in the Peterson household was conscious at five A.M., and Julie's thoughts began to head down a new path. If not Britney, then who was Jess IMing? And why would she lie?

"Have the police come here yet?" Britney continued, interrupting Julie's thoughts.

"The police?" Julie said, her eyebrows lifting. "Why would they come here?"

"I told the police something, and they said they would probably come and talk to you about our computer. I thought maybe they'd have come already."

"Our computer?" Julie asked. Had something happened in her house? She heard the back door open, and knew it was Clay. He'd taken the day off and run to the store to get some milk. Britney glanced quickly at her dad before continuing.

"On the night of Spring Fling, when Jess came over to get ready, she asked to use the computer for a minute. I said sure, and when she came back I asked what she needed the computer for. She said she had to tell some friends she was going to the dance."

Julie's thoughts were spinning. She needed to slow things down and not jump to conclusions. "So someone at school was probably going to be there, and Jess wanted to tell them."

Britney shook her head. "She said I didn't know them—I think she met them on mybulletinbored.com."

"What's that?" Clay asked, pulling out yet another kitchen chair. Sheila started fussing, and Julie picked her up and bounced her while Britney continued.

"It's a place where kids make their own web pages and put up pictures and things—they call the pages boreds, like B-O-R-E-D—get it? Bored.

When you're bored, you go to mybulletinbored.com. Jess and I made a bored a few months ago."

Julie was shocked and exchanged a look with Clay, who was equally surprised. Britney had made a web page? They were very clear with their kids that they couldn't participate in those things unless Mom and Dad gave their approval and knew their passwords. But Julie ignored that for the moment. "Did she say who she met or what their names were?"

"Well, I know she was e-mailing a girl named Emily awhile ago. But before the dance she was talking about two of them, and she wouldn't tell me anything. I thought that was weird. But, well, Jess has been acting kinda weird about a lot of things lately."

"Show us this website," Clay said while Julie was still processing the information. Britney nodded and stood. They followed her to the computer in the living room and watched her go through the steps to bring up the website. Sheila pulled at Julie's hair and Julie shifted her to one hip, slightly annoyed by the baby's distraction. Within a minute they were looking at a picture of Jess in the formal dress she'd worn to Spring Fling. It was eerie, and Britney started to get emotional. Julie pulled her into a hug with one arm, while Clay sat down in front of the computer.

He began opening up tabs and scrolling through lists. Julie didn't have a clue what he was doing. "What was the date of the dance?"

"April 28," Julie said, remembering all the preparations leading up to it. Britney, though still in her mother's one-armed embrace, turned to see what her dad was doing. "Why?" Julie asked.

"That program I installed, Cyberwatch—the program that sends all the kids' e-mail to our in-boxes for us to approve—also records all websites visited and e-mails sent for thirty days."

Julie approved the kids' e-mail every morning, but she didn't realize the program did more than that. Her heart rate increased as he brought up page after page of websites and e-mails.

"Bingo," he said. All three of them leaned forward and read the e-mail.

"Emily and Colt," Britney said as they all read the e-mail Jess sent.

"There are e-mail addresses here," Clay said. "Britney, did Jess use this computer other times?"

"Well, yeah, but I don't know what days."

"Should I call Brad and Kate?" Julie asked.

"Not yet. Let me see what we've got first—the police will take the computer once they realize there's something on it."

He turned to look at Britney. "Think hard about what days Jess used the computer. Jules, get Britney a calendar."

63

"Your wife was unable to come?" the detective asked when he ushered Brad into a room. It was after three o'clock—he'd been waiting for hours. They'd told him more than once he could go home, but he refused.

"She's home with our other children. I think it's best that I'm here alone," he said, trying not to show his concern too strongly. Since reading the journal he'd been a bit dazed.

"I understand," the detective said with sympathy. "These are tough situations. We're still looking over the journal and computer, but some things are lining up."

Brad's stomach sank. "What?"

"Well, over the four days before your daughter disappeared, someone was deleting large amounts of information from your computer's hard drive. We're assuming it was her."

"What does that mean?" Brad asked.

"It means she was hiding something."

"We already know that," Brad said in frustration.

The detective took a breath. "Mr. Thompson," he said. "One of the things we've come to believe is that there is no Terrezza."

Brad said nothing. It didn't make sense, but then again none of this did.

"We have found no evidence, outside of the note left by your daughter, to suggest that this Terrezza even exists. And in one of the journal entries she says Colt told her to leave a note. It's possible that he told her to make up a name so there would be nothing to track. We also found evidence that the instant-message program—a program that Britney Peterson knew nothing about—was a homemade thing and only linked two computers. It was deleted Saturday, and none of the conversations were saved."

"She deleted it after I caught her," Brad said, slowly piecing together the information as a fire built up in his stomach. He'd been right there. Jess had lied to him, and he'd believed it. The monster this already was grew bigger as the seconds ticked by. It was all so . . . organized, so specific.

"We did find one e-mail," Detective Smithton continued. "Something she wanted to save in paper form. The printer had some kind of error the first time she tried to print it, so she sent it again and it worked. But the first attempt stayed in the printer queue." He pulled open a drawer and removed a piece of paper, but he didn't hand it over. "I would consider this an almost miraculous development since she was so painstakingly diligent in removing everything else from the computer. This was a very simple oversight, but it might make all the difference."

Brad stared at the paper, afraid to touch it.

"Mr. Thompson, you need to understand something before you read this," Detective Smithton explained, keeping the paper face down on his desk. "Your daughter not only deleted information, but she emptied the recycle bin and she removed cookies—not something we would expect with an innocent relationship. Even she thought it strange to go to such painstaking efforts to hide these things. But this guy had so much power over her that she did it anyway.

"These kids get to know people through the Internet and often feel more comfortable with them than with their own family and friends. These online relationships are powerful, intoxicating—especially for young girls. We are still working on data recovery to see if we can glean any more information from it, but the IM conversations and e-mails weren't stored anywhere anyway. The mystery now is who he is, whether he really was who Jess thought he was, and if she was planning on coming back home and then didn't."

Brad could hardly breathe and had to close his eyes in order to keep his composure. When he opened them, he looked across the desk at the detective. "She didn't take any clothes, and her birthday is next Wednesday. She wouldn't be gone for her birthday."

"But she didn't come home," the detective said. "And she deleted the program, closed her e-mail, and left a note."

Brad swallowed and stared at the paper in the detective's hand. After a couple of seconds, the detective nodded and handed over the paper. "This is what we found in the printer queue. We do not believe we are dealing with a high school boy, Mr. Thompson. We believe we're dealing with a predator."

Brad took the paper with trepidation and started reading.

——Original Message——
From: coltinator_51@yahoo.com
To: jjk_hollywood@hotmail.com
Sent: Sunday, May 7, 1:14 PM
Subject: Re: Nerves

Jessie,

I can't wait to see you

I can't wait to hold you

I can't wait to tell you how much I love you

I can't wait to take moonlight walks with you

I can't wait to gaze into your eyes

I can't wait to hold your hand

I can't wait to promise myself to you forever

I can't wait to make all your dreams come true

I can't wait to caress your face

I can't wait to tell you how beautiful you are with my own voice

I can't wait to kiss you in a way that makes you realize that you are the only girl in the world that could ever make me feel this way.

I love you Jessie—just hold on to that, okay. I promise all this will be worth it. Please write me back as soon as you get this, I need to know you'll be waiting for me.

Love you,
Colt

64

K ate?"

It was Friday evening. Kate looked up from where she was sitting on the couch, a sleeping Chris in her arms, and was surprised to see her mother standing in the doorway. They'd talked on the phone that morning but Kate had told her again that she didn't need help, that she was fine. Joy's flight back to Oregon had left over an hour ago, and though Kate hadn't thought about it, she'd assumed her mom was on it.

"Mom?" she said, easing Chris out of her arms and onto the couch. She was losing energy fast, the storm pressing in on her. Marilyn still had the other kids, and Justin had gone to a neighbor's house. "I . . . did you miss your flight?"

She stood up and looked at her mother, too exhausted to summon any of the negative feelings.

"I know you didn't want me to come, and I went to the airport and everything, but . . . I couldn't go. I know the timing is bad, but can we talk?"

"Sure," Kate said quietly, although it was the last thing she wanted to do. She didn't have the energy. Unsure of what she was getting into, Kate gestured toward the front porch and Joy nodded, following her. Without discussing it, they sat down on the front steps. It had stopped raining, but the smell of spring was in the air. Kate took a breath, anxious about what was about to take place; then she turned her head and met her mother's eyes.

"I should have taken you up on shopping," she said, trying to smile. "Jess heard what I said to you. She was really mad at me for it." *Would she still be here if I'd let my mom watch the kids so she could stay at Britney's?* Kate wondered if there was any *one* thing she could have done to prevent all this. A hundred "one things" came to mind.

Joy shook her head and held Kate's eyes for several seconds, tears brimming. "I love you, Kate," she finally whispered, looking away as if embarrassed to say it out loud. Kate hadn't expected this. She'd assumed her mom wanted to talk because she was feeling bad about not being included. "I know growing up with me was hard—I wasn't much of a mother, never have been. But I do love you, and I love your kids and . . . can I please . . . can I please stay?" She looked up, and Kate had never seen such humility and sadness on her mother's face. "Isn't there some way I can help you?"

Kate felt tears rise in her eyes again and felt stupid for being so hung up on her mother's faults. She looked away. "I've made my own mistakes, Mom. Big ones. And I'm a hypocrite to be so hard on you."

"Kate," her mother continued. Kate looked at her again, tears coming to her own eyes as she realized that she had never been so honest with her mother; they'd never talked like this. Joy's chin trembled. Her tears were causing her mascara to rebel and make black tracks down her powdered cheeks. "I'm so proud of you."

Kate's own tears overflowed, and when her mom pulled her into her arms, she didn't hold back the tears and she didn't resist. Had her mother ever held her this way? Had Kate ever looked to her for strength? And were her own feelings toward her mother any different than Jess's feelings toward her? "You are remarkable," Joy said into Kate's hair after several minutes had passed. "And I'm so sorry this has happened to you. I haven't prayed for years, but I'm praying with all my heart that Jess comes home, and that you one day will get to look at the woman she has become and be proud of her too, even if you weren't the perfect mother."

65

As the day dragged on, Kate prayed for strength, prayed for calm, but felt as if a storm was pressing in upon her. Jess had been gone almost forty-eight hours. Kate was sitting at the kitchen counter, listening to Marilyn and her mother take care of the kids, feeling as if she were imploding, when the front door opened. She listened to Brad come inside, heard him hug Justin, whisper with his mother, and say hi to Joy as if it were perfectly normal for her to be there.

"We need to talk," he said quietly, when he reached Kate. But Caitlyn overheard from where she was sitting at the table finishing dinner.

"What happened?" Caitlyn asked. "Where's Jess?"

"I need to talk to your mother," Brad said calmly. But it was a forced calm. Kate could feel it and wondered if this internal dread spiraling inside her was what Brad had been feeling all along. While she'd been so sure Jess would walk through the door, had he felt like this? Joy and Marilyn shared a look with one another and then went back to what they were doing.

"But I want to know too!" Caitlyn said, starting to cry. "Why won't you tell us anything? Where is she?"

"I need to talk to your mother!" Brad snapped, causing Kate to jump. She looked around and saw Caitlyn's face crumple. Brad let out a breath and shook his head, but Kate could see the tension in his face, and it helped her snap out of it.

"It's okay, Caity," she said, longing for someone to say that to her. "Let me talk to your dad, and then we'll talk to you."

But Caitlyn ran downstairs.

"I'll talk to her," Joy said, following after her.

"I've got this," Marilyn said, herding the other children into the living room. "We'll watch a show."

Kate nodded and followed Brad into the bedroom, trying to prepare herself but not sure if she could.

66

Brad watched Kate, who was sitting perfectly still on the edge of the bed. He stood awkwardly in the middle of the room and relayed the information he'd received at the police station. He spoke in monotone, afraid to summon any emotion at all for fear that it would reduce him to a bawling child. Kate stared at the floor, making no reaction. When he finished they both remained still, silent and scared.

"I . . . I can't believe it," Kate finally said, her voice barely a whisper.

Brad just nodded. He was finding it harder and harder to feel anything as the details sunk in. Relaying them to Kate had been like telling her Jess was dead. The thought suddenly made him shudder. *Was* she alive? Would they ever see her again?

"Um," Brad said, going through the lists in his mind of what needed to be done. People needed to know this wasn't a runaway; he'd need to explain it to his work, to his family members. Maybe he should call the news stations, even though the police didn't feel they had enough details to garner the media's interest yet. But there were other things that needed first consideration. "We need to tell the kids."

"Tell them what?" Kate said, looking up at him, her eyes frantic, glassy. "Tell them she ran away with some boy . . . or someone, and we don't know where she is or when she's coming home or if—" She pursed her lips together, her chin shaking, and clenched her eyes closed. He watched her, not knowing what to do, and soon her hands began to shake; her whole body began trembling. "How do we tell them that!" she suddenly screamed, causing Brad to flinch. "How do we—" she cut herself off with a sob. Brad finally moved, rushing to her, wrapping his arms around her as she dissolved from the strong capable Kate into hopeless sobbing. She didn't return his embrace, pulling away as if his touch made it worse. But he only held on tighter. "Kate," he said, trying to calm her, aware that the kids on the other side of the door could surely hear this.

But she didn't calm down. She continued crying, the sobs turning into near-screams. Brad pulled her closer, caressing her hair, trying to soothe her. "It's okay, Kate," he said, even if he didn't believe it. "It's going to be all right." She finally gave up resisting and melted into him, like a child, but the tears didn't stop. She dug her fingers into his shoulder, still crying, groaning—reacting to the full terror of this moment. He realized that she really had thought Jess would just walk in the door. And without that hope, what was left for her? Their family was her life.

All the news stories Brad had watched about missing teenagers, all the "Have You Seen Her?" posters he barely looked at in the grocery stores flooded through his mind. If he'd only found the IM that day, if he'd only investigated a little further. Jess had stormed off on Wednesday evening and he hadn't followed up; he hadn't tried to talk to her. Maybe she'd needed more attention, needed to know she mattered as much as the new baby did. And he hadn't given it to her. He hadn't even gone downstairs to tell her good night. He wrapped his arms tighter around Kate, the only other person in the world who knew what this felt like, and felt himself giving in to the horror of it all, too. There was work to be done and calls to be made, but he couldn't hold back the torrent of emotions any longer.

67

Karl Weatherford had fallen asleep, but the ding-dong sound of an e-mail woke him up. He lifted his head from the desk and blinked at the clock. It was three o'clock in the morning. Why was he even here?

After his parents agreed to the website, he and Jamie had spent the next two days finishing it. Though no stranger to this kind of thing, even he was impressed with the comprehensive dual-country marketing plan they had been able to execute in just forty-eight hours. The banner ads were in place, and the e-mail blitzes had begun that morning—well, technically, yesterday morning—Friday. Karl had planted himself in the chair, just sure that within hours of the launch they'd have hundreds of replies, tons of leads. He had realized pretty quickly that his expectations were ridiculous. He'd had one e-mail from someone in New York who said they had been talking to a coltinator_47@yahoo.com in March. Karl replied, asking for more information, but they hadn't responded and it wasn't the information he was looking for anyway.

Then again, what *was* he looking for? What were the chances that someone who had seen Terrezza would stumble onto one of his marketing tactics? The odds were insurmountable. However, he didn't dare tell that to his parents after getting their permission, and after all the money they'd put into it. So he stayed in his chair despite the fact that he was beginning to feel like a fool.

He clicked over to the e-mail account and opened the new message. Maybe the New York guy was responding.

——Original Message——
From: bradthompson@accntcorp.com
To: findTerrezzaskiller@hotmail.com
Sent: Friday, May 12, 2:56 AM
Subject: Terrezza

My name is Brad Thompson. My daughter disappeared two days ago with only a note saying she was going to stay with a girl named Terrezza. We don't know anyone by that name and found a journal where she wrote about someone named Colt and someone named Emily—people she met through mybulletinbored.com. I've been surfing online, trying to figure out what's happened to my daughter, and this website came up on a Google search of the unusual spelling of Terrezza. Please contact me at your earliest convenience. My phone number is 801-555-9436 or you can respond to this e-mail. I'll be right here. I can't sleep.

Brad

Karl blinked and read it again. This hadn't been what he'd been expecting, or even hoped for. He wanted information on how to find the man who had killed his sister, but the ramifications of this man's e-mail descended quickly. He scrambled for the phone, managing to knock it off its base. It clattered to the floor, and he hurried to pick it up.

"What?" his mom said, sitting up from where she'd fallen asleep on the couch. She'd come out of her room for the first time since the funeral the previous afternoon. She looked older somehow, broken, and he wondered if she, or any of them, would ever recover from this. She stayed as his silent companion. Dad and Jamie had gone to their own beds around midnight.

"Some guy just e-mailed me," Karl said, looking at the computer screen and punching the number into the phone. "His daughter disappeared a few days ago and left a note with Terrezza's name. He gave me his number." He finished dialing and put the phone to his ear, his heart pounding, while at the same time asking himself why he was so anxious.

"Hello?" a man's voice said into the phone.

"Hi, this is Karl Weatherford. You just sent me an e-mail about a note with my sister's name on it."

"Yes, I did," the man said, his anxiety showing in his voice. "I thought it might be a long shot, and I don't know if you can help me but—"

"Terrezza left a note, too," Karl interrupted. "Did you read about that on the website?" The exact wording hadn't been on the website—it was one of those pieces of information they held back.

He heard the click of a mouse on the other end of the line. "No," the man said. "I didn't read very far, I . . . I'm not sure I'm up to considering a connection to your sister's case."

Karl nodded to himself, realizing the implication. This man was trying to accept his daughter's disappearance. Linking her to a girl who was already dead wasn't good. He could feel his mother watching him and met her eyes. "What exactly did the note say, sir?"

"It says, 'I need a time-out. I'm at Terrezza's and I'll be back in a few days . . .'"

Karl felt heat rush through his body. Same words. "Sir, the note my sister left almost six months ago was worded exactly like that—except it said she was at Danyelle's. We don't know a Danyelle."

The other end was silent.

"What can you tell me about your daughter's situation?" Karl continued.

"She met him online," Mr. Thompson said, almost hesitantly. "Through mybulletinbored.com, and they e-mailed for almost two months. He posed as a girl first, then introduced her to her cousin, but we think it was the same person the whole time."

"And his name was Colt?"

"Yes, she had an instant message program she used to contact him,"

Mr. Thompson said. "One that was hidden and only linked two computers."

Karl was stunned and didn't know what else to say. "Mr. Thompson," he said, "My sister had that program, too—the e-mail address was coltinator_39@yahoo.com. They started e-mailing almost eight months ago." Karl thought of the other e-mail he'd received. "I got an e-mail earlier today. The person said they communicated with a coltinator_47 back in March. They haven't e-mailed me back with any other information, though."

The other end of the line was silent for several seconds.

"Mr. Thompson?"

"Jess was e-mailing coltinator_51@yahoo.com. She didn't start e-mailing him until April."

The phone line went silent again, and Karl wondered for a moment if Mr. Thompson had hung up. "Is he . . . ?" Mr. Thompson breathed. "Is he counting?"

68

D o it," Monique said, handing over her credit card. Karl looked at her with questions in his eyes. The sun was just coming up, casting the room in bright yellow. Monique could see the sparkly dust particles as they floated through the air.

"Mom, it's so expensive."

"I don't care," she said, pushing the credit card even closer. "If there's three, there must be others, and people are finding you. I don't care how much it costs. Buy all the Internet stuff you need to get the word out." Karl finally took the card. "What else can I do?" she asked.

After the phone call from Mr. Thompson, she'd been unable to sleep. The rage she felt was overwhelming, but she was finally able to see the wisdom behind all this online stuff Karl had wanted to do. Mr. Thompson's idea that this man was counting grabbed hold of her like a vice grip and wouldn't let go. This man was a hunter. Someone else's daughter was facing Terrezza's fate, and Monique might just be able to help stop him.

Jamie's voice caused both Monique and Karl to look in her direction. "I have a friend who did an internship at one of the news stations in Wisconsin. She might know some people."

"Do you think she'd help us?"

"I think she'd try."

Monique nodded, picturing Terrezza's face all over the news, not missing, not even abducted—but dead. Because of this man. Because of

Colt. "Your father does repair work for the *Chronicle's* sports reporter. I wonder if he could help us—make the right contacts, I mean."

Karl finally spoke up. "I've already blitzed a whole bunch of media contacts, but if we could get enough voices behind us and step up the Internet campaign—"

"Let's do all this," Monique said. "Let's do it now." *And then what?* she thought. It wouldn't bring Terrezza back. But quick on the heels of that thought was the reminder that it might bring someone else's daughter home. Maybe that would bring some peace. Right now, she could use all she could get.

69

"Brother and Sister Weatherford," Reverend Adams said as they exited the chapel Sunday afternoon. He grasped Harrison's hand and held on tightly. "How are you doing?"

Harrison nodded. "Every day's a little better than the last." He turned his head to catch Monique's eye and she nodded, though *better* sounded like a really big word.

They hadn't been to church for years. Every time they talked about going it ended up in an argument about which one to go to. Lutheran, the church Monique was raised in, or Baptist, the church Harrison attended as a child.

The minister nodded, his dark face etched with sincerity. "I'm so sorry for your loss." He'd conducted Terrezza's services, and Monique had been touched by his kindness enough that she didn't argue over what church to go to today. She just needed the Lord Jesus in her life right now.

"Thank you," Monique said. "I expect we might be around more often."

The reverend's dark face split into a huge white-toothed grin. "We would sure love for that to be the case. Even through our trials, the Lord does love us, Brother and Sister Weatherford. It would do my soul good to help you find that love in your life again."

Monique felt tears fill her eyes. Thinking of God's love now, after so much tragedy, was difficult, and yet she felt it somehow. How could that be?

"Ours, too," Harrison said. They moved on down the steps, Karl and Jamie trailing behind them. They had been less inclined to come today, since they'd not been raised with religion, but at least they were there. Monique had never seen Karl in a tie before. He looked very handsome.

"That was nice," Jaime said with a smile as they reached the car.

Monique took her daughter's hand and smiled, though the tears were still coming. "It *was* nice, wasn't it?"

Karl just shrugged, but Harrison put his arm around his son's shoulder, something Monique was sure hadn't happened in years. She wiped at her eyes and hoped Terrezza could see that losing her had helped them all find each other a little bit. It was small consolation for the agony of her death, but Monique was grateful that there was some good to come from it—at least a little. She looked toward the heavens and scanned the scattered clouds in the sky. *Be with the Thompson girl,* she said in her heart. *Please help her find her way home.*

70

On Monday, the FBI took over the investigation, now that there was enough evidence to suggest a multistate crime had been committed. They set up a command center in the Thompson house, and the media finally got involved full force. The Weatherfords stepped up their advertising even more, blasting the title "Do you know the Coltinator?" along with Terrezza and Jess's pictures all over the Internet. The phone rang off the hook. That coming Wednesday was Jess's sixteenth birthday; no one could get it out of their heads.

By six o'clock Monday night the FBI had found eight more girls who at one time or another in the last year had exchanged e-mails with Emily, Ashley, Tiffany, or Jenny—every one of whom had introduced the girls to their cousin or brother, Colt.

The missing link, however, was that no one had a physical description of the man. He had sent them pictures that were traced back to a clip-art website. The lack of what he looked like created a double complication. First, they could pass him on the street and not know it. They had no idea how old he was, if he had any distinguishing tattoos—nothing. And second, their fear increased that there may have been girls who had seen him but were never given the chance to tell anyone about it. Jess Thompson had been gone for almost five days. She very likely knew who he was and what he looked like. Would she ever be able to tell anyone about it?

These thoughts were cycling through Karl's head Monday night when his in-box dinged again. The FBI had taken over the account, but they sent him e-mails now and then to keep him updated and let him know what changes to make to the website in order to reflect the current status. He was grateful they had let him stay on as web master and not brought in one of their own. He quickly toggled over to his e-mail account.

——Original Message——
From: shishipartyup@msn.com
To: findTerrezzaskiller@hotmail.com
Sent: Monday, May 15, 11:49 PM
Subject: The Meeting

Mr. Weatherford

I might be the Danyelle you're looking for. I met this guy, coltinator_26, online over a year ago. We were supposed to meet once at a McDonald's and this old guy said he was Colt's uncle, but then he put something in my drink. When I started feeling funny he offered to drive me home. But the same thing had happened to me at a party once, so I knew what was happening. I started screaming and freaking out. He took off. My friend saw one of your ads and thought it might be the same guy—but you can't tell my mom, k, she'll never let me go back online if she knew I was meeting people.

Danyelle (but I never use my real name online)

Karl read the message four times, and chills coursed down his spine. She'd seen him. She knew what he looked like. He grabbed his phone and dialed the Thompson's number in Salt Lake City, wondering if they knew yet. While waiting for the call to go through, he turned toward the doorway and yelled over his shoulder. "We found Danyelle!"

71

Brad and Kate were relieved when Danyelle was found, but they were running out of ideas, and the last six days were catching up to them. Worried about the stress all this might be causing on the baby, Kate went in and met with Dr. Lyon. Everything looked okay, but he insisted she needed her sleep and a proper diet. She agreed and was trying hard to follow his instructions, but it wasn't easy.

Things had been moving fast. The posters were now up, but the media attention was already dying down, thanks to one of the president's cabinet members being indicted on criminal charges. The Thompsons were running out of things to keep them busy.

"It's Tuesday," Brad nearly screamed into the phone at two in the afternoon. "She's been gone for six days."

"I know, Mr. Thompson. We've taken all the information from the Weatherford case; we're analyzing all the e-mails and phone calls you and they have received—we're doing everything we can." The frustration in the detective's voice was almost as thick as Brad's. The difference was that it wasn't the detective's daughter. "We did find a coltinator_45 and a coltinator_50 this afternoon—both girls got suspicious and cut off contact. Their story fits everyone else's. It looks like he became much more careful after Terrezza. He got smarter and took more time to lay his groundwork."

"And what's happened to the others? The ones we didn't find?" Brad asked. "Did they end up like Terrezza?"

"Mr. Thompson, we're doing all we can."

"It's not enough."

The detective was quiet for a few seconds. "And yet it's all we can do."

Brad took a breath and tried to calm down. "And I suppose you're going to tell me, again, that I should keep doing what I'm doing and let you guys do your job."

"And pray, Mr. Thompson."

"I've never stopped," Brad said. He hung up the phone, walked to the couch, and sat down heavily. A woman in the ward had taken Justin and Chris, and the older kids had agreed to go to school, despite how hard it was to do such normal things. Kate was trying to catch up with the housework while she listened to his side of the conversation. Marilyn had invited Joy to stay with her so that Kate and Brad could be alone. However, she'd made sure Kate knew the grandmas were only a phone call away. Kate wiped off her hands and came to sit next to him, placing her hand on his knee. He covered her hand with his own and gave it a squeeze.

He looked at her, intending to thank her out loud for the incredible support she had been, but he was taken aback by the tears falling down her cheeks. She didn't try to wipe them away. His words stuck in his throat. "What else can we do, Kate?" he asked in a quiet voice. "Where do we go next?"

She shook her head and finally wiped at her eyes. "It's Jess's birthday tomorrow," she said. "How do we get through that?"

Brad let out a breath. "I don't know," he said honestly. His oldest child would be sixteen. She was enrolled to take drivers' ed this summer. She was planning to go into the Laurel class at church. She'd be old enough to date. Or would she?

Every day she was gone, the likelihood of her coming home diminished. He remembered following the Elizabeth Smart case in Salt Lake years ago—the parents had such determination that their daughter was alive. They were so sure, and they were right all along. Was Brad sure? He didn't know. Did that mean he wasn't in tune? Did it mean he wasn't going about this the right way? Or was it the Lord's way of telling him that she was already gone from him? The thought made it hard to breathe.

"What about a fast?" Kate asked.

"I've fasted every other day," he said, feeling defeated. "The ward fasted on Sunday."

"What if we did a fast that was stake-wide? We could contact all our family, friends, everyone, and ask that they do a special fast on Jess's birthday. One of the missing-children agencies that sent us some information talked about a town where the entire community prayed every hour on the hour for an entire day."

"Did the child come home?" Brad asked. But he knew the answer. He'd read the same story. The girl's body had been found two months later in a ravine a hundred miles from their home.

Kate didn't say anything.

Brad clenched his eyes shut and forced the sorrow and guilt away. He couldn't give in to the despair; he had to keep moving forward. "It would give us a focus, wouldn't it?"

"How else do we make it through that day?" Kate asked. She shook her head. "And that much faith and prayer can't be a bad thing, can it?"

"We have to accept something," Brad said softly, feeling as if he were betraying Kate and Jess to say it out loud. "She might not come home."

Kate nodded, and the tears that had dried somewhat returned. "I know," she whispered.

Brad nodded, and he took her hand again, feeling guilty for bringing the worst possibilities to the forefront of Kate's mind. "I think the fasting and praying is a great idea," he said. "We'll give it everything we've got."

72

W

"e're going to Canada in the morning," he said. She didn't look up from where she sat on the one chair in the room. Her knees were pulled up to her chest, her arms wrapped around them. She spent most of her conscious time that way, a vain effort to try to feel protected. *Canada,* she thought. *I'm never going home, am I.*

She smelled tuna but didn't look up, assuming it was dinner. Most of the meals had been like that, something from a can or a package. The cabin had a coffee pot and a microwave, but no fridge. She'd never have guessed she'd miss vegetables so much, but it seemed ridiculous to even think of something so trivial.

The last five days had been unreal, and she could barely allow herself to think about them. She'd heard of this kind of thing on TV, and Britney had even warned her about it. But never in her wildest dreams did she ever imagine it could happen to her. She felt so stupid. To make things worse, tomorrow was her sixteenth birthday.

"What do you want to drink?" he asked. She could feel his eyes on her, feel his intensity. He always watched her with such tension, like he was waiting for something.

She didn't answer in words—she only spoke when she needed to use the bathroom—but she shook her bent head. She wasn't drinking anything tonight.

"Suit yourself," he said. Then she heard the sound of porcelain sliding along the wooden table. She lifted her head to see a plate of tuna and crackers. How would she be able to not drink after a meal like this? And she was so hungry. She put her head back on her knees, praying and pleading for help, though it made her feel foolish. Why should anyone help her after everything she'd done? All the lies, all the anger. She deserved this to happen, and she didn't deserve help now. But a very small part of her rebelled against those thoughts every time she got lost in them. A very small part of her told her not to give up, not to give in, that she was not yet lost.

And now she'd decided not to drink anything. That was strength, if only a little.

She'd known since the second day that there was something in the drinks he gave her—the only drinks she was allowed to have. Hours afterwards the room would go fuzzy; then she'd come to and know without remembering that something had happened to her. The first time he touched her when she was awake she completely freaked out, clawing at his face and leaving two long slashes down one of his cheeks. He covered her mouth to keep her from screaming, even while reminding her that no one could hear her. He told her over and over again that it was okay, that he loved her. When he let her go, she scrambled into a corner of the one-room cabin and cried until she couldn't breathe any more. Then he offered her a Pepsi, and she drank the whole thing—grateful for the chance to disappear. Since then he'd left her alone—until she passed out from the next beverage she couldn't help but accept.

She tried one day not to drink anything, but she couldn't stop from getting thirsty. And then she thought that if she drank enough, maybe she'd never wake up. But she always did, and he was always there telling her how beautiful she was, how happy they would be, how much he loved her. The sink in the cabin was agonizingly close, but the one time she'd tried to get a drink from the tap, he'd backhanded her so hard that she didn't need the drugs to cause her to lose consciousness. It was the first time in her whole life anyone had hit her—but it wasn't her last. Anytime she didn't do what he asked, or tried to do something she shouldn't, he hit her again, then followed up with the reminder that if she'd just follow the rules he wouldn't have to hurt her. He said that he hated that she made him do those things.

She looked up at him, and he smiled at her smugly, as if he knew exactly what she was thinking. She looked at the tuna and crackers and found herself wondering what her family was eating tonight. She wondered what they were doing, if she'd ever see them again. She felt tears come to her eyes but blinked them away. He told her that her family wouldn't want her back, that they were mad. He said he was the only person in the world who could love her now.

He was lying . . . she hoped. Tomorrow was her sixteenth birthday, she thought again, and she was determined not to let the drugs keep her hazy and unable to think straight. If she was ever going to have a chance to get away, it would be tomorrow, when they were traveling again. The part of her that was still praying, the part that believed there was still something good inside her, held fast to the belief that she would somehow be given a gift. She just had to be ready for it and recognize it when it came.

She pushed the plate away, despite how hungry she was, and put her head back on her knees. *Please, Heavenly Father, I'm sorry. Please help me now,* she said over and over again. *Please.*

73

Wednesday morning at six o'clock Joy, Marilyn, the Thompson children, and several of Brad's siblings came from the various houses they were staying at to join them in the first prayer of the day. Brad's brother in Vermont was listening through Brad's cell phone and his sister in Ohio was on the home phone when thirty-two people kneeled down in the Thompson living room. Brad offered the prayer, filled with expressions of gratitude for Jess and requests for her safety. Around Salt Lake City, and in the homes of friends and family across the nation, other people who loved Jess did the same.

After that initial prayer, those in the group returned to their homes, but at seven o'clock they stopped where they were, went onto their knees again, and offered the second prayer of the day. Kate fixed breakfast while Joy and Marilyn helped with the kids. No one was going to school today.

At eight fifty-two the phone rang and Brad picked it up on the first ring.

"We've finally got a name," Agent Gardner of the FBI said. "We've been talking to Danyelle, doing some investigation, and we found him. Drake Colton Shepard, forty-seven years old, born in Canada, came to the U.S. as a teenager. He's lived everywhere since then and works on computer systems. He's been a tech support for a software company for the last five months. Last Tuesday he didn't show up for work, and he hasn't been back since."

Drake Colton Shepard, Brad repeated in his mind. The man who ruined their lives. Kate came out of the bathroom and stared at him. She'd been talking to Sharla while brushing her hair, but told her to go check on the boys who were playing outside. Then she listened to Brad's end of the conversation. The detective hesitated, and Brad spoke again. "Thank you," Brad said. "Anything else?"

"Not yet," he said. "We have a few confirmations of his crossing the borders over the last few years, and we're tracking down his DMV info so we can do a more detailed border check. How about on your end?"

"Nothing new," Brad said, trying to hide his disappointment. "I sent the poster out to a few more people in Canada—they're putting them up all around the border crossings. The border patrol keeps taking them down, so people go out every morning and put more up in their place. With it being Jess's birthday today, people are going all out." But it never felt like enough.

"That's really good," the agent said. Brad ignored his tone, which seemed to say Brad was trying to catch a whale with a fishing pole. He didn't care. He was doing whatever he could. Anyone who offered to help was his new best friend. "I'll call you when we find anything else."

"Thank you," Brad said.

He hung up the phone. Kate was looking at him with concern, and he relayed the information.

"And they're sure it's him?" Kate asked.

"So far it's all matching up."

The clock in the living room chimed that it was nine o'clock. "I'll round up the kids," Kate said. The hourly prayers had included the children, but it was time to more completely explain to them what was going on. With all the extra people around they hadn't explained things the way they would have liked. With the family kneeling in a circle, Joy and Marilyn included, Brad looked at each of his children—all of them still scared and yet somewhat numb. How did a child process this when Brad himself could barely believe it was really happening?

"Do you guys know what today is?" he asked.

"Jess's birthday," Caitlyn said, her eyes filling with tears again. She'd taken this the hardest. Thank goodness for Joy, who seemed to take special care of Caitlyn.

"Yes, and we're having a special fast day. The entire ward, lots of our friends, and all our aunts, uncles, and cousins all across the country are fasting for Jess."

"So she will come home!" Justin spouted, his simple faith allowing him to smile. Brad could read in his eyes that he had no doubt his sister would come back.

"That's right," Brad said, wishing he were so sure. "We're going to pray for Jess every hour today." He caught Kate's eye for just a moment. She'd expressed to him last night how bad she felt that she couldn't fast. But with the pregnancy she was unable to go without food. He had reassured her it was okay—the Lord knew her heart. Kate had limited herself to simple meals as a way to offer some kind of meaningful sacrifice.

"Prayers don't always work," Sharla said. "We've been praying for days."

Kate and Brad shared a look before Kate spoke up. "Prayers always work," Kate said. "Even if we don't get what we are asking for, prayer makes our hearts feel better, and I think Jess will feel how much we love her wherever she is."

The kids seemed to accept their mother's explanation. They all folded their arms and bowed their heads.

"Our dear Father in Heaven," Brad began. "We ask that this day Thou wilt be with Jess, that Thou wilt bless her with peace and wisdom. That if it be Thy will, she might be returned to us, and . . ."

74

I need to use the bathroom," Jess said. It was still the only sentence she'd spoken since the first day—after the pleading and begging to take her home.

"Two minutes," he said without looking up from the TV. It wasn't TV, really. It was just a DVD. They didn't get television, so he watched movies all day. He was really into Sylvester Stallone. He looked at her, and she met his eye just briefly enough for him to communicate that trying anything would not be worth the price she would pay. She already knew that.

She stood up from the chair and small table she'd been sitting at and walked toward the bathroom, catching her reflection in the mirror over the sink. Two days ago he'd forced her to dye her hair black. For all the years of hating her red hair, the black was definitely worse. She looked like a gothic freak. Seeing the mottled bruising on the side of her face made her wince. Her eyes looked different too. But then, they would, wouldn't they?

She shut the door behind her and staved off the tears. The bathroom of this little cabin was the only privacy she had. He kept the windows covered, but the little plaque on the door reminded her of the one at the hotel in Disneyland a few years ago, so she thought the cabin was rented. She kept hoping that someone would come to check on them—a maid or something—but no one did. Every time she fell asleep, or felt the drugs pulling her away from time and space, she prayed she'd wake up and realize this had been a nightmare. But it was her life now—he told her that over and over again. After so many days, it was hard not to believe it. Dances and baby-sitting felt light years away.

She quietly removed the back of the toilet and set the cover on the seat. Her heart was pounding. He'd already broken the lock to the bathroom door—he could come in anytime. She peered into the stained porcelain and cringed.

Jess had awakened that morning with the continued belief that she would be given a gift that day. She refused breakfast and a red cream soda when he offered it but noticed he looked unhappy about it. She didn't want him to get mad but knew she couldn't accept the drinks. She also wondered how she'd get away if she was dehydrated. She already felt sick she was so thirsty and hungry.

By ten they were packed up, and she was so thirsty her tongue was sticking to the top of her mouth. It took all her willpower to stand her ground. That was when she remembered.

It had been almost two years ago, but the memory suddenly became strong. It was a family home evening lesson, and Mom had gone over a list of things to do in an emergency. One of them had been about getting water out of the back of the toilet. All the kids had been totally grossed out. Caitlyn had said she'd rather die. Jess had never imagined the lesson might save her life.

She reached into the pocket of her jeans, the same jeans she'd worn every day, and pulled out the paper she'd printed the day she left, the list of all the things Colt couldn't wait to do with her. All lies. It would make a crude straw, for sure, but it would work, and she had to get some fluids. That same lesson that involved drinking out of the toilet had offered another grain of truth. No matter what it takes—survive.

Her mother had taught her that—the mother Jess had wanted so badly to get away from. All day those words replayed over and over in her mind as if her mom were whispering it into her ear the way she used to whisper the talks Jess gave in Primary. When she thought of that, she also pictured her dad—always proud of her, always supportive. Why hadn't she talked to him?

She rolled the paper in her fingers. *Whatever it takes,* her mother's voice said in her head, *survive.* It surprised her that the water didn't taste awful, but the idea of drinking out of the back of the toilet was disgusting enough to make her gag. When she'd drunk as much as she could, she lifted her necklace over her head and looked at the medallion. She could only hope that he wouldn't notice it was missing. She took the medallion off the chain, then put the necklace back on and the medallion in the front pocket of her jeans. Then she carefully replaced the lid, flushed the toilet, and came out of the bathroom, startled to find him standing right outside the door. Had he heard her replace the lid? Did he suspect something? But he was smiling, so she assumed he hadn't. Surely she'd have felt his fist if he knew. She ducked her head and didn't meet his eyes.

He held out a shiny silver box about the size of her math book. He shook it slightly as he pushed it closer to her. "Open it," he said.

She didn't dare disagree with him, and she took the box. He was insane to think his deception and what he'd done to her were no big deal. But she had to play the game a little longer. She undid the bow and pulled out a red hoodie sweatshirt. It said Edmonton Oilers across the front in black embroidered letters. She'd never heard of Edmonton Oilers.

"Your first taste of Canada. That's who Wayne Gretzky played for before he went to America."

She had no idea who Wayne What's-His-Name was, but she forced a smile. "It's really nice," she managed to say.

"Put it on," he said.

"That's okay, I think I'll—"

"Put it on," he repeated in a tense voice. She hurried to put it on over her T-shirt, not willing to risk upsetting him, not willing to risk being hit so hard the room spun and went black.

He beamed. "You're so beautiful, Jessie," he said, stepping closer. She shrank back, and his face darkened. "When are you going to accept how much I love you?"

She pulled the hem of the sweatshirt down and avoided looking at him. "It's really nice," she said again.

He was quiet for several seconds, and she shifted from one foot to another. "We're leaving," he then said. "Check-out is at noon."

He went on to explain what would happen to her if she tried anything. "I know you think you've got a plan," he said. "I can see it in your eyes." She felt herself shiver. He'd been a step ahead of her the whole time, but it had only been today that her head felt clear enough for her to really think. "You can't thwart destiny, Jessie. We're meant to be together." He went quiet until she looked up at him again. Then he smiled.

She just nodded. "Can I wash my face?" she said. "I don't want to break out or anything."

He fairly beamed that she was speaking to him. "Oh yes, yes, certainly. I'll get the washcloth wet for you." He still didn't trust her to use the sink. He grabbed a washcloth from the rack, got it wet, rubbed it with soap, and handed it to her.

"Thank you," she said as she took it.

"You're welcome, Jessie," he said, reaching out and running his hand over her hair and down her back. It made her want to throw up, but she didn't pull away.

She scrubbed at her face, slow and deliberate, careful not to get the soap near her eyes. Her contacts were the kind she could wear day and night for almost a month, but she'd already been wearing them for three weeks when she'd left home. If something happened to them, she'd be unable to see very well. After almost a full minute of watching her every movement, he got another washcloth wet and handed it to her. She washed off the soap slowly, and he turned back to the room. She watched his back in the mirror and quickly pulled the medallion out of her pocket. He didn't notice. She held it tightly in her left hand as she finished rinsing her face. Then she bundled the washrag around the pendant and dropped them both on the counter. He finished zipping the large duffel bag that held all his clothes and supplies.

"You'd better drink something. It will make things easier for you."

She felt a tremor roll up her spine. What did he mean it would make things easier for her? "Okay," she said, as if defeated. He smiled again, and his big fat face relaxed. She could tell he thought he was winning.

They left the cabin for the first time in a week, and she looked around quickly without being too obvious. All she could see were trees, brush, old snow and the dirt road. He had a hand clamped on her arm as he led her to the car, opened the back door, and pushed her inside. When he got in the front seat, she pretended to take a big drink from the water bottle he handed her. His face relaxed, and she felt reassured in her choice to play the game this way. She replaced the lid, but didn't tighten it all the way before placing it on the seat and gently knocking it over. She glanced at it only long enough to see the drips of water disappearing into the seat cushion. He glanced at her continually in the rearview mirror. She tried not to notice and looked out the window. A few minutes later, with the water now seeping into her pants, she picked up the bottle and watched his eyes in the mirror measure that it wasn't full. She feigned another drink, then dropped it to the seat again. He relaxed even more as she lay against the door, closed her eyes, and waited for whatever came next.

75

I'm so hungry," Keith said, throwing himself dramatically on the couch as if to imitate a starving man.

"You can eat, Keith," Kate reminded him. "We told you this morning that we don't expect you to fast all day."

"I know," he grumbled, but he made no move toward the kitchen. It was almost two o'clock. Kate couldn't believe he'd made it this long. Sharla, who had always had a difficult time fasting, had chosen to eat around noon. Half an hour later she broke down and cried, sure that her eating was going to ruin everything. They'd had a long discussion about fasting, about faith—and they'd prayed again.

The phone rang, and as always, the household held its breath. Brad came out of the study where he'd been online again. He picked up the phone on the second ring. Kate was glad he'd taken the role of spokesperson. Though she was doing better, she was still completely frazzled and couldn't handle talking to people. "You're kidding," Brad said into the phone. "Yes, we're here—come over."

Kate hurried toward him. He hung up the phone and turned to look at his wife.

"What?" she asked.

"They found Jess's medallion."

"What?" Kate said, feeling her face blanch. "Where?"

"It was in a pile of towels left in a cabin outside of Columbia Falls, Montana. The maid cleaned the room this morning and found it. The manager remembered hearing something about a missing girl with a silver religious token. She called the police."

Kate staggered back until she caught herself on the counter. Her mind was a blur of thoughts.

Brad smiled, though his chin quivered. "We're so close," he said.

Kate nodded, speechless. Jess was alive—she had to be. She'd somehow managed to drop the medallion as a clue. It had her name on the back. Brad reached for Kate, and they clung to one another as the first good news washed over them.

By the time Agent Gardner showed up at the front door, they had their overnight bags ready to go, and half their family gathered in the living room. Agent Gardner handed over a large piece of paper with two photographs side by side. Kate and Brad stared at the enlarged picture of the medallion, front and back.

Love you
Jess
**
Dad
&
Mom

"That's it," Kate breathed, remembering how excited she'd been to give it, and how much Jess had seemed to appreciate the personalization. Now it was part of bringing her home. Kate had done something right!

Brad handed the picture to Kate, then hoisted a bag onto his shoulder. In addition to their own items, they'd packed clean clothes for Jess— pajamas and a few of her other things.

"Uh, what's this?" Agent Gardner asked.

"We talked about it. We're going up there. We want to see the cabin."

"I don't know that it's such a good idea," the detective said. "We don't know what we're going to find and—"

"They're on their way to Canada," Brad said. "You know they are. If they find her, we'll be there."

"Uh—"

"Are you really going to try to stop us?" Kate asked.

The detective looked between the two of them and finally shook his head. "No, I'm not."

"Good," Brad said. "Where is this cabin?"

76

Jess was dreaming. She knew it, and she hoped she'd never wake up. In her dream she wasn't alone anymore. She was surrounded by people—hundreds of them. And she knew every face, every voice. It was as if every person she'd ever met were gathered together. She didn't know what the occasion was, but she was so glad to be there. After six days she would give anything to be with any one of them. There were teachers, cousins, friends, kids from school—everyone.

And yet, would they even want her now? He said they wouldn't—he, the man who called himself Colt, though she never thought of him that way. Even after all this time, it was hard to admit that Colt and Emily were really this monster. As strange as it sounded, she missed her friends.

A bump in the road shook the car, jolting her from sleep. The dream shut off like a switch, and she whimpered inside. She needed those faces—even if it was only in her mind. She didn't open her eyes, hoping he would think she was still asleep. Besides, if she opened her eyes, she'd see his reflection in the rearview mirror—watching her, smiling at her. She belonged to him, he said. He owned her.

The seat was soaked from her water bottle, which was still dripping into the cushions. She'd left it on the seat so he'd be able to see it, so he wouldn't get suspicious. A few minutes later she felt the car drifting to the right, and she opened her eyes, thinking that because he was turning he wouldn't be looking into the mirror so intently. She glanced at the rearview mirror. He wasn't looking at her. She quickly shut her eyes again—but not before she saw something . . . just for an instant.

The negative of it was imprinted on her eyelids, and she nearly forgot to breathe. *It couldn't be,* she said to herself. But it had been her face she saw, hadn't it? Or was she just seeing things? She waited until he made another turn, and she opened her eyes again—chiding herself as she did so. What did she expect? To see the same paper again? It had been miles ago.

But it was there. On a tree this time. She wanted to study it, but instead she snapped her eyes shut. Her heart began to pound. The paper had her picture on it, the one from Spring Fling, with the word **KID-NAPPED** written in big bold letters. They knew! They were looking for her.

She wanted to cry, but instead she forced herself to remember that dream, the one with all the people—everyone she'd ever known. She wanted to transport herself there so badly she could hardly stand it.

Another turn. She opened her eyes again. No posters. But there was a sign that read, "Waterton Crossing, 1 mile." Had he seen the posters?

She felt the car slow and pull off the road. They drove for a couple more minutes on road much rougher than the highway before coming to a stop.

This is it, a voice said in her mind.

This is what? she asked back. Why were they stopping?

She kept her body limp, as if she'd really drunk the water, and she nearly fell on the ground when he opened the door she was leaning against. He caught her, but she felt sure he noticed her muscles were tense—very undrugged-like. It was colder here than it had been outside the cabin, and she worried that he'd notice her pants were soaked. But she didn't let the fear talk her out of this. *Faith,* she told herself, parroting at least a hundred Sunday School lessons in her mind, *not fear.*

"You're waking up?" he said. "That's too bad, Jessie. The trunk would have been a lot more comfortable if you weren't." She didn't react to his words as he put his arms under her armpits and started dragging her out of the car. She waited until only her legs were in the car; then she bent her knees and, using the seat as leverage, pushed as hard as she could. Both of them flew backward. He landed on the ground with a grunt, cushioning her fall, and she didn't waste a moment in trying to get away. They weren't on the highway anymore, and there was nothing but trees and patches of snow surrounding this side road. But she didn't care. All that mattered was getting away. She'd figure out later where she was, and if she ended up lost and dying in the mountains, that was better than this anyway.

But she didn't move fast enough. His hand latched onto her ankle and sent her face first into the gravelly road. She screamed and kicked for all she was worth. He was strong, and she felt his other hand grab farther up her leg as she clawed at the loose gravel, struggling to find anything to give her an edge. Her hand closed around a handful of dirt and rocks. She twisted and threw it into his face. It was enough. His grip loosened, and with a couple of swift kicks, she was free from his grasp. She scrambled to her feet and ran headlong into the trees that lined the roadside, crashing through a pile of crusted, crystallized snow. The ice particles got underneath her pant leg, but she didn't care. Her wet pants were already soaking up the cold. She kept running.

"Jessie!" she heard him scream, and she looked over her shoulder enough to see him coming after her. She made a sharp right, avoiding another pile of snow. She couldn't see very far ahead, and she felt branches slash at her face, but she kept going. He was fat. He was old. Surely she could outrun him.

"Jessie!" he sounded farther away.

She pulled off the red hoodie sweatshirt as she ran and threw it to the side so that the color wouldn't make her easy to spot in the trees. The cold air hit her hard now that she had only her T-shirt on, but she didn't let it faze her. She pumped her arms as hard as she could, did her best to ignore the coldness around her, and wished she'd taken Britney's advice to lose a few pounds. "Please help me, please help me, please . . ."

"Jessie!" He called again, closer this time. Her breath caught in her throat, and she made another sharp turn. *Keep moving,* the voice said again. *Don't stop.*

"Jessie!"

77

Brad hung up the cell phone and glanced at Kate in the passenger seat. "They've informed the borders to be on the lookout. They're pretty sure he's heading for the Waterton crossing in Glacier National Park. It's only been open since May first, it's pretty remote, and the park isn't very busy this time of year."

"That's good," Kate said. "Did they recover anything else from the room?"

Brad shook his head. "Not that they would tell me. They were there the whole time—a few miles from the main resort. He paid in cash."

Kate nodded, refusing to think of what that cabin might have been for Jess. "She's got to be okay," she whispered.

Brad reached over and took Kate's hand. What could he say? They drove in silence for another twenty miles, until they passed a road sign that welcomed them to Idaho Falls. Had they been driving for only three hours?

"We missed the five o'clock prayer," Kate pointed out.

Brad glanced at the dashboard and frowned.

"I'll say it," Kate offered. Brad nodded. They were seven minutes late, but hundreds of other people had been on time.

"Our Father in Heaven, we come to Thee again this day, the sixteenth birthday of our daughter Jessica, and ask that Thou wilt guide her footsteps, lead her to safety, and bring her home to us. We pray that she might know our love for her, forgive us our failings, and have faith in Thee during her times of trial. We pray for . . ."

78

There was no more air to breathe. Jess was barely moving, but kept going for fear that he was right behind her. Instead of running straight, she turned left and ran that way for awhile, then turned left again. Before she knew it, she was completely lost. She didn't know where she'd been or what direction she was heading, but she didn't care. Lost was good.

With racking breaths, she dropped to her knees, placed her palms on the wet, cold ground, and let her head fall forward. Her throat was so dry she couldn't swallow anymore. Her tongue felt huge in her mouth. She worried she would choke if she tilted her head back. There was a patch of crusted snow not far to her left, and she stumbled over, digging through the dirty top layer before grabbing a handful and shoving it into her mouth. Her thoughts were swimming as she let the snow melt enough for her to swallow, but not so much that she didn't realize the miracle that had just happened. She'd gotten away, and she had found water. "Thank you," she said between gasps for air and swallows of melted snow. "Now, help someone find me."

She waited until she could get air; then she got very still and listened. Was he following her? Was she near the road? Was there any other human in this forest?

The sun was going down, and the sky was gray. Though it was mid-May and spring at home, this place—wherever it was—still seemed trapped in wintertime except for a few patches here and there of new grass and some trees with tiny leaves popping out on their branches. What were the chances that someone would find her? Had she escaped only to die in the mountains? It was so cold, and all she could hear was the rustling of wind through the old leaves still stuck to the dead-looking trees. She would freeze to death if she didn't find shelter. *Survive!* she told herself. *Do whatever it takes to survive.*

She bowed her head and prayed for guidance. She'd never prayed like she had the last twenty-four hours—once she'd gotten that drug out of her system. Prayer was truly all she had. After seeing the posters, she wondered if her family was praying too. The connection was powerful, and she prayed even harder.

When she finished, she felt no miraculous guidance, but she got up and kept moving. If she could find her way back to the road, maybe a car would drive by. She didn't even know what direction she was heading or which direction would be her best choice, but she wrapped her arms around herself and kept walking. She found a rock with moss on one side—north. But what good did *north* do her if she didn't know where she was?

When she encountered a trail of some kind, her heart nearly leapt. A trail had to lead somewhere. She looked to the left and to the right, unable to tell which was the better choice. "Choose the right," she told herself, knowing it was silly but needing some kind of help. She went right and walked as fast as she dared, her eyes darting back and forth in fear that he'd melt out of the trees at any moment. The sun continued to go down, and she got colder. All too soon it was dark, and she'd lost feeling in her toes and face. *Survive!* she said again. *Just keep moving.*

Then she stopped in the middle of the trail. She took a deep whiff and smelled campfire smoke. Smoke meant people. At nearly the same moment, she heard something behind her, and she took off toward the smoke like a shot. Maybe it was a falling branch or an animal—she didn't dare look back to see if it was him.

She moved as fast as she dared, stumbling over a rough path she couldn't see, the smell getting stronger, her legs getting weaker, until she was barely moving again. She heard something. A voice? She froze. Was it him? She listened again, trying to control her ragged breaths enough to hear over them. The voice laughed. It was feminine—a woman—but still seemed very far away. Her mother's admonishment from when she was a child rang in her ears. "If you ever get lost, find another mommy. She'll help you find me."

"Help me," she tried to yell as she stumbled forward, but it came out as little more than a hoarse whisper. She moved ahead and tried to work some saliva up in her mouth. She looked around for more snow, but in the darkness she couldn't see any and didn't want to risk getting off the trail. "Help me!" she yelled again. This time it was almost audible.

"Please," she said, as the tears started to fall. She was so close, but she didn't have any idea where he was. She had to find that voice, yet she couldn't afford to go silent and still long enough to listen for it again. The smell of campfire was stronger than ever, but she couldn't tell exactly what direction it was coming from.

"Help me!" she yelled again. This time it was full force, surprising even herself. "Help!" she yelled again. She tripped over a tree root. It sent her careening into another tree. Her knee crunched against the bark, closely followed by her forehead. Once on the ground, her hand wrapped around a thick stick. She used it to help get herself on her feet again; then she grabbed onto a tree and lifted the stick, hitting it against branches in hopes of alerting someone. "Help me," she said and tried to take a step. Her knee rebelled and nearly sent her to the ground again. She steadied herself and realized she'd run as far as she could.

"Please, Heavenly Father," she whispered, staving off her panic.

Then she took a deep breath, leaned against the tree, and shouted toward the sky. "Help me!"

She fell against the tree, her lungs still lobbying for air. She heard movement, leaves being shifted. She closed her eyes. If it was Colt, so help her, she'd die before she'd let him take her again.

"Oh!" she heard a startled woman's voice say. Jess opened her eyes to see the glaring light of a flashlight. It moved from her face, and Jess squinted up to see a burly looking blonde staring at her in the darkness.

Jess dropped the stick, afraid it might look like a weapon. With her head bleeding, the last thing she needed was to scare this woman away. She opened her mouth while trying to figure out what words she would say.

The woman beat her to it. "Jessica?" she asked. "Jessica Thompson from the posters?"

79

Brad, go to the Columbia Falls police station as soon as you get into town."

"We wanted to go to the cabin," Brad said into his cell phone. It had been a very long, very fast drive, and yet the miles didn't seem to go by quick enough.

"Brad," the detective said. "Go to the police station. It's located at 130 Sixth Street."

"Okay," Brad said, as dread filled his chest. He wanted to ask more questions, but he didn't dare. He wasn't sure he wanted to know what had changed their plans. He clicked the phone shut and relayed the information to Kate.

She nodded and stared straight ahead. Had they found something? Would they act this way if they'd found Jess alive? Forty-one miles later, at nearly midnight, he pulled up to the boxlike building. He and Kate shared a look; then he leaned across the seat and took her into his arms. They said nothing—all the words too scary to say out loud. He wanted to tell her it would be okay, but would it?

They stepped out of the car and walked slowly inside. The station seemed awfully busy for a small town. They stood in the doorway, waiting for someone to approach them. It only took a moment for a female officer to come forward. "Mr. and Mrs. Thompson?" she asked. They nodded, and Kate sought Brad's hand. He held on tight as they followed the officer down the hall toward a big brown door. Brad swallowed as they pushed the door open.

In the corner someone was wrapped up in a blanket. The head was down, the knees pulled up. Black matted hair was the only thing showing above the grey blanket. For an instant Brad thought it was the man who'd taken Jess, but then the head lifted. He froze. Her face was bruised, her hair a different color, but beneath the scratches and the dirt was his girl.

"Jess?" he said in a whisper. Kate caught her breath and squeezed his hand even tighter.

Jess looked at them, just staring as if not recognizing who they were. Then her eyes filled with tears.

"You came," she said quietly.

The sound of her voice released their hesitancies. They both rushed forward, unable to reach her fast enough. They wrapped their arms around her, and the three of them sobbed. There were so many questions Brad wanted to ask, but he pushed them away. "Dear Father in Heaven," he managed to choke out. "Thank you."

"Please take me home," Jess said after five of the most powerful minutes of Brad's life. Both Brad and Kate pulled back, looking into the face of the daughter they had worried they would never see again. She looked from one to the other. "I'm so sorry."

Kate shook her head. "It's okay, sweetie," she said, caressing Jess's cheek. "We are just so happy to have you back."

Jess looked skeptical.

"You know you're safe now, right?" Brad asked. "You know that everything's all right?"

Fresh tears filled Jess's eyes, and she shook her head as if unable to accept that things could ever be all right again. "I just want to go home—can we just go home?"

"Yes," Brad said with a sharp nod of his head. Kate looked at him, and the tears filled his eyes again as she took his hand. They had their second chance.

Epilogue

J ess," Kate said with a laugh. "Don't fidget. It makes your head move."
Jess stopped, but only for a moment. Then she started up again,
pleating and repleating the skirt of her homecoming dress. Kate pinned
up one more curl into the elaborate updo she'd been creating for over half
an hour and sprayed the entire creation with more hairspray than was
likely FDA approved. It looked great, if Kate did say so herself.

After they had brought Jess home in May, a sister in the ward had
fixed Jess's hair, taking it from black to a nice dark auburn that looked
beautiful against Jess's olive skin. With it pinned up, and her makeup just
right, Jess looked exquisite. Once finished, Kate pulled up a chair and sat
down with a considerable lack of grace, on account of her seven-months
pregnant belly. Per doctor's orders, Kate had gone onto partial bed rest at
five months. Yet, at her appointment yesterday, her blood pressure had
still been a few points higher. She was attempting to prepare herself for
the next few months as best she could and had saved up all her "vertical
time" in order to see Jess off tonight.

"Are you okay?" Kate asked, placing a hand on her belly as the baby
kicked and squirmed.

Jess just shrugged. But then she stopped herself and looked at her
mom. Kate knew it was part of Jess's therapy that she not hold back her
feelings. It was also part of Kate's progression to take the time to listen—
really listen. "I just . . . I feel so weird doing this, going to the homecoming dance like every other teenage girl."

Kate smiled and nodded. "I can only imagine," she said softly. "You don't have to go if you don't want to." She'd said this about fifty times since Jess had come home to find her bedroom stuffed with balloons, floor to ceiling, two weeks earlier. She'd had to pop them all in order to figure out the message. She'd waited for the other kids to come home; then they all had a popping-party while Kate lay on the couch upstairs. But once the fun was over, insecurities had risen up.

"I know that," Jess said. "And I want to go. It's just . . ."

Kate squeezed her daughter's hand. "I know," she said, reaching out and caressing Jess's face.

Jess nodded. "I'm so different," she said.

Kate nodded again. She *was* different. Different from the Jess who had gone to Spring Fling. Different from the girls around her. She'd been through a lot, and those things had changed her. Kate couldn't imagine what it was like to balance out the before and after. Throughout the summer Jess had attended therapy three times a week. She'd gone back and forth on whether she wanted to finish high school or just take the GED when she turned seventeen. Her whole life—all the basic expectations—had changed. She'd had to become accustomed to the way the eyes of everyone in a room followed her when she entered, and the way they tried to hide the fact that they were whispering about her—retelling the bits and pieces they knew about what had happened. Jess hated being the center of attention, and yet people avoided her at the same time.

"Jess," Kate said, wishing as she had a million times that she had just the right thing to say. "You're an amazing girl, and you look beautiful. You'll have your cell phone, so Dad's only a phone call away. But remember how much fun you had at Spring Fling?"

Jess nodded, and her face relaxed a little bit. In July, Britney asked if Jess wanted to run with her in the evenings as she got ready for cross-country. Jess's knee had healed by then, and she'd enjoyed it. When Britney started training with the cross-country team in August, Jess did too. In the two months since then, Jess had slimmed down some and made friends with the other members of the team, who seemed to help buffer her from all the curiosity sent her way. That kind of support had made all the difference. Jess decided to give high school another shot, and yet it still hadn't been easy. Kids asked her questions constantly, some treated her like a celebrity, and others acted as if she had an infectious disease.

Jess had handled it all with as much grace as a sixteen-year-old girl could, but she still struggled to find her place amid everything that had happened—things that Kate and Brad still knew very little about. What they did know was bad enough, but Jess guarded her experience very closely, and Kate did not push. It hadn't been easy to change the way she parented, but it *had* been working. That was enough.

As Kate searched for something else to say, Jess straightened, squared her shoulders, and lifted her chin. It was a trick her therapist had taught her, preparing to face the situation. And every time Kate saw it, her pride in her daughter soared. She thought back to her mother's words, "I hope one day you can look at the woman Jess has become and be proud of her too." Perhaps Jess was not a woman just yet, but Kate was very, very proud.

"I can do this," Jess said with a smile and a nod.

"And we're only a phone call away," Kate reminded her as she stood.

"Right," Jess agreed, taking a breath and standing. The dress they'd picked out was peach chiffon, with a full skirt and cap sleeves. It looked beautiful with Jess's coloring. Kate stood, reached out, and gave her daughter a long hug, not wanting to let go.

"Now," Kate said, pulling back. "Are you ready to face the Thompson masses?"

Jess skewed up her face in feigned consideration, then elaborately nodded her head as if she were being sent to the front lines. "I think so."

Kate nodded and opened the door to the hallway outside the master bedroom, where she'd been helping Jess get ready.

"You look like a movie star!" Justin said, clapping his hands. The other kids oohed and aahed, especially Caitlyn, while Brad snapped pictures as fast as he could. Kate's mom and her husband, Gary, now living in Ogden, were standing to the side and remarked to one another just how beautiful she looked.

"Okay, now let's get one over by the fireplace," he said. "Monique just called, wanting to know where her pictures are."

Jess smiled and complied. The entire Weatherford family had flown to Salt Lake City two weeks after Jess's homecoming—just two days after Drake Colton Shepard had been arrested by the Canadian Mounted Police in Edmonton, Canada. He had twelve current e-mail addresses numbered fifty-seven through sixty-nine, looking for his next victim. The Weatherfords and Thompsons had celebrated his capture together, but Kate wouldn't have guessed how powerful the Weatherfords would become to Jess. Monique and Jess especially had developed a special friendship, which had continued with phone calls and e-mails ever since. A year ago, having another woman be that close to her daughter would have made Kate jealous and territorial, but she couldn't deny that Monique filled an important role in Jess's life. If that's what Jess needed, then it didn't matter where it came from—though Kate wondered if things would be different if she'd had a different kind of closeness before any of this had happened. She looked at her own mother, who caught her eye and smiled, reminding Kate that there was always hope between a mother and daughter.

Jess had recently talked about perhaps going to Ann Arbor for college, and the Weatherfords had offered to have her stay with them. The idea sounded horrible to Kate, who couldn't imagine Jess moving a couple thousand miles away. But she had smiled and reminded herself that this was Jess's life, not an appendage of her own. One thing Monique said over and over again was that it wasn't how we handle our success in life as much as how we overcome our trials. *That* really proves who we are.

Though that advice was intended for Jess, Kate found it great wisdom in regard to her own life as well.

A knock at the door caused everyone to pause, and Brad hurried to open it. Nick Tolson, a boy who ran with Jess on the cross-country team, stood at the threshold, trying not to look nervous. Brad shook Nick's hand and invited him in. With all the kids and grandparents gathered together, the room was full.

"Let's get a shot of the two of you," Brad said eagerly.

"*Dad!*" Jess said under her breath and behind her smile.

Brad ignored her. "By the fireplace."

They complied, and Brad took several shots of the two of them standing together while Kate sat down on a kitchen chair, knowing she needed to get back to bed soon.

That Jess was home at all was miraculous. That she had healed enough emotionally to go to the homecoming dance like other girls her age was further proof of God's tender mercies.

"We need to go," Jess said behind her teeth after the ninth picture.

"Okay," Dad said; then he looked at her date. "Will you take a picture of us, Nick? One of her family?"

Kate stifled a laugh at the look on Jess's face, but Jess didn't argue, and they all piled around her while Brad showed Nick how to use the camera. Then Brad hurried to his place on the right side of Jess, with Marilyn standing beside him. Kate stood on the left next to her mom and Gary. When the kids had filled in every other inch, they all smiled.

"Okay," Nick said, his nervousness wearing off a little bit. "Say . . . uh . . . families are forever."

They all paused for a brief second, then each of them broke into a wide grin. Joy squeezed Kate's shoulder.

"Families are forever!"

Nick snapped the picture and looked up. "Perfect."

Author's Notes

The Crimes Against Children Research Center did a study in 1999 based on 1,500 American teenagers aged eleven to seventeen who used the Internet on a regular basis. Regular basis was defined as at least once a month for six months. Statistics found that in a one-year period of time, one in four children were exposed to some type of pornographic imagery, while one in five were the victims of sexually driven comments and invitations. One in seventeen were threatened or harassed, and one in thirty-three were asked to meet someone in person. Only 25 percent of these children told a parent, and only a very small fraction of those reports were ever forwarded to the police or any other online agency. Perhaps the most disturbing portion of this study was that most of the teenagers involved were not bothered by sexual content online or with being asked for personal information. Only one-third of the households with children surveyed had filtering programs on their computer.

It is true that many sexually directed comments come from other youth, even friends, but the fact remains that the Internet opens our homes to every other home with the Internet. As portrayed in this story, the Internet provides a forum in which many teenagers feel comfortable being themselves. It's easy to believe the person on the other end is just like them and in need of friends.

So what can parents do to protect their children from Internet hazards? I believe there are three keys: education, supervision, and software.

Education. Rather than banning children from the Internet, teach them how to use it. We live in a technological age that is only becoming more advanced. To function in this society, our kids are expected to have familiarity with the computer and the Internet. Instead of cutting them off from the advantages of the Internet, make sure they understand that the Internet has both good and bad available, and just as with books, movies, TV, and friends, they need to be careful in the choices they make. Children should be warned to never give out personal information and to choose screen names that keep their gender, state of residence, and age unknown. Yet, even after teaching your children, don't assume they would never break these rules. They are children, and they don't understand the full spectrum of the situation they are in—that's why they have parents (!)—which leads us to the second part of the plan of protection.

Supervision. Nothing can take the place of parental awareness. Keep your computer in a common area of the house where you can see it at any time. Pay attention to what websites your child goes to and search the history on the hard drive on a regular basis. If you find that you have no history, someone has deleted it. Establish time limits and be sure you know the screen names and passwords of the web sites your kids frequent. Talk to your kids about what they do online, and monitor programs they download. Be prepared to take away computer privileges and even remove Internet service should children abuse their online privileges. Be sure you know enough about computers to be an effective steward. Discuss with your kids your expectations as far as site content, chat rooms, graphic levels of online games, information required by some memberships, posting pictures of themselves online, and e-mail options. Establish boundaries and then follow up to be sure they are staying within those parameters you have set. An ounce of prevention is worth a pound of cure. For help in establishing and enforcing the rules you make, consider utilizing the final suggestion for keeping your children safe: software.

Software. There are two main types of software to assist parents in being cautious online. *Filtering software* will block certain sites and keep pornographic materials from being viewed or downloaded. As the parent, you can adjust the levels of filtering and ban certain sites. *Monitoring software,* on the other hand, records everything done online, can track computer usage time, and can list web sites accessed. Both software options are great tools for parents; different products range from being simple to requiring a great deal of computer proficiency to set up. Ask your friends, research different programs, and find one that best fits your needs. Once it is installed, keep an eye on it. Kids are notoriously smarter than we are when it comes to technology. With a little help from a friend they can disable the software you put in place, so be alert and aware of that risk.

Of course, nothing is a guarantee. Just as crossing the street puts our kids at risk of being hit by a car, being online puts our kids at risk of becoming a target of an Internet predator. However, we teach our children to look both ways, to obey the laws, and to use caution as they go into the world. We know they must learn to cross the street some time, and therefore we arm them with the knowledge and understanding necessary for them to do so safely. The Internet is no different. As with many aspects of parenting, knowing our children and establishing a trustworthy relationship will go a long way. Nothing takes the place of a savvy and aware parent, and nothing gives children more security than knowing their parents love them and want to care for them.

For more information on Internet predators and how to protect your children, try the following web sites:

http://www.isafe.org/

http://www.cleartraffic.com/keeping-kids-safe.htm

http://www.ed.gov/pubs/parents/internet/index.html (a resource published by the United States Department of Education)

About the Author

Josi S. Kilpack is the author of several contemporary LDS novels for women, including *Unsung Lullaby, Surrounded by Strangers, Tempest Tossed, Star Struck, To Have or To Hold,* and *Earning Eternity.* She and her husband, Lee, are the parents of four children.